"What a delight to be reacquainted with classical pianist Lottie Braun and her cast of characters! Author Jane Tucker delivers another intriguing story in "Lottie's Hope."

—RJ THESMAN, author of Life at Cove Creek Series

Lottie's Hope

JANE M. TUCKER

ST. JOSEPH, MISSOURI USA

Lottie's Hope

One

*D*on't call us, Mr. Arnold. We'll call you."

"But I can bring this house into the 1980s—"

Lottie closed the heavy front door on the dapper little salesman and slumped against it. "That man couldn't build a sandcastle at the beach, much less my room addition. Please tell me we have another choice."

Miranda didn't blame her employer for sounding discouraged. So far they'd seen three contractors, none of them suitable. One wanted to talk to the man of the house. Another was more interested in financing the project than discussing design. The third—well, Peter Arnold's enthusiasm for paisley drapes and country blue walls marked him as a decorator, not a builder. She couldn't suppress a chuckle. "Can you imagine this gorgeous old house with pink wall-to-wall carpeting?"

Lottie shuddered. "Old-fashioned or not, I love these hardwood floors." Her gaze fell to the polished walnut staircase. "Helen kept this house in beautiful shape. If only it had a room big enough for a grand piano."

"But it doesn't." Miranda consulted her clipboard. "Which brings us to our last construction company. This is the one Ed Williams recommended. Apparently, the owner is a friend of his."

"That's a good sign," Lottie said. "Ed and Martha have to live next door to this room addition. They'd want to point me in the right direction. What do you think of this company?"

Miranda looked up with a frown. "They didn't impress me much. When I called, the guy acted like he was too busy to answer my questions."

7

Lottie's blue eyes lit with humor. "You probably caught him by surprise. Not everyone knows as much as you do about construction."

"Surprised or not, he should have had answers." Miranda frowned. "He wasn't even sure he could make time to see us because they already had a Saturday appointment. No business is secure enough to turn away a customer." She glanced out the window. "Speaking of which, they're here."

"Oh, good." Lottie pulled the lace curtain aside and peeked at their last option. A big white pickup truck stood at the curb, Harms & Sons Construction printed in block letters on the door. She threw Miranda a startled glance. "Harms? Their name is Harms?"

Miranda nodded. "Why? What's wrong?"

Lottie shrugged. "I once knew a family named Harms. But it couldn't be them. They weren't from Iowa."

The wistful note in her voice caught Miranda's attention. In her year as Lottie's assistant, she had never seen the great pianist drop her guard. Which made it all the more surprising when Lottie opened the door and stared at the contractor with slack-jawed recognition.

Tall and dark-haired, with broad shoulders and blue-gray eyes, the man returned her stare with a look of polite boredom. "Jason Harms, ma'am. We spoke on the phone?"

Lottie flushed to the roots of her wavy white hair. "Come in. We're expecting you. This is my assistant, Miranda Charles." She reached out to draw Miranda into the conversation. "Actually, she's the one who called...." Her voice trailed off as she stared toward the street.

Miranda had to crane her neck around the man in the doorway to see what had caught Lottie's attention. As she watched, the passenger door of the truck swung closed, revealing a man who could only be Jason's father. Tall and lean, with a silver crew cut and weather-beaten skin, he strode across the lawn carrying a notebook in one hand and a tool box in the other. When he reached the porch, he set his burden down and looked straight at Lottie, who smiled radiantly back.

"Well, hello there," she said brightly.

"Hello, ma'am." His tone was distant, almost wooden. "I'm Sam Harms. I'll be helping my son today."

Lottie's welcoming smile froze. "Of course. Come in." Her voice, usually so smooth, sounded hoarse. She cleared her throat. "I'll let my assistant take over from here. She's in charge of the project."

Miranda stared at her employer, trying to puzzle out what had just happened. Lottie looked devastated. What did she know about these men? Could they be trusted?

Jason Harms cleared his throat. "Can we get started? We've got a schedule to keep."

Miranda matched his brisk tone. "Right this way." She led the men down the hall, away from Lottie, talking business all the way.

♫

Lottie sank onto the bench in the entry hall, her thoughts in a whirl. That man was Sammy Harms. She was sure of it. So what if she hadn't seen him in forty years. He hadn't changed that much. And his son— well, the likeness between them was uncanny.

What was Sammy doing in Collison? Had he lived here long? Did he still play the drums? Her brain teemed with questions.

Most of all, why was he treating her like a stranger?

Long minutes later, she heard the sound of work boots stomping back down the hall. "All finished?"

The men looked preoccupied. "We're moving outside, ma'am," Jason said. "We'll need more measurements to give you an accurate quote." He turned to Miranda, who followed close at their heels. "No need to come. We'll bring you a bid in a couple of days."

Miranda looked like a storm cloud as the door swung shut behind them. Lottie was amused in spite of herself. The Harms boys always did know how to irritate women. "They're a charming pair."

Her assistant smiled ruefully. "Unfortunately, they know their stuff. You'd be a fool not to hire them."

"Did they..." Lottie hesitated. "Did they say anything about me?"

A pucker appeared between Miranda's black eyebrows. "What kind of thing?"

Lottie turned away, embarrassed. "Forget it. I can't imagine why I said that." She glanced at her watch. "Would you look at the time? I've got to get moving. I planned on putting in a few hours at the office."

Miranda took her cue. "I'd better get out of your hair. I'll just put this clipboard in my office before I go."

Lottie watched her petite assistant climb the stairs to the tiny room that served as an office. The arrangement wasn't ideal, but it was necessary. Collison College had outgrown its campus, and office space was scarce. At least, that's how the matter had been explained to Miranda. Lottie had her doubts. Surely there was always room for one more secretary's cubicle.

"What else can I do for you?" Miranda asked when she came back downstairs.

"Tell me what you liked about Harms and Sons."

Miranda thought a moment. "I could tell from their walk-through that they're competent builders," she said slowly, "but it's more than that. They seem to understand old houses. The son pointed out architectural details that he'd want in the new room, while the dad knew what kinds of problems you'll have with wiring and plumbing. I think the two of them work well together."

Lottie thought this over. "So you really think I should hire them?"

"Yes, I do."

Lottie walked her assistant to the back door and watched her hurry down the brick path. Miranda looked oddly formal for a Saturday in a blue business suit and low-heeled red pumps, with her abundant black hair confined to a bun at the nape of her neck. The girl's choice of wardrobe screamed, "Take me seriously," but no amount of shoulder pads or ruffled blouses could disguise how young she was.

As Miranda's Toyota hatchback puttered down the alley and disappeared, Lottie sighed. Most of the time she didn't think about getting older. Fifty-three was only a number, and she had the energy of a much younger woman. But after this morning she felt downright ancient. Ancient, faded, and forgettable.

For some reason Sam Harms' sudden appearance had knocked her sideways. She puzzled over this fact as she stood at the stove, heating a can of tomato soup for lunch. Over the years she'd run into other men from the Neverland Band, and those encounters had not troubled her. She'd ignored most of them, of course. Those men would have been pretty hard to explain to anyone who knew her now. Her official biography said nothing about playing piano for a down-at-the-heels traveling swing band. As far as her fans knew, Lottie Braun grew up on a little farm in Iowa until she enrolled in the Dayton Conservatory of Music at age fourteen. It would never do to let the public learn the truth.

This morning Sam had given her a dose of her own medicine, looking straight through her like she was no more important than a hat rack. They'd been friends, darn it! She'd been the one to introduce the lonely fourteen-year-old boy to her Aunt Eva, the woman who adopted him, and gave him a way out of the life he hated.

She carried the steaming pan of soup to the table and picked up a spoon. Come to think of it, she and Sam were related now: First cousins, because of good old Aunt Eva. Not that it mattered. Lottie hadn't seen any of her family in forty years. Apparently, Sam didn't plan to be the first to break the ice. No loss, she told herself. She must have dozens of relatives in this county. Surely not all of them wanted to pretend she didn't exist.

Maybe they do, her conscience whispered. Maybe they sit around at family reunions and gossip about what you did to Helen.

She shooed away the treacherous thoughts. Helen's letter had been clear. Nobody knew their secret. Nobody. She raised her eyes to the ceiling. "Helen?" she murmured. "Does that include Sammy Harms?"

Miranda didn't expect a crowd when she decided to jog around Collison's historic downtown in the early afternoon. On weekdays, when she drove through on her way to work, the place looked deserted. Today, though, the shops were full of customers, and a line of cars circled the courthouse square in search of parking.

A busy farmers' market occupied the sidewalk, forcing her to run along the curb, behind booths that overflowed with bright vegetables and fragrant baked goods. One or two dogs on leashes wagged friendly tails as she passed, but a fat gray goose with a gleam in its eye chased her down the street, hissing angrily.

"Look out!"

Miranda hit the open car door and went down like a sack of flour. First her tail bone, then her head bounced on the pavement before she came to rest next to sleek red sports car.

"Are you hurt?"

She opened her eyes to find a man crouching over her, a look of concern in his warm brown eyes. She tried to ignore the way the scenery whirled as she sat up. "I'm fine."

"Thank God." The man looked relieved. "I didn't see you when I opened my door."

She nodded. "I was trying to outrun a goose."

His mouth turned up in a lopsided grin. "Good idea. Geese are mean."

"Of all the fool—" The driver came around the hood of the car and stopped next to Miranda. "Oh. We meet again."

She winced. "Hi."

Jason Harms did not look pleased to see her. "You should watch where you're going."

She narrowed her eyes. "No kidding."

The other man looked curious. "Wait. You two know each other?"

The contractor gave a long-suffering sigh. "This is Lottie Braun's secretary."

"Ohhhhh." The other man's face lit with recognition. "The one with all the questions." He turned his interested gaze on Miranda. "I'm Mitchell Harms. Everyone says I'm the nice brother."

She couldn't help smiling at his friendly tone. "Miranda Charles." She scrambled to her feet. "Well, I'll be going now."

Her knees shook too badly to start running again, so she settled for a fairly steady walk. Once she turned a corner she let herself limp, then sank onto a park bench and rested her aching head in her hands.

She was almost relieved when the red sports car followed her around the corner and stopped at the curb. The tinted window glided down to reveal Jason Harms at the wheel. "Get in," he said. "I'll take you home."

She waved him away. "Don't you have a schedule to keep?"

There was a short pause. "It can wait."

"Uh-huh."

He flung his door open and came around to stand in front of her. "Look, you're obviously in pain. My car did the damage, so I'll make sure you get home." He opened the passenger door and held out his hand. "Come on. I'll help you up."

Her aching head overrode her usual sense of caution. She complied with the gentle pressure of his hand and settled with relief against the soft leather seat.

"Good." He shut the door behind her and got in the driver's side. "Now, where do you live?"

"Division Street, in that big complex of townhouses."

He put the car in gear and pulled away from the curb. "I know the place. The units are tiny."

"It was all I could find."

He nodded. "The best places in Collison never go on the market. Take your boss's house, for example."

She rolled her head to one side to look at him. "How do you know it didn't go on the market?"

"I practically grew up there. My family was good friends with the Parkers." He glanced at her. "It's a great old place. I always wanted to live there myself."

"Wouldn't it be strange, adding to a house you know so well?"

He shrugged. "I'm not thrilled about working for that woman, but at least I know we'll do right by the house."

She stared at him. "What do you mean, that woman? She has a name."

"Yeah, I know. The great Lottie Braun." He shot her an ironic glance. "I just don't get it. She was too good for little old Collison while her sister was alive, but now she wants to settle down here?" He shook his head. "How long do you think that will last?"

Miranda had wondered the same thing, though she wasn't about to admit it. "You make it sound like she's doing something illegal. If you're as close with the Parkers as you say, then you probably know Lottie's sister gave her the house."

"Yeah. That's another thing I don't understand."

Her head was beginning to pound. "You can let me out here."

He pulled up to the curb and came around to help her out of the deep bucket seat. "Easy does it. You're going to be sore tomorrow."

"I'm fine." She yanked her arm away. "Thanks for the ride."

He stepped back and nodded politely. "Chalk it up to good customer service."

He was gone before she could react, tearing away in that ridiculous sports car. "You don't have the job yet," she yelled as he roared out of sight.

Lottie stared out her office window at the deserted campus three floors below. The green quadrangle, hemmed in by six limestone buildings, looked cool and inviting in the afternoon heat. White sidewalks divided the lawn into neat triangles that met in the center at a sprawling marble fountain. Next Saturday the grass would no doubt be trampled underfoot by hordes of returning students, but for now it looked like the cover of a college recruitment brochure.

The quad hadn't changed since Lottie was a little girl. She and Helen had splashed in that marble fountain on hot summer Saturdays while they waited for Pop to finish his business in the county seat.

The peace on the quad carried into the Performing Arts Building. Lottie had passed one or two people on her way to the third floor, but for the most part the place was deserted. Not that she minded. With a week to go before classes started, she had a lot of work to do in a small amount of time. In the past, as a visiting professor, she had worked with piano performance majors and delivered a few guest lectures. She hadn't taught general music courses, and while she was extremely well-versed in music theory, she was finding it difficult to develop a semester's worth of lesson plans.

She did not feel comfortable asking the other professors for help.

They weren't a warm bunch. In the week since her arrival, none of them had said much to her beyond, "Hello." Worse yet, they didn't seem to talk among themselves. Aside from the Monday morning staff meeting, she hadn't seen any two of her colleagues in the same room together. Lottie was accustomed to professional rivalry, but this general sense of alienation was something different. Katherine Snelling, the department dean, set the tone for everyone else. Formal and serious, she approached her duties with the gravity of a prime minister, weighing every word she spoke as if lives hung in the balance. The result was a pompousness she probably didn't intend. Still, it was off-putting.

Maybe things would change when the other piano professor came back from her summer in Europe. Surely two pianists would have enough in common to forge a good working relationship.

She leaned back in her chair and pinched the bridge of her nose. This wasn't working. The warm August air, the whir of her desk fan, and the scent of mowed grass outside the open window all were conspiring to put her to sleep. She stood and stretched, leaning to one side and the other, then paced to the other end of the room and took her seat at the baby grand piano. A little Beethoven would wake her up.

Six measures into the second movement of the *Pathetique*, a prickle went up her spine. A glance over her shoulder confirmed she was no longer alone. A plump, red-faced woman stood in the doorway, holding a red milk crate full of books. Beads of sweat stood out above her upper lip, and her chest heaved in an effort to catch her breath. "Who are you?" Lottie said, without breaking tempo.

"Rhonda Kennedy." The stranger blew a lock of frizzy yellow hair out of her eyes. "What are you doing in my office?"

Lottie stopped playing and turned around on the piano bench. So this was her fellow piano professor. "Your office?" she said with raised eyebrows. "This office was assigned to me."

Rhonda Kennedy took a firmer grip on her box of books. "I'm afraid there's been a mistake. Katherine promised I could have this office after Alicia retired."

Lottie stared at her opponent. The busy dean had not bothered herself with something as small as assigning Lottie's office. Instead Elaine Woodward, the department secretary, had handed her a key and a room number, and sent her on her way. The office, with its long windows, high ceiling, and scarred wood floor, had come as a lovely surprise. She wasn't about to give it up without a fight. Rising to her full five-feet-ten, she approached the angry professor with unhurried steps. When she stood too close for comfort, she looked down at the shorter woman. "What's the old saying? 'Possession is nine-tenths of the law.' I'm not moving until Dean Snelling says so."

A whiny note entered Rhonda's voice. "Katherine will take my side. You'll see."

Lottie nodded. "Maybe. For now, though, you'd better take those books back where they came from before you drop them."

Rhonda threw her one last outraged glance and retreated. "This isn't over," she called over her shoulder. "We'll settle it tonight."

The door swung shut, cutting off Rhonda's shrill voice.

Lottie closed her eyes. So much for forging a partnership. After an introduction like that, she'd be lucky to avoid an all-out war.

With a sigh, she gathered her lesson plans off the desk and filed them in her book bag. Rhonda was right about one thing. The whole department would be together tonight at Alicia Maynard's retirement reception. Hopefully the angry professor had enough sense not to ruin the occasion with an argument over office space.

Fat chance.

Two

*M*iranda felt better after a long hot shower. She had a goose-egg on her head and a purple bruise at the base of her spine, but she'd live. In the future, she would limit her running routes to residential neighborhoods.

She settled on the couch with the Saturday newspaper and a pen. The classified ads were full of tantalizing sale notices, and second-hand treasures were her weakness. She'd circled three ads when the doorbell rang.

The lady from next door stood on the porch, an anxious smile on her pink face. Her mauve track suit and faded red dye job completed the impression of a human petunia. "I saw you come home a little while ago," the lady said. "You were limping."

Miranda nodded, her gaze on the covered dish in her neighbor's hands. "I went for a run, and had a little accident." She opened her door a little wider. "Would you like to come in?"

"I'd love to." The lady stepped inside and held out the dish. "I thought you might want something warm and comforting, so I made goulash." She perched on the edge of the couch. "I'm Rosie, by the way. Rosie Carlson. I live next door."

"I've seen you." Miranda set the dish in the kitchen and rejoined her guest. "I'm Miranda Charles."

"Yes, I know." Rosie Carlson gave a matter-of-fact nod. "My son manages these townhouses. I hear you're Lottie Braun's secretary. I think it's wonderful she's come home to Iowa."

Miranda gazed at her well-informed guest. "Y-yes, I suppose it is."

A mournful look crossed Rosie's face. "If only Helen had lived to see this day. She was a dear one, that Helen." She raised bright eyes to Miranda's face. "Have you met her daughter Patti?"

"No, I haven't had the pleasure."

"Oh, it won't be a pleasure, honey. Patti's always been too big for her britches. I don't imagine she's real excited about an aunt who outshines her." Rosie gave Miranda a reassuring look. "But she'll probably stay in Chicago. She was never too keen on Collison."

"I see."

"You're very pretty," Rosie continued. "Do you mind if I ask where you're from?"

Ah. They'd reached the point of the conversation. "California, actually."

"California?" There was a little silence as Miranda's guest digested this information. "But you look so…foreign."

Miranda gave her guest a measuring look. Experience had taught her that she didn't owe an explanation to everyone who asked.

Rosie wilted a little under her gaze. "I'm sorry, sweetie. I've offended you, and I didn't mean to." She got to her feet. "I know I seem like an awful old busybody, but I'm just so darned curious about everything. I'll leave you be."

She was almost to the door when Miranda spoke. "My family is from India."

Rosie looked back with a relieved smile. "How interesting. I wondered if that was it, but you don't have a dot on your forehead." She gave an apologetic shrug. "I knew some Indian students when I worked in the college cafeteria, and they all had the dot."

"That's a Hindu caste mark. My family are Christians."

Rosie's eyes widened with pleasure. "You're a Christian? How nice. Are you looking for a church?"

Miranda bit her lip. "Not really."

Rosie closed her eyes. "Oh, there I go again, prying into your business. Enjoy the goulash." She reached for the doorknob, then paused. "One last thing, dear. Wasn't that Jason Harms who dropped you off?"

Denial was futile. "He offered to take me home after his car door caused my accident."

Rosie gave a satisfied nod. "Well, Jason always was a nice boy."

And with that parting comment, she was gone.

♫

Helen's house was a five-minute drive from campus if the traffic light at College and Park was green. Lottie rolled down the windows to air out the hot car, and caught a whiff of charcoal smoke from someone's backyard grill. Two girls on bikes coasted down the sidewalk, their hand brakes squeaking as they reached the street corner. Peace reigned on this August Saturday.

A block from home, the faint thrum of an electric bass disturbed Lottie's tranquility. The bass grew louder as she reached her street, when a heavy drumbeat joined in. She gritted her teeth and turned onto the alley behind Helen's house. They were at it again. If the past five nights were any guide, she'd soon be treated to wailing guitars and the opening stanza of "Wild Thing."

She punched her garage door opener with unnecessary force and parked the Mercedes inside, ignoring the scruffy teenagers in the garage across the way. They played on, blissfully unaware of the musical desecration they were unleashing into the atmosphere. She walked out of the garage with her head bent, studiously ignoring her young neighbors. She didn't want to catch someone's eye and be forced to wave. They might mistake mere good manners for approval.

The kids were still practicing an hour later when she left for Alicia Maynard's reception. She had to admire their tenacity. What a shame they weren't improving.

The President's Mansion stood on a narrow, brick-paved residential street at the edge of campus. Its historic neoclassical design won the admiration of all, but the mansion's beauty did not quite make up for its lack of parking.

By the time Lottie arrived, the street in front of the mansion was lined with cars. She parked her Mercedes on an equally narrow street two blocks away and thanked her lucky stars she had chosen low-heeled shoes. She strolled up the tree-lined sidewalk in deepening shade and caught the scent of roses on the breeze. All around her, other people in suits and summer dresses were moving toward the same goal. When she reached the mansion, the receiving line stretched half-way down the front walk.

"I'm surprised at the size of this crowd," said a lady in a shiny red dress.

"Alicia's been here forever," her companion said. "She knows everyone."

The lady in red laughed. "Yes, and has nothing good to say about most of us."

"She loves the students. That's what counts."

Lottie caught herself eavesdropping and looked around. There must be somebody she could talk with while she waited in this crowd. Elaine Woodward stood several feet back, near the end of the line. Lottie considered joining her, but the thought of trying to hold a conversation with the dour department secretary was too daunting. With a sigh, she turned around and settled in to wait.

"Coming through, folks. Make way for the handicapped man." Nathan Bartholomew rolled up the sidewalk in his lightweight wheelchair and stopped beside Lottie. "Well, if it isn't Collison's newest professor. How did they rope you into coming to this? You've never even met the old battle-ax."

Nathan was a brilliant musicology professor with a nasty reputation for plain speaking. His dark good looks and sarcastic wit were a hit with the students, though his colleagues seemed less impressed. Lottie gave him a cool stare, which he returned with interest. "Katherine made it clear this was mandatory for the whole department."

He gave a derisive snort. "And you took her word as law? Everyone knows the Great Lottie Braun doesn't socialize with common folk."

The barbed comment hit home, but she knew better than to show it. Instead she said lightly, "Is that why nobody talks to me? I was beginning to think I was invisible."

"We know when we're outranked," he said. "I saw you play with the Chicago Symphony, back in '68. The program was Rachmaninoff's *Concerto Number Two*, and you chose Kabalevsky as an encore. I never liked Rachmaninoff much, until that night. And Kabalevsky? I had to go home and look him up in the library."

She chuckled. "I find that hard to believe."

He rolled his wheelchair back and forth impatiently. "Why isn't this line moving?"

"I have no idea." She looked at him curiously. "How do you plan to get up those steps?"

He shot her a sarcastic look. "I thought you might carry me." When she didn't rise to the bait, he added, "There's a side entrance with a ramp. I'm just killing time out here so I don't have to go inside and drink watered down punch."

"I'll make a note of that. Avoid the punch."

"I hear you snagged a house in Maple Hills. How did you luck into that?" he said.

She hesitated, unwilling to bring Helen's legacy into this casual conversation. "Why do you ask?"

He looked disgusted. "I'm not prying into your personal life. I just happen to be in the market for a house, and I'm not having any luck."

The lady in red turned around with an apologetic smile. "I'm sorry, but I couldn't help overhearing. Maybe you should try a different realtor. Diana Deering is the best agent around."

Nathan glared at the woman. "That's who I've got. All day today she drove me around, from one lousy property to another, none of them remotely suitable. All I need is a house I can get around in, preferably in Maple Hills."

"Don't worry," the lady said. "She'll come through for you." She turned to Lottie. "So, you're Lottie Braun."

"I'm afraid so," Lottie said. Out of the corner of her eye, she watched Nathan roll away and greet another guest. "And you are?"

"Marla Penworthy, Class of '67. I'm on the board of directors now." Mrs. Penworthy leaned closer. "If you don't mind my asking, how was your first week on the job?"

Lottie's eyes widened. "It was fine."

"That's a relief." Mrs. Penworthy lowered her voice. "Katherine

Snelling was pretty upset when the board voted to hire you without consulting her. We had to act fast, before you took another position. It wasn't our fault Katherine chose that week to go on vacation."

Lottie schooled her features into a polite mask. She didn't care for gossip, no matter how enlightening it might be. "I'm looking forward to the school year," she murmured. With a nod toward the house she added, "It looks like the line is moving now."

"Oh, dear!" As Marla hurried forward, Lottie caught Nathan's ironic gaze. She raised her chin and looked away. Playing the Great Lottie Braun would be a hard habit to break.

♫

After all she'd heard about Alicia Maynard, the tiny, bird-like woman who gripped Lottie's hand in both of hers came as something of a shock. Alicia's shapeless black dress hung loose from her shoulders, and a thick layer of pancake makeup gave her face a grayish cast. The scent of Jean Nate and cigarettes surrounded her like a cloud.

"I'm so glad to finally meet you," Alicia said in a gravel-coated voice. "I'd just about given up the idea of retiring before you threw your hat in the ring. 'Alicia,' I said to myself, 'If anyone can keep that department from going to pieces after you leave, it's Lottie Braun.'"

"What a compliment," Lottie murmured. "You've left some pretty big shoes to fill, you know."

"Nonsense." Alicia's cackle ended in a wracking cough. When she caught her breath, she waved an arm toward the party guests. "They're all here to see you, Miss Braun. I'm yesterday's news." She leaned forward with a conspiratorial smile. "Tell me, is it true you had an affair with Sinatra?"

Lottie detested that story. "The gossip columns had a field day with that incident," she said finally. "I met him once, at a club in New York. Frank and his friends were charming, but once they understood I wasn't a party girl, they gave me the brush-off." She hadn't minded. The spotlight around the Rat Pack was much too bright.

Alicia looked deeply satisfied. "A night on the town with Ol' Blue-

Eyes. Now, that's what I call glamorous."

Once she got past the receiving line, Lottie looked around for a friendly face. Nathan Bartholomew was rolling through the buffet line, his plate on his lap, joking with the pretty student at his side. Across the room Rhonda Kennedy poured her grievance into Katherine's listening ear.

She was searching for a group to join when someone touched her arm. She turned to find a young African-American couple smiling at her. Calvin Jefferson, the college band director, said, "I was hoping you'd be here tonight, Miss Braun." He put his arm around the woman next to him. "I'd like you to meet my wife, Teresa."

Teresa shook hands with enthusiasm. "It's an honor, Miss Braun. I'm a big fan."

"Teresa teaches in the English department," Cal said proudly.

Lottie raised her eyebrows. "Literature or composition?"

"Composition," Teresa said. "Creative writing is my favorite subject."

As the conversation progressed, Lottie began to relax. Cal and Teresa were easy to talk to, and Lottie appreciated their obvious affection for each other. Maybe the evening would not be a complete waste of time. When Teresa walked away to talk with a friend, Lottie turned to Cal. "I understand you want to develop a jazz major for the music department."

Cal fiddled with a button on his suit jacket. "Yes, I do. I feel it's time we widened our offerings to attract a wider variety of students." He frowned. "Unfortunately, Katherine doesn't see it as a priority."

"I gathered as much from last week's staff meeting. Have you thought about including piano students, or would you concentrate solely on wind instruments?"

Cal's face lit up. "Of course, I'd include pianists. Strings, percussion—the whole department."

"Tell me more."

As Cal warmed to his favorite topic, Lottie decided she liked this intense young man. He had ambitious ideas and the drive to accomplish them, qualities she respected. She said as much when he paused for breath and was rewarded with a brilliant smile.

"That means a lot coming from you," he said. "I guess the rumors I heard about you were wrong."

"Oh?" she said. "Where on earth would a jazz professor hear rumors about me?"

"I do a lot of research in Kansas City. You made a real splash there last year." His tone was light. "The students I met called you aloof, unbending, impossible…"

She chuckled. "Stop flattering me."

Cal laughed. "I could tell they loved every minute of it. Can I ask you a strange question?" He leaned closer. "Is your full name Charlotte?"

She looked him straight in the eye. "No. My mother christened me Lottie." She glanced around, caught a stranger's eye, and smiled. "Looks like I'm wanted elsewhere," she said to Cal. "I hope you'll excuse me."

As early as she could, Lottie made her excuses and fled the brightly lit mansion. She reached the street and slowed her pace to let the night air cool her flushed cheeks. Parties were always tiring, but this one had nearly worn her out.

Cal's question was no coincidence. The look on his face told her that. How much did he know about Charlotte Brown? With any luck she'd convinced him she knew nothing of the mythical child prodigy.

She unlocked the car and threw her evening bag on the passenger seat. Charlotte Brown was the loose thread in the fabric of Lottie's history. If Cal—or anyone—tugged that thread too hard, the whole thing would unravel.

Lottie gave herself an impatient shake. Forty years she'd guarded her secrets. She'd last another forty if she had to.

The melodramatic thought made her lips twitch. "Lottie, my girl, you're overwrought," she told herself. "What you need is a good night's sleep."

A warm bath, a glass of milk, and a long rest under expertly ironed sheets. The pretty dream comforted her all the way home.

Then reality set in.

♫

She drove up the alley at a snail's pace, her progress impeded by the junk cars parked on either side. The garage across from hers pulsed with light and sound. She honked at the small group of teenagers in front of her garage, and they moved away, but not before a tall boy wearing jack boots and a Mohawk tapped her hood with his fist.

In a flash she moved from annoyance to fury. She pulled the car into her garage and sat there, shaking, resentful of the noise that filled her ears. Every night this week she'd put up with the caterwauling. Every morning she'd risen to face the day, bleary-eyed with lack of sleep. It was time somebody taught those kids some respect.

By the time she got out of the garage, the boy with the Mohawk had disappeared. Without him, the crowd looked pretty tame: a few boys in T-shirts and jeans and some girls with gigantic earrings under shellacked hairdos. She stood in the doorway as the fight drained out of her and looked over the watchers' heads at the boys in the band.

The lead guitarist bent over his strings, picking out the intro to another number. His brown hair parted in the middle and flopped over his forehead in two wings that hid his face, but the tension in his shoulders spoke of concentration. Behind him, a squarely built boy in a shiny leather jacket adjusted the amplifier as a long-haired drummer riffed in the corner.

She almost overlooked the other person in the garage. Pale and slender, the girl with shoe polish black hair slouched against one wall, her black-rimmed eyes slanted toward the lead guitarist.

The band had a groupie.

She cracked a reluctant smile and headed for the kitchen. Good lord, she was getting soft in her old age.

At midnight, after six renditions of "Wild Thing," she wasn't smiling.

At one a.m., during the longest drum solo she'd ever heard, she thought about the damage she could do to a drum set with a fireplace poker.

At one-thirty, she padded to the kitchen in her slippers and picked up the phone. "Hello, police?"

Three

Despite her late night, Lottie woke up early Sunday morning and went for a walk before breakfast. Collison was deserted at that hour, save for the birds and squirrels. Sunlight filtered through the trees, a warning of the August heat to come. A dog barked as she passed its yard. A woman in curlers scooped the Sunday paper off her doormat.

When she returned home, Ed Williams was watering the flower beds next door in a V-neck undershirt and plaid shorts. His black socks and leather sandals made Lottie smile.

"It was finally quiet last night," Ed said with a conspiratorial smile. "I've wanted to call the police on that boy all summer, but Martha won't let me. She says the poor kid deserves to have some fun."

Lottie raised her eyebrows. "Surely we all have rights."

"That's what they taught us in law school." He shrugged. "Neighbor relations are tricky, though. Sometimes you have to pick your battles."

"Speaking of tricky situations, have you heard from Patti? Does she have any plans to collect her mother's furniture?"

The lawyer shook his head. "I haven't been able to reach her. To be fair, she's got a full-time job and a baby to feed. She's probably pretty busy. While you're waiting, you might consider moving everything into a storage unit."

"I'd rather not. Would it be all right if I tried to call her?"

"It couldn't hurt." He set the hose on the ground. "Wait here. I've got her information in the house."

He hurried into the tidy bungalow and returned with an index card. "This is her current address and phone number, as far as I know."

"Thanks." She took the card and turned to go.

Ed cleared his throat. "Uh, Lottie?"

She stopped. "Yes?"

He looked a little sheepish. "Martha and I wondered if you'd like to go to church with us."

"Church?" She looked at him in surprise. "You mean today?"

He nodded. "We'll understand if you aren't interested. It's just that Helen used to ride along with us after David died. Martha misses that."

"Helen went to your church?"

He nodded. "David was on the elder board for years."

"I'll go. Can I meet you there?"

It was charming, Miranda thought, the way people knew each other in a town the size of Westmont. This was the way to spend a Sunday morning, eavesdropping on local gossip and sorting through auction lots in the shade of a dilapidated Victorian house.

"So, they're finally tearing down the Hoffman place," one man said as he kicked a tire on a Model T Ford in the driveway.

"It ain't fit to live in," said another. "Otto only used two rooms the past five years. Since they couldn't get him to move out, his sons closed off the upstairs and confined him to the first floor. That worked fine till a pipe froze last winter. Flooded the place pretty bad."

Miranda looked at the big shabby house with its boarded-up windows. It must have been beautiful in its day.

The first man shook his head. "He should have gone to the nursing home with his wife when her mind started to go."

"Makes sense to me," his companion replied. "Too bad she outlived him. How much do you think this wrench is worth?"

Miranda moved on to a table in the shade of an oak tree. She was sorting through a box of gadgets when another conversation caught her ear.

Two middle-aged women tidied a box of linens as they talked. "What'll we do with the stuff that doesn't sell?" said one.

"Some of it goes to the dump. Catholic Charities will pick up the rest."

The first one sighed. "Mother and Dad took such good care of their belongings. I hate to see them sold off to the highest bidder."

"Now, Annie, we've been through this." The second woman sounded impatient. "Everyone took the things that meant something to them. Nobody wanted the rest. And the money will go to keep Mother comfortable at the nursing home. Now, don't start crying again!"

Miranda moved on to the house, where an antique rocking chair caught her eye. She examined it from a little distance, noted the lot number and moved on, careful not to look interested. Near the rocker, a grimy pair of stained glass windows lay propped against the wall. With a little elbow grease, they'd be a breathtaking addition to Lottie's new room.

The rocker came up early when the auction started, and several bidders entered the fray. Miranda jumped in when others began to drop out, and won the day with a bid just under her limit. She tried the same technique with the windows, but ended up in a bidding war with someone on the other side of the crowd. Even though she went much higher than she should have, she finally had to admit defeat. At least she'd managed to drive the price up for the other guy.

Lottie pulled into the gravel lot of the little church south of town and parked the Mercedes between two dusty pickups. The brick building looked new and charmless, without stained glass or a steeple. Judging by the parking lot, there would be a sizable crowd.

She sat behind the wheel a moment to give her heartbeat time to slow down. She couldn't recall the last time she'd gone to church. She raised her eyes to the roof of the car. "This is for you, Helen. You have to give me credit for trying."

Ed and Martha waited at the door to usher her down the sanctuary aisle. They passed Sam and Jason Harms, and their reverently bowed heads made Lottie feel even more of a fraud.

Unlike the church of her childhood, this one had no organ, only an upright piano where a lady in a flowered dress played a prelude of hymn tunes. She was proficient at best, but just for this morning Lottie resolved not to criticize.

The first hymn brought on a flood of memories. She swallowed around a lump in her throat as the words swelled to the rafters:

"Blessed assurance! Jesus is mine.

Oh, what a foretaste of glory divine.

Heir of salvation, purchase of God,

Born of his spirit, washed in his blood."

For a moment she was a little girl again, standing between Pop and Helen in the old church at Westmont, and the old sense of security replaced her customary restlessness. Perhaps this wouldn't be so hard.

After the hymn, she settled into her seat, prepared to suffer through a dry sermon. A slight, unassuming man mounted the steps to the pulpit and greeted the congregation. "Please turn in your Bibles to Mark chapter two, verses one through twelve."

All around her, people found their places in Bibles they must have brought from home. Lottie felt like a school child, caught unprepared by the teacher. "Nobody told me," she wanted to say. "I'd have brought one if I'd known."

Martha slid her open Bible onto Lottie's lap and leaned over to share with her husband as the minister began to read. The story involved four friends who cut a hole in a roof and lowered their paralyzed friend down into a house where Jesus was teaching. Jesus saw the man, and said, "Son, your sins are forgiven."

The minister paused there to begin his sermon. He spoke in simple terms about Jesus, painting a picture of a humble, loving Savior with the power to forgive. Lottie warmed to the idea of a God who knew what she'd done and still loved her. She envied people like Helen and Parson, who could believe God existed.

The sermon ended, and Lottie returned Martha's Bible with a sense of relief. The congregation stood for the benediction, then came alive with movement and conversation. Martha placed a hand on her arm. "I hope you'll stay for coffee hour."

Lottie stared at her in dismay. "Oh, I'd better be going..."

Martha's grip was surprisingly firm. "This will only take a few minutes." She stepped into the center aisle, pulling Lottie behind her. "There are a few people I'd like you to meet."

They made slow progress toward the fellowship hall, impeded by regular churchgoers who wanted to meet the new lady. "Welcome," they said again and again. "We hope you'll come back."

One man asked if she was *the* Lottie Braun.

"I suppose I am," she replied with a bemused smile.

An elderly lady with pinkish-red hair stopped to say hello. "I'm Rosie Carlson," she said. "I saw you last night at Alicia's reception. Did you have a nice time?"

Lottie smiled. "I certainly did, Mrs. Carlson. It was lovely. And you?"

Rosie wrinkled her nose. "I'm never quite at home in the President's Mansion. It's too fancy for this old lunch lady. Say, I met your secretary yesterday. She lives right next door to me. She's a nice girl, and so pretty. What I wouldn't give to have those big brown eyes!" She laughed. "Of course, they'd look pretty strange in my pale Irish face."

Lottie smiled and nodded as Rosie's words flowed on. She was fully capable of snubbing the chatty lady, as she'd done last night to Mrs. Penworthy. But the memory of Nathan's jeering smile, and her own resolve to change her ways, held her back.

Rescue came in the form of Jason Harms, who set his hand on Mrs. Carlson's arm. "You don't mind if we borrow Miss Braun for a minute, do you? Dad has some business to discuss with her."

Rosie patted Jason's hand. "And I've got some business to discuss with you, young man. What do you mean, running over nice young women who are out getting exercise?"

"Well, I—"

"You must learn how to treat a girl if you're ever going to find one, young man."

As Rosie warmed to her subject, Jason looked as trapped as Lottie had felt. She was about to attempt an intervention when Sam stepped up next to her. "My son's got a way with old ladies, Miss Braun. Don't you worry about him." He glanced at her. "If you don't mind, I have a list of questions about that room addition. Jason was going to give you a call about them this afternoon, but this'll save us some time."

Lottie nodded. "Lead the way."

As she followed Sam to the door, she cast a look over her shoulder at Jason. He had managed to extricate himself from Mrs. Carlson and was talking with the minister. "Your son is a serious young man, isn't he?" she said to Sam's back.

"He can hold his own." Sam glanced back at his son and smiled. "That conversation will take a while."

Sam's pickup was not far from Lottie's car in the fast-emptying parking lot. He opened the driver's side door and pulled out a thick manila folder. "There are a few points I'd like to explain, if you've got a minute."

She squinted at him in the bright sunlight. "Shoot."

He propped one foot on the truck's running board and opened the folder. "How soon are you prepared to break ground?"

"As soon as possible."

"Good. Sooner the better, if we want to get the job done before winter."

Lottie watched with interest as Sam warmed to his subject. He talked with expertise about the time it took to let concrete footings cure and what might happen if the ground froze too early. She hadn't seen this side of him in their Neverland days. Back then he'd been an angry orphan forced to play in his brother's band. She'd been the enthusiastic one, eleven years old and in love with performing.

He caught her staring and cut his explanation short. "We'll get that bid to you tomorrow, Miss Braun. If you accept it, we'll start work as soon as possible."

Miss Braun. "In that case, you're hired."

He blinked. "You don't have our bid yet. You don't know how much this is going to cost."

"I know you'll give me good value."

"That's true, but—"

"I do have one condition."

"What's that?"

She caught his gaze and held it. "You tell me why you're acting like we don't know each other, Sammy."

He glanced away, across the gravel lot to the highway beyond. After a long silence, he turned his gaze back to hers. "Do we know each other?"

"What's that supposed to mean?" Really, she could throttle the man.

He shrugged. "You haven't been home in forty years. I figured I'd better not assume anything."

She stared at him in disbelief. "You could have assumed I'd know an old friend."

"When you didn't acknowledge your own sister?"

His words plopped like stones into a dark pond. "I see."

"Why did you stay away?"

She couldn't meet his eye. "Why do you think?"

"I never really believed they made a snob out of you at that music conservatory."

She glanced at his baffled expression. "Is that what Helen said?"

He shook his head. "I got that from the folks down at Westmont."

"I…I can see how it would look that way."

The tension left his voice. "I always thought there was more to it than that. I knew how much you loved Helen as a kid. I couldn't see you cutting her out of your life without good reason." He watched her, waiting for an answer she could not give.

She pulled at a loose thread on the hem of her blouse and wound it around her finger. She couldn't think about this without feeling nauseated. "Did Helen ever tell you why?"

"No. She and Parson wouldn't talk about the old days."

With an effort she met his measuring gaze. "Then I can't tell you either. You see that, don't you?" She had the sense she'd been measured and found lacking.

He gave a short nod. "It's none of my business, I guess. We'll work with you either way, of course."

She strove to match his impersonal tone. "Of course."

"We'll get a set of plans to you in a day or two."

"I'll be expecting them." She turned to go, her feet crunching on the gravel, then paused. "Sorry about calling you Sammy. I'll bet you outgrew it years ago."

He nodded. "Nobody's called me that since I was a kid."

Miranda pointed to her new purchase. "It's the rocking chair."

The clerk brought the chair to the table, and Miranda handed over her check. With one arm around its back and the other under the seat, she turned—and nearly bumped into Mitchell Harms.

"Whoa." He put up his hands in mock-defense. "You're getting revenge for yesterday, right?"

She couldn't help smiling. "What are you doing here?"

He held up his auction number. "Buying for the company. We use stuff from old houses in our projects."

Her smile widened. "That's awesome." She glanced behind him, then caught herself, but not before he noticed.

His eyes lit with fun. "Jase doesn't do auctions."

"Well, I…" She looked around, stuck for words. Nodding at the rocker she said, "I'd better get going. This weighs a ton."

His teasing look turned to concern. "That thing's as tall as you are. I hope you're parked nearby."

"I'll be fine." She didn't want to admit she'd left her car in an empty lot two blocks away.

Between last night's injuries and the weight of the rocker, Miranda had a harder time than she expected. After a block, her arms screamed for a rest. She lowered her burden to the ground and sat down, glad she'd bought a chair. She wasn't sure when she'd be ready to stand up again.

"Need a ride?"

Mitchell sat in the cab of a beat-up pickup truck, its back end full of auction items.

She gave a reluctant nod. "Are you sure you've got room for this?"

"I'll make room."

He jumped out and opened the tailgate. Before she could do more than stand, he'd lifted the rocker over his head and dumped it into the truck bed. "That oughta do it."

Miranda climbed in the cab. "You did well, from the looks of things."

"Got almost everything I wanted. There's a pair of stained glass windows back there that took some doing. Someone else wanted them pretty bad. Dad's going to have a fit about the price I paid, but they're worth it."

She suppressed a smile. So he was her unknown opponent. "I'm sure they are."

"I'm related to those folks," he continued. "Well, sort of. My dad was adopted by the owner's sister."

Miranda glanced over her shoulder. "It's a lovely old house. What a shame they're tearing it down."

He shrugged. "It should have been condemned ten years ago, if you want the truth. Uncle Otto was lucky the roof didn't cave in on him. Give me a new build any day."

"Then why do you remodel old homes?"

"I don't," he said quickly. "That's Dad and Jase's business. I just work there temporarily, helping them out with the legal side."

He was a young man on the move, or at least he wanted her to think so. She pointed. "Here's my car."

Even with Mitchell's help she couldn't wedge the rocker into her Corolla. After several failed attempts, he offered to carry it home in the pickup and deliver it later.

As she parked behind her townhouse, she felt a fresh wave of gratitude for Mitchell's generosity. She locked the car and walked briskly up the path between the two buildings. "Hi, Mrs. Carlson."

Rosie looked up from sweeping her porch. "Hello, honey. How was the goulash?"

♫

Lottie drove home with a lighter heart. She and Sam had reached an understanding that, while not warm, would at least allow them to work together reasonably well. She gathered from the distant way Jason addressed her that he was in the dark about the Neverland days. She was willing to bet the young man had never even seen his dad behind a drum set.

Too bad.

She passed another drummer as she rolled down the alley to the garage. In fact, the entire garage band slumped on the back steps of the house across the way, four half-grown kids in full summer boredom. The lead guitarist sat on the steps, bangs over his eyes, one skinny arm draped around the black-haired waif. Behind him, the bass player leaned against the house, while the long-haired drummer kicked a hacky-sack around the yard.

An unfamiliar sense of remorse welled up in her when she saw the little group. Someone had spoiled their fun, and that someone was Lottie. What would Helen do at a time like this?

The answer came in a flash. Helen would give them food.

Excited by this idea, she hurried around the end of the garage and nearly tripped over a giant orange cat sunning itself on the warm brick path. The cat yowled in protest, but didn't run away. Lottie squatted next to it and held out a hand for inspection. "What's your name, big fella?"

The cat blinked and nudged her hand. When she scratched behind its ears, it began to purr.

"Marmalade," she said softly. "You look just like a big jar of marmalade."

A minute later she stood and stretched, and made her way more slowly to the house, with Marmalade following behind. He rubbed against her ankle as she unlocked the kitchen door, then sat and looked up at her with pitiful eyes. Anyone could see the big cat wasn't starving, but Lottie poured a bowl of milk for him, just in case.

She stood on the porch for a moment, watching Marmalade lap up the milk. Across the alley, the kids from the band still sat, watching their friend bounce that silly beanbag on his foot. She stepped into the kitchen and opened a cupboard. What did she have that would brighten their day?

A few minutes later she stepped off the porch and made her way across the yard, a peace offering in her hand. When she reached the alley she stopped and called, "Hello."

The lead guitarist looked up.

She stepped forward. "I thought I'd come meet my fellow musicians." She'd rehearsed that line. "I'm Lottie Braun."

No reaction.

She tried again. "I'm a concert pianist. I've heard you practicing your...music."

The drummer dropped his hacky-sack and left it in the dirt.

"I live behind you?" She felt like the new kid at school.

The guitarist leaned back on his hands. "Yeah?"

Lottie held out the box she'd taken from her pantry. "You guys look hungry. I brought you these."

He took the box and gave it a puzzled stare. "Thanks."

She half-turned to go, then stopped. "Oh, and sorry about last night. I just couldn't take the noise anymore."

Nice job, Lottie, she thought as she marched back across her yard. That's exactly what Helen would have done.

A buoyant sense of satisfaction carried her into the kitchen to start her own lunch. As she gathered the components for a bologna and cheese sandwich, she couldn't help stealing glances out the window. She was spreading mayonnaise on white bread when a new thought pricked her balloon.

The kids didn't look happy.

Rather than open the box of wheat crackers, the guitarist had thrown them into the bushes. As Lottie watched, they got up and plodded into Tommy's house.

"How's that for ingratitude?" Lottie said around a bite of sandwich.

The kids' odd behavior bothered her, but she knew better than to dwell on it. She set to work in the sewing room, refining her lesson plans for the first week of classes. The built-in table that housed Helen's sewing machine was not an ideal desk, but it made up for lack of space with an odd sense of inspiration. Helen's creative spirit seemed to hover in that room, with its drawers of patterns and the framed examples of her work on its wall. One of those little framed dresses belonged to Lottie, a remnant of a happier time, when Helen had been both her mother and her sister.

Around four o'clock someone knocked at the kitchen door. A man in a delivery uniform stood outside. "Pizza for Lottie Braun?"

She gave him a blank stare. "I don't understand. I didn't order this."

The man checked his order slip. "This is the right address, lady."

She looked at the flat cardboard box in his hand. It did smell good. "I…I guess I'll take it."

The second pizza arrived fifteen minutes later, from a different restaurant. "What is the meaning of this?" she asked.

The man shrugged. "I don't know, lady. I'm just the delivery guy."

She met the third delivery man in the alley. "Don't even get out of your car," she said firmly. "I didn't order a pizza, and I won't pay for it."

He was sympathetic. "Looks like you've been pranked, ma'am. If I were you, I'd call all the pizza places and tell them not to fill those orders."

Marmalade joined her as he drove away. She stood with the cat rubbing against her legs, and glared at the house across the alley. So much for making peace.

She got out the Yellow Pages and made her phone calls, but not fast enough to keep one last pizza man from ringing her doorbell. "Large pizza with olives and extra anchovies?"

She took one whiff, paid the man, and had him deliver it to the band.

The house was quiet after that, but Lottie couldn't settle down to work again. She packed up her materials with an exasperated sigh and headed to the kitchen for a piece of pizza. She might not have ordered the darned stuff, but she wasn't going to waste it.

She was just about to bite into her second piece when the front doorbell rang. She narrowed her eyes. A joke was a joke, but this had gone on long enough. She charged through the house, bent on venting her anger, and swung open the door.

A young woman in overalls stood on the porch. She held, not a pizza box, but a metal pan full of brownies. "I…I can come back later," she said in a timid voice.

All the anger whooshed out of Lottie, leaving her deflated. "No, of course not. Come in." She stood back to let the girl enter. "You live next door, don't you?"

The girl pushed a wisp of red-gold hair out of her eyes. "Well, sort of. I'm living there temporarily while I help my grandpa. I'm Jessica McCall." She held out the brownies. "I made these for you."

Lottie drank in the scent of the still-warm pan and paused. The brownies smelled a little odd. She met Jessica's hopeful gaze and smiled. "How thoughtful." A chuckle escaped her. "These would have come in handy earlier this afternoon."

Jessica's smile deepened. "You mean with the kids?"

Startled, Lottie glanced up. "The kids?"

"I saw you talking to them from my kitchen window. It wasn't hard to guess what happened when the pizzas started showing up. I've pulled that prank before."

Lottie groaned. "Payback for calling the police on them last night. They probably think I'm a scary old lady who yells at kids to stay off her lawn."

Jessica laughed. "Grandpa used to do that."

Lottie gazed thoughtfully at her pretty neighbor. "Won't you come in and sit down? I could use some company." She led the way to the kitchen and set down the pan. "Would you like a brownie?"

The girl hesitated. "All right," she said finally.

"How about a glass of water to go with it?"

"Sounds good." Jessica plopped onto a chrome kitchen chair and looked around. "Cool house. I wish my grandpa's place was this nice."

"My sister was a wonderful housekeeper."

"Mrs. Parker was your sister?"

"Yes." Lottie set the snack on the table and sat across from her guest.

"She was a nice lady." Jessica sipped her water. "She always made Patti play with me when I was little, even though Patti was older."

"That sounds like Helen."

"Patti didn't want me around, of course, so it didn't go very well. I guess it's the thought that counts."

"Adults can be pretty tone-deaf when it comes to children. Look at me and the kids across the alley."

"They're all right, once you get to know them." Jessica bit into her brownie and made a face. "These are awful," she said with her mouth full.

Lottie took a bite, chewed slowly and willed herself to swallow. "They're not so bad," she told the crestfallen girl. "What's your secret ingredient?"

"Wheat germ." Jessica wrinkled her nose. "I guess healthy brownies were a dumb idea."

Lottie rushed to reassure her guest. "I don't know anything about baking, but when I try a new piano technique, it usually takes me a few tries to get it right."

"So you think I should try again?"

"Yes, I do. And bring me a sample of the next batch."

"Thanks." Jessica crossed the kitchen and set her glass in the sink. "Sorry about the brownies. I'll throw them out at home."

"No, leave them here," Lottie said quickly. "They're bound to come in handy somehow."

Lottie walked her guest to the door. "I'll bring your pan back when the brownies are gone."

"That's fine." Jessica stepped onto the porch. "My feelings won't be hurt if you end up throwing them out." She pointed to an envelope on the doormat. "Looks like you dropped some mail."

Lottie picked up the envelope, and frowned. It was long and white, with "LOTTIE BRAUN" on the front in block letters. No address, no stamp. She carried it to the sewing room and used a stitch ripper to slit open the top. She shook the contents onto the desk and gasped. "What in the world?"

Four

Ten-Year-Old Wins Talent Contest.

In the fading light from the sewing room window Lottie re-read the *Des Moines Register* article for the hundredth time. There it was in black and white, a short account of Charlotte Brown playing "Flight of the Bumblebee" to win the big prize. And at the bottom, a faded picture of Charlotte, a thin child with pale braids and a smocked dress.

Charlotte Brown. Lottie's stage name for three years. The name she had shed like a snake skin when it became inconvenient. The name that saved her in the end.

"From this point on, you're Lottie." Aunt Eva had said as she put her niece on the train to Ohio. "Charlotte belongs to the past."

Charlotte had traveled with the Neverland Orchestra. *Charlotte* had run off to have fun instead of babysitting a sweet little boy. *Charlotte* had climbed that tree and crawled back in the window too late to do any good. Charlotte Brown, killer, boarded the train in Los Angeles... and Lottie Braun, innocent Iowa farm girl, stepped off.

Charlotte had been dead a long time now. Once in a while the rumors surfaced, especially when she performed in the South, but they were easy to squash. A confident denial usually did the trick. There wasn't a lot of proof the little girl had ever existed, and none of it pointed conclusively to Lottie. She examined the photo once more. That pale, thin face might belong to any Depression-era child.

Someone had made the connection, or at least a lucky guess.

41

Lottie held the envelope under Helen's sewing lamp. The return address was some kind of business logo made of linked initials. O.O.? D.O.? O.D.? It was unreadable.

She sat up straight and rubbed her aching neck. Who would go to such lengths to stir up trouble? Nathan Bartholomew? He knew where she lived. Rhonda Kennedy? Not clever enough. She closed her eyes. There was one other possibility.

First thing tomorrow morning she'd have a talk with Cal Jefferson.

Miranda poured water into the coffee maker's reservoir and flipped the switch. In ten minutes she'd have a pot of hot, fragrant brew. That first cup of coffee almost made it worth getting up in the morning. She opened Lottie's refrigerator to reach for the cream, and the smell of cold pizza hit her nostrils.

"What on earth?" She leaned down to peek inside. Sure enough, two flat cardboard boxes took up all the room on one shelf. She looked up as Lottie walked into the kitchen. "Did you have a pizza party yesterday?"

"No." Lottie glanced toward the refrigerator. "I had a craving for it, that's all."

For two large pizzas? "Did you have a craving for brownies, too?"

"They were a gift from my next-door neighbor." Lottie gave Miranda an admiring look. "You're all dressed up. Are you expecting visitors today?"

Miranda glanced down at her high-necked dress and heels. "This is how I always dress for work."

Lottie smiled. "I appreciate your professionalism, but it's probably not necessary if you're going to be alone all day."

"But I…" She liked dressing up. It made her feel less like an impostor.

"Think it over." Lottie handed her a scrap of paper. "Ed Williams gave me Patti's phone number. I called her yesterday, but got no answer. Would you please try today?"

"What do you want me to tell her?"

"Ask if she's made plans to take care of her mother's things." Lottie paused on her way out the door. "Oh, and help yourself to the pizza. It's really rather good."

Lottie stuck her head around Cal Jefferson's door. "Got a minute?"

He put up a finger and continued writing. "Have a seat. I'll be right with you."

She settled into a chair on the visitor's side of the desk and studied the pictures on the wall. A signed photo of Charlie Parker caught her eye and she leaned closer to examine it.

"You like that?" The pride in Cal's voice was unmistakable.

She nodded. "Where'd you get it? You're too young to have seen him yourself."

"My daddy played trombone in the Kansas City jazz scene back in the day. He gave me that picture when I first took up the saxophone. Said I should shoot for the best."

"Good advice."

"I wrote my dissertation on Bird and the development of bebop." He leaned forward in his chair. "Did you ever meet the man, Miss Braun?"

"I never had the pleasure. If I have my time line right, I was at the Dayton Conservatory during his heyday." She laced her fingers together. "We didn't play jazz."

His eyes were bright. "Not even for fun? Outside school?"

Her voice was light. "I'm surprised you think anyone could play jazz just for fun. It takes years of serious study, doesn't it, professor?"

He laughed. "You got me there. What about swing, or big band?"

She raised her eyebrows. "No. Did you drop by my house yesterday?"

His eyes narrowed. "Now, that's a strange question."

She regarded him steadily. "Did you?"

"Miss Braun, I don't even know where you live." His voice was soft, bitter. "Why? You missing some valuables?"

The question surprised her so she almost laughed. "Nothing's missing, I assure you." She handed him the newspaper clipping. "Someone

43

dropped this on my porch last night. Do you recognize it?"

Cal took the clipping. "Ten-Year-Old Wins Talent Contest." He glanced at Lottie. "Is this you?"

"You first," Lottie said. "Is it yours?"

He scanned the article. "I never saw it before."

She plucked the paper out of his fingers. "The other night you asked if my name was Charlotte, like the girl in the clipping. Why?"

"I've heard stories. Folks I interviewed for my dissertation talked about a little girl who could really swing on piano. She supposedly ran around with a two-bit band during the war." He shrugged. "Charlotte Brown, Lottie Braun. You have to admit the names are pretty close."

She kept her voice soft, flat. "'A little girl who could really swing.' That's pretty flattering. If it was me, why would I deny it?"

He chuckled. "Look, I don't have an agenda. I just wanted to know."

She slipped the clipping into her pocket. "Well, now you do. And if you happen to know who left me this little gift, you can tell them, too."

Lottie took the stairs to the third floor and stood at the top, waiting for her breathing to slow. "Two-bit swing band," she murmured. "I wonder what Johnny would say about that?"

Johnny Columbus, co-founder of the Neverland Dance Orchestra. He'd been like a brother to her. Wayward and unreliable, and oh so much fun. No one in his band ever made the big time. No one but Lottie.

"Two-bit," she said again. "Ouch."

She unlocked her office and slipped the newspaper clipping into a file folder. Cal seemed to believe her, and that was a relief, but she still didn't know who had left the letter on her porch. She frowned. "I could use a little help here, Helen. Who should I trust?"

The squeak of crepe-soled shoes told her she had company. Rhonda Kennedy stepped out of the stairwell, looking less flustered than she had on Saturday. "Katherine wants to see us," she said, then turned and went back the way she'd come. Lottie followed more slowly. The fight could not start until both sides were present.

When she reached Katherine's office, Rhonda was mid-tirade. "...I worked my butt off for five years with that woman, and did I complain?

No. I deserve some kind of award, and I want that office."

Katherine held up a hand and Rhonda subsided into silence. Turning to Lottie, Katherine said, "I didn't realize you had taken over Alicia's office. Can you tell me how that happened?"

"Elaine Woodward handed me the key," Lottie said. "I had no idea I shouldn't take it."

Katherine looked pained. "This mix-up is my fault. Elaine is new around here. I should have given her more guidance about your office. I'm sorry, but I did promise Rhonda she could have the one you were given. You two will have to trade places."

The triumph on Rhonda's face was ludicrous. "We'll switch today."

Lottie squared her shoulders. She'd been dealt harder blows. How bad could the other office be?

♫

Miranda spent the morning arranging travel for Lottie's fall engagements. This was one of her favorite tasks. She kept a Rolodex full of contact information for airlines and hotel chains and enjoyed chatting up the booking agents to get the best deal for Lottie's money.

Living in Collison added a piece to the travel puzzle as the nearest decent airport was Chicago O'Hare, four hours away. One commercial flight per day from Collison to O'Hare wasn't nearly enough. Lottie would end up with long layovers unless Miranda could come up with a solution.

She tried Patti's phone number mid-morning, but nobody answered. Not surprising, since Patti worked full-time. She tried again an hour later with the same result.

At lunch time, she bypassed the pizza in favor of the salad she'd brought from home. She sat on the shady front porch, munching on cucumber slices and reading *House Beautiful* magazine.

"Hello, neighbor." Martha Williams waved from her front porch next door.

Miranda waved back. "The brownies look wonderful," she called.

Martha looked confused. "Brownies?"

"Lottie said you brought her brownies."

"It wasn't me."

Miranda thought a moment. "Come to think of it, she must have used the word *neighbor*. I assumed she meant you. Sorry."

Martha walked across the yard and joined Miranda on the porch. "I understand why you were confused. I can't think of anyone else in this neighborhood who has the time to bake for a new neighbor. When my kids were young, this street was full of young families. Now anymore, seems like I'm the only person at home during the day."

Miranda nodded toward the house to Lottie's north. "I see a girl at that house sometimes. Maybe she baked the brownies."

"Who, Jessie?" Martha sounded disapproving. "I don't think so. With an upbringing like hers, I doubt if she knows how to bake. Her mother was always a little wild."

"I see." Miranda didn't, but she didn't want to ask more questions.

Luckily, she didn't have to. "The house belongs to Jessie's grandfather. He had a heart attack a few months ago, and Jessie came down to take care of him."

"That's nice."

Martha grimaced. "I guess it looks that way. Ed and I think she's taking advantage of her grandpa. He went straight from the hospital to the nursing home a few weeks ago, but Jessie is still here, and we're pretty sure she's not paying rent."

Miranda felt a little sorry for the absent Jessie. From what she'd seen, the red-haired girl looked fairly nice. She had no idea how to stop this neighborly gossip session, so the mailman's cheerful whistle came as a welcome distraction. "Looks like the mail is here."

Martha smiled at the mailman. "Hi, Bob. I'll take our mail and save you a trip."

"Thank you, ma'am." The man in blue handed each woman a stack of envelopes and went on his way, whistling.

Martha started down the porch steps. "You tell Lottie we're here for her. Anything she needs, she can count on us."

"Will do."

Miranda took her bowl to the kitchen and set it in the sink. She paused to sniff the brownies and wrinkled her nose.

She grabbed the pile of mail and headed upstairs, sorting as she went: Two pieces of junk mail. A newsletter from a children's hospital in North Carolina. A letter from a D. Davenport. Probably a fan.

She threw out the junk mail and set aside the newsletter for Lottie to read at her leisure. Lottie received similar mailings from children's hospitals all over the country, and Miranda had learned to treat them with care.

The letter from D. Davenport proved interesting.

Dear Ms. Braun,

I've spent months trying to contact you. Congratulations on your watertight contracts and excellent lawyers. They have made my job much more difficult. Thanks to your appointment to Collison College, I finally know your address.

You may have heard of me. I have written a number of well-received biographies about music superstars, most notably Elvis Presley. I am currently working on the background information for a book about you and would like to talk with you at your earliest convenience about the information I have discovered.

I would prefer to have your cooperation with this project. However, with or without your input, be advised I will go ahead with my research.

Please contact me as soon as possible.

Donna Davenport

Miranda read the letter twice before she set it aside. Donna Davenport was a tell-all celebrity biographer and a regular on the talk show circuit. Why would she be interested in a concert pianist? No doubt Lottie would give her lawyer an earful over that one.

Lottie stared in dismay at the windowless room. No wonder Rhonda wanted to change offices. More of a glorified practice room, it was only big enough for one console piano, a desk, and a bookcase. Now she understood what the fight was about. A piano professor could barely function with only one piano.

The tricky part about moving in was figuring out which books to keep in the inadequate office and which to take home. She could count on Miranda to find a place for everything and to deliver a book at a moment's notice if need be, but the lack of space still irked her. She unpacked her most essential materials and set the other boxes next to the door.

The ancient desk chair creaked as Lottie sat down. She reached for the telephone, and the chair gave a miserable moan. "Hello, Miranda. I need to give you my new office extension." She leaned over to check the dial. "It's 2585. All right? How's everything going?"

"Interesting," Miranda said. "You got a letter from Donna Davenport, the author. Do you know who she is?"

"Not really. Can you read the letter to me?" Miranda complied, and Lottie gave a low whistle. "That is interesting. I'll check in with my lawyers this afternoon. Thanks."

She hung up and stared at the receiver for a moment. "Donna Davenport." She reached into her book bag and retrieved the envelope with the clipping inside. Sure enough, the return address read, "D.D."

She left a message for the lawyer who handled her professional matters, and finally settled down to get some work done.

At lunch time, Lottie pulled a foil-wrapped packet of cold pizza out of her desk drawer and spread it in front of her on the desk. She was good and tired of pizza, but she was a child of the Depression. She could not throw away perfectly good food. Her mouth was full of pepperoni when Rhonda pushed the door open as far as the box of books behind it would allow and set a folder on the desk. "I've divided up the private piano lessons. You'll have two of Alicia's students, as well as your two Carolina transfers. The freshmen don't take privately until second semester."

Lottie swallowed. "Only four students?"

Rhonda looked down her pudgy nose. "The other six wanted to take from me."

"I guess we should discuss the group lessons, then."

Rhonda opened the folder and pointed at a schedule. "With all my private lessons, I'll only have time for the Tuesday morning group. You'll have to take the Thursday and Friday groups."

Lottie frowned. "I have several weekend performances this semester, so I'll be traveling on a lot of Fridays. I do have time on Tuesdays, if you'd like to trade for the Friday group."

Rhonda looked irritated. "Sorry, no. I guess I can sub for the Friday group when you're out of town."

"All right." Lottie gathered the remains of her lunch. "Is there anything else?"

"You've been assigned to the Women's Auxiliary Committee. They plan certain social events throughout the year and put together care packages for finals week. That sort of thing." Rhonda smiled sweetly. "It's a good place for a new professor. You'll meet all kinds of people."

Committee work? Inwardly Lottie cringed. She was much better at solo tasks. "All right."

Rhonda's smile was smug. "That's it then. Good luck."

No sooner had Miranda settled in for the afternoon than the front doorbell rang.

"Drat," she muttered under her breath. "I don't have time to chat with Martha again."

She considered pretending she wasn't home, but the Toyota in the alley gave her away. With a last regretful look at her desk, she turned and made her way back downstairs.

Jason Harms stood at the door. "I guess you heard we got the contract."

She stared at him. "No, I didn't."

"Ms. Braun sealed the deal with my dad at church yesterday." He held up a roll of paper. "I have blueprints."

"Already? Isn't this pretty fast?"

"We're efficient," he said, then added more truthfully, "Actually, my dad's really fired up about this project for some reason."

She stood aside, interested in spite of herself. "You can spread those out on the dining room table."

He strode across the entry hall and through the living room. "We've come up with a plan to add the room to the side of the house, instead of straight back. It will fit better on the lot and look more like a natural extension of the house. My brother is at the county clerk's office now, checking the easements to make sure we can do it." He glanced over his shoulder as he spread his drawings on the table. "Do you need to take notes for your boss?"

"I'll remember." She tilted her head, her eyes on the drawing. "I wondered if the lot was deep enough for what Lottie wanted to do. It makes a lot of sense to bring it out to the side."

He pointed to the sewing room. "All we lose is this little room here, which she shouldn't miss. It becomes the entrance to the music room."

"You're remodeling the bathroom, too." She glanced up and caught his watchful gaze. "I like it."

His face relaxed into a faint smile. "Good."

She pointed at the plan. "Have you considered reorienting the bathroom to the end of the hall, instead of its current location?"

"Moving all that plumbing costs money."

"But it saves space. In a house this age, you'll probably have to replace the pipes anyway."

He frowned at her. "Who's designing this thing, you or me?"

"You are, of course." She glanced away. "I'll show these plans to Lottie when she gets home."

"You do that." He rolled up the drawings. "If she wants to make any changes, you can leave a message for me at the office."

"Okay. Um, thanks for driving me home on Saturday."

"No problem. Do you often run alone?"

She felt her defenses go up. "Are you going to lecture me about safety?"

He shot her a look she couldn't quite read. "No."

"Because I've got a rape whistle on my key chain."

His lips twitched. "I'll keep that in mind."

♫

Miranda met Lottie at the door when she arrived home in the afternoon. "Jason Harms brought over some blueprints for the addition. They're very good."

Lottie held up one finger. "Hold on. I've got groceries in the car. Come help me bring them in."

Miranda followed her boss down the brick path to the garage. When they reached the alley, the kids were setting up their instruments in the garage across the way. Miranda nudged Lottie. "Looks like you're in for a night of it. Maybe this would be a good time to talk to them."

"Not now." Lottie started for the house, her arms full. "I need to figure out what to say."

Miranda watched her walk away. Lottie always knew what to say. Didn't she?

"Did you reach Patti today?" Lottie asked as they reached the kitchen.

"I tried, but nobody answered." Miranda set her bags on the counter. "How was work?"

"Complicated. Rhonda Kennedy is finally home from Europe, and the first thing she did was demand that we trade offices. The one I had to take is tiny and unworkable."

"Don't they have anything else you could use?"

Lottie shook her head. "The P.A.B. is bursting at the seams. I brought home some files to leave in your office and a box of books that won't fit on the shelf."

Miranda shook her head in disgust. "How can they treat you that way?"

"I'm low man on the totem pole."

"Hardly."

Lottie knelt to fill a lower cupboard with cereal boxes. "I've also been volunteered for some kind of social committee that sounds like a lot of extra work. I'll probably be bringing some of it to you for help."

"That's why you pay me." Miranda stuck a bag of peas in the freezer. "Sounds like you'll be busy."

Lottie looked up from her seat on the floor. "Miranda, you were in college not that long ago."

"Yes?"

"Do you think college kids are good judges of character?"

"Most of them. Why?"

"I'd bet money Rhonda Kennedy has cherry-picked the most promising students for her private lessons. I don't think they were given any say in the matter."

"Why would she do that?"

"If all the students excel, the teacher's reputation is boosted. Nobody looks at how gifted they were in the first place. I guess I'm wondering if the students will see through her."

Miranda thought this over. "The more perceptive ones will. Do you mind working with less gifted students?"

Lottie leaned back against the cupboards. "I don't know. I've never done it before. As an artist-in-residence, I worked with the best of the best."

"I wish you luck, then. Let me know how I can help." Miranda picked up a box of dry cat food. "Where do you want this?"

"I'll take it." Lottie whisked it into the cereal cupboard and closed the door. "Now. Let's see those plans."

Miranda talked her through the proposal, pointing out the advantages of using the sewing room as the entrance and enlarging the bathroom. "Jason has been very thorough," she said, surprised at how involved she felt.

"I said to put the room out the back, not on the side."

"But there's a lot to be said for building to the side…"

"This will never do."

Startled, Miranda took a step back. "You don't like it?"

"I hate it." She stabbed a finger at the plans. "I never said they could take out the sewing room."

"But they surveyed the lot, and there isn't enough room to extend it out the back. You're too close to the alley. There's more space in the side yard."

Lottie pressed her lips together. "Someone out there must be clever enough to do what I want. I guess I'll have to reopen the bidding."

Miranda stared at her employer. "I…I'll talk with Harms and Sons tomorrow, I guess."

"Good." Lottie said. "Then that's it for today." When Miranda hesitated she added, "Go home."

Disappointment stole Lottie's appetite. She hated to admit how much she wanted to work with Sam. Not only was he trustworthy, he was also a direct tie to Helen and Parson and the life they'd all once lived. But she couldn't give up the sewing room, not for anything.

Dinner turned to sawdust in her mouth, so she stuck her plate in the refrigerator and escaped to the garden. Hard work was the best antidote for depressing thoughts.

She grabbed a trowel and a pair of gardening gloves from the garage and set to work thinning out a massive patch of mint behind the garage. She knew it was mint by its leaves and its scent, but she knew it required taming because Aunt Cora had told her so. It was odd, the scraps of knowledge she retained from her childhood.

Marmalade found her kneeling in the mint and sat next to her to wash his paws. She reached over to scratch between his ears and was rewarded with his jet engine purr. "You're a simple old soul, aren't you, big fella?"

He bumped his head against her hand.

She stood up. "I know what you want. Wait right here."

In the fading light from the kitchen window, she poured a helping of cat chow into a bowl and added a bit of milk. Why not spoil the old boy a little?

When she returned, Jessica had joined the cat on the porch steps. She nodded at the bowl of food. "So you're the reason he's stuck around so long."

Lottie set it down. "I can't be the only one who feeds him. Not at that size."

"You're right. I feed him, too." Jessica raised her sweet blue gaze to Lottie's face. "He's a pretty good listener."

She looked so unhappy that Lottie found herself saying, "I'm a good listener, too."

As soon as the words were out, she regretted them, but it was too late. Jessica took the invitation to pour out her troubles. "I've been trying to fix up my grandpa's house and get it on the market. He went from the hospital to a nursing home after his stroke, and I'm the only one left to take care of things." She sighed. "The house has big problems. It needs new faucets and the roof leaks. I'm not sure who to talk to about it all, and even if I did, Grandpa couldn't pay much."

The girl's troubles were bigger than Lottie imagined. "If you don't mind my saying so, aren't you awfully young to deal with such a mess?"

"I'm twenty-five." Jessica sighed. "But I do look young. That's part of the problem. People don't take me seriously."

Lottie thought this over while she scratched Marmalade behind his ear. Sam's advice would come in handy in a case like this, but they weren't really on speaking terms. "Have you met Ed Williams?" she said finally. "He's a lawyer, so at least he could advise you on your options."

"You mean the guy who lives over there?" Jessica nodded toward the Williams' house. "I don't think he'd help me."

"Why not?"

"Mr. and Mrs. Williams never liked me much." Jessica grabbed the porch rail and pulled herself to her feet. "Anyway, I should go."

"First, let me give back your pan." Lottie went into the kitchen and came back with the pan. "Have you made any more brownies?"

Jessica shook her head. "I can't afford to buy the ingredients. Well, I'll see you later."

Lottie watched her neighbor stroll across the lawn, her red-gold curls floating in the breeze. She looked deceptively delicate, but Lottie admired her pluck.

Five

 ainy days were the bane of the construction business. With their scheduled job at a standstill, all the permanent employees of Harms and Sons crowded into the tiny business office. Sam poured a fresh cup of coffee and resigned himself to a day of paperwork. Out of the corner of his eye, he watched his oldest son slam down the phone. "What's wrong, Jase?"

Jason wheeled around. "That was Miranda Charles. You know the addition for the Parker house? Well, the Great Lottie Braun rejected our plan. She wants to start the bidding all over again."

Mitch chimed in from his perch on the bookkeeper's desk. "Too bad! How will we meet up with the lovely Miranda?"

"There's no need to be sarcastic, son." Sam poured a packet of sugar into his cup and picked up a stir stick. "Did she say why?"

"She wants to keep the little sewing room intact. It doesn't make sense, Dad. That's a terrible space. If she wants a sewing room, I'll build her a better one upstairs."

Sam pictured the cramped room tucked in behind the stairs. On Saturday he'd noticed Lottie's things laid out on Helen's sewing table. "Give it a little time, Jase. Maybe she'll come around."

Jason snorted. "Patience is your virtue, not mine."

"Well, it's time to change that. You won't last long in this business if you pick fights with your customers."

"She won't be our customer if she re-opens the bidding." Jason drummed his fingers on his desk. "How much time are we talking about?"

Sam squinted at the rain on the window. "A day or two, at least. Meanwhile, the rain's not supposed to let up until tonight. This would be a good day for you to do a little business at the lumberyard." This was his code phrase for taking a few hours off. He worried about the boy's long days.

Jason reached for a roll of blueprints. "Later, Dad."

Mitch jumped off the desk. "I'll go to the lumberyard."

"Don't move, Mitch." Sam pointed at his younger son. "I need you to pull a plat map for the Anderson job. You can go down to City Hall, rain or no rain."

♫

Lottie caught Katherine at the coffee pot. "I'd like to talk to you about my office. It really is unsuitable as a piano studio."

Katherine held up a hand. "There's nothing I can do. I know you've only been here a short while, Lottie, so you wouldn't know what a space crunch we're in. This old building isn't big enough for the job it has to do. We all feel the pinch."

"Pinch?" Lottie chuckled. "That office is more like a vise grip."

Her little joke went unappreciated. "Frankly, I'm tired of hearing about that office," Katherine said. "Why don't you and Rhonda work together to share the one decent office allotted to the piano program? Have you thought about doing that?" She walked away before Lottie could form a reply.

Lottie climbed the stairs to the third floor, her cheeks burning from Katherine's unjustified reproof. If there was one thing she couldn't stand, it was a chronic complainer. To imply that she was one was unfair. Rain drummed on the skylights as she crossed the atrium, reinforcing her mood.

She fumed until she reached the detested office. There, with the door closed, she gave herself a talking-to. "You've worked in closer spaces than this, my girl," she muttered. "Planes. Trains. Student apartments shared by four girls. You're a Braun and a Hoffman. You can make this work." That last part sounded more like Pop than Lottie. She liked it when his stubborn Iowa philosophy made its way into her thoughts.

She looked around with a critical eye. What the room lacked in space, it made up for in ceiling height. The standard-issue desk took up more room than necessary, too. If she replaced it with something smaller, another piano would fit next to the first one. The P.A.B. might have no extra space, but it had plenty of pianos.

After a phone call to Miranda, she walked down a flight and asked Cal about finding another piano. He directed her to the group practice room. "There are always a few too many in there." He added, "I can't believe Rhonda stuck you with the closet. You've got to watch that woman like a hawk."

Lottie put her head around Katherine's office door. "Will there be a problem if I change some things in my office? I want to hang shelves."

For the first time, Katherine's smile looked genuine. "Be my guest."

Miranda arrived with a tape measure and a lot of questions. "How wide do the shelves need to be? Painted or stained? Plain metal brackets or decorative?" She was just as thorough with the desk. When she finished, she measured the space and filled a legal pad with notes. "This will take a little time," she said. "I assume I can use the tools I saw in the garage?"

Lottie shook her head. "They're not mine. They belong to my niece."

Miranda looked blank. "I can't do anything without tools."

"Buy what you need. I own a house now. I should probably have some tools of my own."

Her assistant smiled. "So you'll be doing your own home repairs?"

"Not as long as I have you. You're turning out to be very talented."

Miranda regretted changing into jeans and tennies. Stilettos would have been helpful to reach the boards she wanted. "Why do lumber yards always put the warped ones within reach and the straight ones up above?" she grumbled under her breath. She picked up her red umbrella and went in search of help.

Down the row stood two men in canvas aprons, absorbed in conversation. They watched her approach with a touch of resentment. "Can one of you help me reach some boards?" she asked.

The older man followed her back to the two-by-eights and pointed to the stack on the floor. "There's plenty to choose from right here, ma'am."

"They're warped. I want to see the ones up above."

He scratched the back of his head. "The thing of it is, we don't usually sell small lots."

"Are you saying you won't sell me a couple of boards?"

He wilted under her glare. "I'm just saying we usually don't."

"So noted." She pointed. "Now, about that upper stack."

Reluctantly he sauntered away to find a ladder. A minute later he returned and set his foot on the first rung. She stopped him. "No sense bringing me boards I don't want. I'll climb up and check them myself."

"That's not our policy…" he began, but she'd already reached the upper stack.

It took three tries, but she finally found what she was looking for. Climbing down the ladder, she said, "Skip the first two. I'll take the third, fourth and fifth boards."

He looked at her warily. "You want me to get them now?"

"If you won't, I'll get someone who will."

With a hefty sigh, the man climbed the ladder and pointed. "You want me to start here?"

"The next one down."

As Miranda watched him work the boards loose, someone came up the aisle and stopped beside her. She turned to find Jason Harms looking at her curiously. "Mind if I ask what you're up to?"

She returned her gaze to the man on the ladder. "Building a set of shelves for Lottie's office."

He looked interested. "Hold up a sec, Hank."

The man on the ladder paused. "This lady work for you, Jase?" Miranda noticed the respectful change of tone.

Jason squinted upward. "No, I work for her. Or I'd like to, anyway."

He turned to Miranda. "Let me build those shelves."

"I don't need help. I know what I'm doing."

"I'm sure you do, but if you give the job to me, maybe I can win your boss's trust."

She thought this over. "Why are you working so hard to get the room addition?"

He shrugged. "Call me sentimental. It really is a great old house. Now, can I build those shelves or not?"

"I guess I could use the help." She showed him her page of instructions. "Let me show you what I want."

They bent their heads over her yellow legal pad as she explained Lottie's dilemma. "This has to be finished as soon as possible. She can't give student lessons until she has two pianos."

"Can we get in this afternoon?"

She looked at him in disbelief. "You can't tell me you don't have other work to do."

He broke into a grin. "Believe it or not, the rain canceled all my plans."

Lottie spent the morning in meetings, each longer than the one before. Even lunch was a meeting of sorts, as she met Marla Penworthy to discuss the Women's Auxiliary. "I have to admit, I was a little surprised you signed up for this," Marla began. "Surprised and delighted, of course."

"I didn't have a choice. It was presented as part of my duties."

Marla raised her eyebrows. "Katherine told you that?"

"No. Rhonda Kennedy did."

"Ah." Marla shook her head in disgust. "You'll want to be wary of Rhonda. She spent too long in Alicia's shadow. On the bright side, you couldn't be on a nicer committee. We really do help the freshmen feel at home."

Consider yourself warned, Lottie thought as she walked back to her office. Rhonda was going to be tricky to work with.

The smell of paint was the first thing she noticed when she reached the back hallway on the third floor. Light spilled from her doorway, but she had to edge past her desk and two pianos to reach it. Companionable voices carried on a conversation, interrupted periodically by the sound of a hammer.

She stopped in the doorway, torn between hope and anger. Jason Harms stood on a ladder, wielding the hammer, while Miranda inspected his work, a paint brush in her hand. "Careful," she said when she caught sight of Lottie. "The wall is still wet over there."

The room, now painted a crisp blue, looked a hundred times better, and the dark-stained wooden shelves were exactly right. Lottie looked at her assistant. "Can I talk to you in the hall?"

"What have you gotten me into?" she said when they were alone.

Miranda's eyes widened. "What do you mean?"

"I didn't ask for a professional to do this job. How much is it going to cost me?"

Miranda looked guilty and defiant by turns. "It's free. All the materials are scraps, and Jason is donating his labor. He wants a chance to change your mind about the music room."

Lottie stared at her assistant. "It means this much to him?"

Miranda nodded.

She felt herself softening. "It's not about his workmanship, you know."

Jason spoke from the doorway. "If it's about the sewing room, I'll try to work around it."

She yielded completely.

Miranda wanted to laugh at the shock on Jason's face. "I did not expect her to give in like that," he said.

"Lottie is easy once she gets her way." She dipped her paintbrush and tapped it on the rim of the can. "Besides, she wants to work with your company."

He grinned. "Of course she does. We're the best in town."

"That's not what I mean." She paused, brush poised in mid-air. "On

Saturday, when you two came to the door, it was almost like she recognized you. Did you notice?"

"Yeah, I did." He shook his head. "I figured it had something to do with my dad. He has this effect on older women."

Miranda rolled her eyes. "Okay, now you're laughing at me." She stretched to reach an upper corner. "I'm sorry I brought it up."

"I'm not kidding. Ever since Mom died, single women over forty have beaten a path to his door."

"Does he go out with them?"

He shook his head. "He's not ready yet. It's only been three years."

She turned to stare. "That's plenty of time for a lot of widowers."

"You didn't know my mom. She was something special."

"Sounds like it."

The conversation lagged while they concentrated on work. Miranda finished painting and stepped back to admire the job.

"I still don't know how to bypass the sewing room," he said.

"Why don't you dismantle the built-in cabinets and install them in the new addition? They're what she really wants."

"That's so simple. Why didn't she say so in the first place?"

"I don't think she knows. Every time she talks about that room, though, she brings up those cabinets."

He set down the drill and picked up a pencil. "Maybe I should design a new cabinet. I can make a better one."

She reached over and plucked the pencil out of his grip. "Don't you dare. This is about memories, not workmanship."

"How did you get so smart?" He grabbed for his pencil and caught her fingers instead.

She pulled away, startled, and the pencil clattered to the floor. "I…I notice things. That's all."

He scooped up the pencil and stuck it in his pocket. "You're nicer to Miss Braun than she deserves."

"That's not true," she said sharply. "Lottie's got more integrity than anyone I've ever met. What makes you such an expert on her, anyway?"

"I know a snob when I see one."

Miranda stared at him with something close to disgust. "There's two sides to every story, Jason. When people break with their families, there's always enough blame to go around."

"All right, all right." He put up a hand in self-defense. "I think we'll have to agree to disagree."

♪♫

As satisfied as Lottie was with the developments in her office, she still had nowhere to work for the afternoon. She ended up in the faculty dining room, drinking iced tea and studying a textbook on music history. She wouldn't be teaching the course, but it didn't hurt to refresh herself on the subject.

Rain fell all afternoon, pattering on the roof and making rivulets down the plate glass windows. Lottie caught herself watching droplets fall into puddles, her mind far away from the Baroque period on the page in front of her. Rainy days made her think of Dayton, not so much because it was a wet climate—it wasn't—but because the dreariest days of her life had happened there.

Madame D'Abri had met Lottie's train from Los Angeles in a torrential rainstorm. Inside the station house, the intrepid Frenchwoman had taken her by the shoulders and subjected her to a long, searching look. What she saw must have pleased her because she gave a decided nod. "You will do," she said.

In the taxi, Madame sat with hands folded primly in her lap. "The term has already begun," she told Lottie, "but I have no doubt you can catch up in all your subjects. You will sleep in the girls' dormitory. You will take instruction daily from eight o'clock until noon, with practice hours in the afternoon." She glanced at the girl. "Mail call will occur daily at three o'clock. Sundays are visiting days, just as they were when your Aunt Cora lived at the conservatory. Students may line up to use the telephone beginning at one o'clock. You are to keep your calls to five minutes or less."

Madame's gaze softened slightly. "The dormitory provides very little privacy. If you need to be alone—once in a while—you may come to my rooms. I am not certain why you have come to me so abruptly, but whatever trouble you are in, I believe it will pass. Take heart, child."

Comforted by Madame's words, Lottie had begun her studies determined to make her family proud. For a while she worked her heart out without expectation of mail or phone calls, knowing she would not be easily forgiven. After a month or two, her hopes began to rise. Surely Madame would write and tell Aunt Cora how hard she worked, and how well she behaved, and Aunt Cora would write back that all was forgiven.

No letter ever came. She held out hope for weeks and weeks and spent hours imagining the myriad ways a letter could get lost in the US postal system, but by her fifteenth birthday she had accepted the truth. Aunt Cora was not planning to write to her. Neither was anyone else.

Lottie was on her own.

"Would you like more iced tea, ma'am?"

Lottie dragged her thoughts back to the present and glanced up at the waitress. "Yes, please."

The waitress filled the glass and walked away.

Lottie gave herself a mental shake and turned her attention back to the Baroque period. No sense dwelling on the past. Her life had not turned out too badly.

She had nearly finished another chapter when Nathan Bartholomew rolled to a stop next to her chair. "Reading my textbook, Miss Braun? Are you trying to flatter me?"

She didn't look up. "I'm trying to live up to your example."

He gave a grunt of disbelief. "You hardly need to prove yourself."

"Prove myself?" She gazed at him without really seeing. That's exactly what she'd done. Prove herself, over and over, until performing became the objective instead of the means.

"Lottie."

She blinked. "What did you say?"

Nathan looked nettled. "You weren't listening."

She smiled and closed the textbook. "I think I'll pack it in for the day. Are you going back to the P.A.B.? Come along, and I'll let you drop some more pearls of wisdom along the way."

The rain had given way to late afternoon sunshine. They strolled across campus, Nathan dropping one-liners and Lottie responding with mild amusement. She found his black outlook tiring, every joke a little jab at someone or something.

They reached the faculty parking lot, and Lottie stopped next to the Mercedes. "Well, here's my car. See you tomorrow."

"Very good." Nathan began to roll past, but stopped when he reached her front bumper. "Uh-oh."

Lottie followed his gaze. "What's wrong?"

Her left front tire was flat as a pancake.

♫

Sam rang Lottie's doorbell and listened to the chime echo through the house. He stuck his hands in his pants pockets, then removed them and dropped his arms to his sides, only to stick his hands in his pockets again. After a minute or two he rang the bell again, but nobody seemed to be home.

"Meow!"

A giant orange tomcat watched him from under the porch swing. Sam looked away. He didn't want to encourage the animal. Unwilling to give up, he rang the bell once more, then jogged down the steps and around the house. A look inside the garage confirmed it: Lottie's car wasn't there. Disappointed, he trudged back to the front yard. He'd spent all day figuring out what he wanted to say. Now it looked like he'd have to wait until tomorrow to say it.

Just as he reached his car, a tow truck drove up the street and stopped. The passenger door opened and Lottie jumped out. "Thanks again, Max," she said to the driver, who saluted and drove away. Hiking her book bag higher on her shoulder, she started up the walk.

Sam watched her walk toward the house. She hadn't even seen him. He cleared his throat. "Uh, Lottie?"

She turned. "Oh, hi."

"Can I talk to you for a minute?"

She hesitated, her eyes watchful. Finally, "You might as well come in."

Not a promising start, but he'd take it. "What happened to your car?" he asked as he followed her up the walk.

"Flat tire."

"You picked a good garage."

"That's reassuring." She unlocked the big front door and led him into the living room. "Have a seat. I'll be with you in a minute." She pointed at her wet shoes. "I need to change."

He sat on the overstuffed couch and looked around. Helen's furniture sat in the same place it always had, with the same framed pictures on the walls. Even the books sat on the bookshelves in the same order. Over the years he'd borrowed several of those titles from David.

Lottie came back into the room in jeans and a checkered shirt, her wet shoes exchanged for a pair of red Keds with a hole in the toe. She perched on an easy chair and looked at him expectantly. "Now, what can I do for you, Sam?"

An unexpected stab of panic shot through him. All day he'd been picturing the little girl he used to know, not this distant, self-possessed woman. Well, he'd come too far to back out now. Better dive in and get it all out there. He cleared his throat. "When my wife knew she was going to die, she sat me down and gave me a list of instructions for her funeral. Nancy had written down which hymns to sing and the scriptures she wanted." He glanced at Lottie. "She even told me which suit I should wear, so I went home from the hospital and got it out of the closet to make sure it didn't need dry cleaning. Just by looking at it I knew it was miles too big." He set his hands on his knees. "I lost a lot of weight that year. So I called Helen for help."

"Sam, you don't have to—"

"I stood in the middle of the sewing room in that baggy suit while Helen measured and pinned. She ordered me to keep still, so I fixed my eyes on that little purple dress on the wall, the one she made for your birthday the year you joined the band." He paused, remembering the moment. "Helen poured all kinds of love and comfort into that needle and thread. I felt it back when we were kids, and I felt it again that day."

Color rushed into Lottie's face. "Then you understand why I have to keep the sewing room."

"I understand why you want to keep it." He looked straight into her eyes. "But I don't think Helen would want you to. She gave you the house to live in, not to turn into a shrine. If you need to keep her stuff, put it somewhere else and build that music room."

She drew a sharp breath. "You're missing the point. I can't keep her stuff. I can only keep the room."

"What do you mean?"

"Helen willed everything but the actual structure to Patti. Patti owns the little purple dress, and the sewing machine, and all the patterns. When that angry young woman gets around to clearing out this house, I get the feeling she won't be asking me what I want for a souvenir. And once she's finished, what will I have left of Helen?"

He looked at her with grim understanding. "Just the sewing room."

"She lives in that room, Sam."

"Patti won't care about her mother's sewing stuff." He leaned forward, eager to convince her. "If you put away the things you want, she'll never miss them."

She raised her eyebrows. "How can you be so sure?"

"Patti Parker's one goal in life is to stay as far away from Collison as she can get. She doesn't want her mother's old things cluttering her big city life."

"Sam, what would you give for a souvenir of your mother?"

He went still.

She looked at him with steady understanding, one orphan to another. "I'd give my right arm for something from mine."

He refused to believe she was right. "Patti's got a whole houseful of Helen's stuff. She won't care about a dress she never wore and a couple spools of thread."

"Can you promise me that?"

He hesitated. "No."

"I thought not."

They stared at one another, neither willing to budge. Inwardly Sam kicked himself for thinking he could change this stubborn woman's mind.

The phone rang, breaking the tension. Lottie got up to answer it, and Sam rose, too. "I'll let myself out," he said quietly.

"No, stay." She hurried toward the phone. "I have something to tell you."

Ill at ease, he sat down again while Lottie answered the call. What had possessed him to tell her that story? He'd never felt the need to tell it to anyone else. And it hadn't even changed her mind. He felt like a fool.

Lottie came back with an odd look on her face. "That was Max from the garage. He found a pocket knife blade stuck in my tire with the handle broken off."

"So you ran over a knife blade on your way to work?"

"Not exactly." She clasped her hands tightly in front of her. "The blade was embedded in the side of the tire."

He stared at her. "That sounds like a matter for the police. Criminal mischief, or something like that."

"I'm not going to bother the police. This is the kind of thing a kid does on a dare."

In the faculty parking lot? In the pouring rain? He opened his mouth to raise these points, but the hopeful look in Lottie's eyes made him swallow the words. "That's a possibility."

"Anyway," she said brightly. "Before the phone rang, I was about to give you an update on the room addition."

His heart sank. She'd hired someone else already.

"Your son seems to think he can redesign the plan so I can keep the sewing room."

He got to his feet. "When did he tell you that?"

"When I saw him a few hours ago, remodeling my office at the P.A.B."

Sam stared at her, thunderstruck.

"He talked my assistant into letting him do my office for free, to convince me to go with Harms and Sons. I told him I'd sign the contract, provided he could find a way to work around the sewing room." She gave a satisfied nod. "Jason's quite a businessman. I'm glad we could come to terms."

♫

Lottie stood at the window and watched Sam drive away. He'd been so sure he could talk her into parting with the sewing room. She felt a guilty pleasure in shaking his self-confidence. Jason deserved the credit for that, of course. He was the one who sealed the deal by promising to keep her sewing room. No doubt Sam would have some choice words to say to his son about making rash promises to the customers. Too bad she couldn't be a fly on the wall for that conversation.

Sam had been rather nice about her flat tire, wanting her to report it to the police. She couldn't take the matter too seriously. Like it or not, luxury cars attracted attention, and sometimes people played out their envy in mean-spirited ways. She couldn't take that kind of thing personally.

She walked into the sewing room and sank onto Helen's work chair, which did not creak or groan. It would be perfect for her office, if only it belonged to Lottie.

What was it Sam had said? If you put away the things you want, Patti will never miss them. That sounded like wishful thinking. Even if he was right, she couldn't cheat her niece that way. Not if she wanted a relationship with her down the road. And she did, in the worst way.

Patti might let her buy a few items, like the desk chair. A young woman with a child probably didn't live in a big enough house for all this stuff, especially in Chicago. Maybe she'd like to sell a few pieces, and walk away with some cash in her pocket.

Lottie sighed. Maybe, maybe, maybe. The truth was, she wouldn't know what Patti wanted until she decided to show up and explain. She reached for the card Ed Williams had given her. This was as good a time as any to try again.

The phone rang three times before Patti picked up, sounding breathless. "Hello?"

Lottie opted for a matter-of-fact tone. "Hello, Patti. This is Lottie Braun. I'm calling to ask—"

The line went dead before she could finish her sentence.

Miranda dug one last screw out of the tiny plastic bag and picked up the Allen wrench. "The desk is almost finished." She attached the screw and sat back on her heels to admire it. "Looks pretty good, don't you think?"

Jason set down the metal file cabinet and turned to look. "Not bad for a kit from Jack's discount store. Where did you learn to put stuff together like that?"

She shrugged. "This is no big deal. You have to follow directions and not get frustrated."

"Well, that's impossible for a lot of people." Jason picked up the desk and moved it into place against the wall. "A perfect fit. Now all we have left is cleanup."

They stacked paint cans in one corner and loaded a trash barrel with packaging from the desk. Miranda used a clean paint rag as a dust cloth, and Jason borrowed a vacuum from the scruffy janitor on the night shift. When everything was spotless, they stood back to admire their handiwork.

Two pianos sat side by side on the long wall of Lottie's office. Across from them, in the corner, the new desk and adjacent two-drawer file cabinet would give her room to work. The built-in shelf that ran the perimeter of the room provided far more space for books than the tiny case they'd taken out. With her height, Lottie would only need a small step stool to reach anything she needed. "It's not ideal," Miranda said, "but we've made it pretty efficient."

Jason glanced at her. "You came up with the smart ideas. I just carried them out."

She felt a little thrill of pleasure at the compliment. "You do good work. Lottie won't be sorry she hired you."

After one last glance around, they turned out the light and shut the door. Jason pushed the trash barrel down the dim hall, with Miranda close behind. "Goodnight," Jason called to the janitor, who was mopping the bathroom.

"Night, man."

The freight elevator took them down to the back door, where they dumped the trash barrel and set it back inside. Then they started for the parking lot.

With the project finished, Miranda found herself suddenly tongue-tied. She glanced at Jason, who seemed to be having the same problem. He caught her eye and they laughed. "It's a nice night," he said.

Miranda thought this over. The cloying humidity was doing unpleasant things to her hair. "Is this as nice as Iowa gets?"

"No, August is the worst. You'll like it when the heat breaks."

"I hope so."

"What are summers like where you grew up?"

She smiled, remembering. "Summer in San Francisco is not like anywhere else. The wind off the ocean keeps it cool, and we have lots of fog...." She trailed off, her attention caught by a man in the parking lot, searching the ground with a flashlight. "Jason, isn't that your dad?"

He nodded. "Hey, Dad. What's going on?"

Sam switched off his flashlight and stuck it in his belt. "Uh, hi, Jase. I was hoping I'd catch you. Nice work landing the Braun contract."

"Thanks." Jason sounded confused. "You know, you could have just left me a phone message."

"I hear you promised you'd keep the sewing room." Sam's tone was disapproving.

Jason smiled. "I've got that figured out."

"Oh yeah?"

"We're going to dismantle the built-in cabinets and use them in the new room." He nodded toward Miranda. "Miranda says that's what Lottie really wants."

Sam looked at her with fresh respect. "Did you run that past Lottie?"

She smiled. "I called and talked to her, and she likes the idea."

"Well, I guess you've got it all worked out."

She didn't contradict him.

"I'll be on my way, then." Sam started for his truck, then turned back. "Jase, we need to start on the music room next week, if we're going to pour a foundation before the freeze."

This time Jason looked surprised. "We've got a few other projects in line ahead of it."

"Hire an extra crew."

"Dad, we can't start a project that big on one week's notice."

Sam opened his truck door and climbed in. "We can if we work hard enough." He slammed the door and drove away.

Jason turned to Miranda with a puzzled look. "My dad's never let a job jump the line in his life. I don't know what's gotten into him lately."

Miranda stared after the truck as it turned the corner. "I wonder."

Six

ottie stood in the middle of her office and looked around in wonder. Gone was the cramped utilitarian space of yesterday. A warm, inviting, fully furnished studio had taken its place. Not only could she work here, she'd look forward to it. She sank into her new leather desk chair and pulled a framed photo out of her bag. Time to add a personal touch.

Cal stopped in a few minutes later. He gave a low whistle as he took in the new office. "Lookin' good, Lottie. Those kids knew what they were doing yesterday."

She felt like a proud mama. "They're both pretty talented."

"I'll say." He laughed. "Boy, won't Rhonda be steamed!"

He wasted no time in spreading the news, a fact made clear by the stream of visitors that came through her door over the next few hours. Unsurprisingly, Rhonda was the first. She took in the two pianos with a critical eye. "You'll have to be careful about spacing them," she said. "If they touch at all, they'll affect each other's sound."

What nonsense. "I'll be sure to watch that." Lottie hoped her tone wasn't too dry.

Katherine arrived with Elaine Woodward. "This is beautiful," Katherine said, her tone less chilly than usual. "You single-handedly turned the worst office in the department into the—" she stopped herself. "Well, one of the best, anyway."

Her honesty made Lottie smile. "It is pretty good."

Elaine's praise was more subdued. "We'll have to make sure that piano isn't wanted elsewhere."

Katherine laid a hand on Elaine's arm. "I'll take care of that personally, Elaine. Lottie must have two pianos."

For a split second, Elaine looked furious, but in a blink she was smiling again. "I know that as well as you do, Katherine. Let's not forget I raised a concert pianist."

Nathan Bartholomew rolled up to the door. "Am I invited to this party?"

Katherine and Elaine parted ways to let him in. "What do you think?" Katherine asked him.

Nathan looked unimpressed. "This is what all the fuss is about? It's tiny." He shot an accusing look at Lottie. "I rode that dirty freight elevator to get up here."

She hid a smile. "It is just an office, I suppose."

The photograph on Lottie's desk caught Katherine's eye. She picked it up for a closer look. "That's Vladimir Horowitz. I don't know who the other man is." She glanced at Lottie. "Arthur Fiedler?"

"No. You wouldn't know him. He was a personal acquaintance."

Nathan peered at the picture. "So, you know Horowitz?"

"Hardly. That was taken at the 1969 Grammy Awards. He won Best Classical Performance. I was a runner-up." It wasn't an interesting story. "Nathan, have you found a house yet?"

His face darkened. "I've got another appointment on Friday. That Deering woman swears she's got something up her sleeve." He looked at the secretary. "You're new in town. Who was your real estate agent?"

Elaine looked startled. "I rent."

"Good luck, Nathan," Katherine said. "Come on, everyone. I'm sure you've all got work to do." She swept them out the door ahead of her, then turned back. "I'm meeting with Cal Jefferson at three to discuss his ideas for a jazz curriculum. Would you be willing to join us? I have a feeling you could make a contribution."

Lottie smiled. "I'll be there."

Miranda rolled a page of file tabs into her Selectric typewriter and paused to think. How did one label a file for a two-inch pocket knife blade inside a plastic bag?

"File it under Miscellaneous," Lottie had said this morning. Since this was her standard instruction for everything but sheet music, Miranda had learned to ignore it. Now she typed *Flat tire* and the date, and detached the label from the page. She would store the bill from Max's Garage in the same place.

As she set the blade inside its folder, she wondered all over again about the knife's owner. Lottie believed he was a kid bent on mischief, but Miranda wasn't so sure. Random acts of violence didn't fit Collison's squeaky-clean image. But who would deliberately harm Lottie? Miranda couldn't imagine.

One thing was sure. Someone in town had a pocket knife with a missing blade. Find the knife, find the culprit.

The image of Sam Harms with a flashlight in his hand popped into her head. He'd certainly been searching for something in the staff parking lot. But why would he trouble himself with Lottie's problem?

Miranda dropped the file into place and shut her desk drawer, but questions lingered in her mind.

She was typing up lecture notes when the doorbell rang. Mitchell Harms stood on the front porch, holding a takeout bag in one hand and a pile of envelopes in the other. "Hey, I brought lunch." He held up the envelopes. "And your mail."

Miranda reached for the mail. "Lunch? Is that all?"

He looked confused. "What did you expect?"

"A finalized construction bid."

He gave her a rueful look. "Once again you've confused me with my brother. He'll be along later with a big, complicated bid full of square feet and dollar signs. You'll love it."

She couldn't help smiling. He was so right.

"You have to eat, don't you? Do you like Chinese food?"

Her smile grew wider. Something in that bag smelled delicious. "Come on in."

Mitchell set cardboard cartons on the kitchen table while Miranda sorted the mail. "I took a chance and ordered the Szechuan pork," he said. "It's the kind of spicy that makes my ears turn red."

She was only half-listening, her attention on a letter from the Los Angeles Philharmonic Orchestra.

He looked over her shoulder. "What's that?"

"An invitation for Lottie to play with the L. A. Phil. They want to give her some sort of lifetime achievement award."

"That'll be fancy. Will she take you along?"

"She won't go at all."

He raised his eyebrows. "Because?"

"Everyone knows Lottie doesn't play L.A."

"I didn't."

She hurried to correct herself. "Me neither, until I went to work for her. But Lottie's fans know she won't go near California."

"Huh." He handed her a bucket of white rice. "Sweet and sour shrimp, or beef and pea pods?"

"You went all-out."

"Well, I don't know what you like yet."

Something in his tone made her look up. "Mitchell, you're a really nice guy…"

He winced. "And I'll make some girl very happy someday, right?"

"I'm sorry."

He gave her a reassuring smile. "Don't look so concerned. I was kind of expecting this."

"You were?"

He rolled his eyes. "The look on your face when I didn't have the bid said it all." He pushed a crab rangoon toward her and picked up his chop sticks. "Now, let's change the subject. How 'bout those Cubbies?"

She laughed. "You're going to hate me."

He feigned a look of astonishment. "You mean you're not a Cubs fan?"

"I don't even like baseball."

"Clearly, this would never work out." He shuddered. "Let's never speak of this again."

Once they cleared the air, they ate lunch in good harmony. Mitchell put himself out to be charming, and Miranda let herself be charmed. When she walked him to the door with the leftovers, he leaned over and kissed her cheek. "Thanks for letting me down easy."

She gave him a playful push. "You weren't serious."

He yanked the front door open with a flourish, his hand over his heart. "You'll never know how serious I was."

He was so busy playacting, he nearly mowed down his brother, who stood on the porch. Jason steadied him with a none-too-gentle grip on his arm. "Dad's looking for you, Mitch."

"I'm going." Mitchell shook off Jason's hand. "There's no law against taking a lunch break."

Jason watched his brother stride across the lawn, then turned to Miranda. "I've got the construction bid."

"Great. I've been waiting for it."

She stood back to let him inside, but he declined. "I'll just leave it with you." He nodded toward Mitchell's departing car. "I'd have sent it with him if I'd known he was having lunch with you." He pushed the envelope into her hands and headed down the steps. "Call the office if you have questions."

Speechless, she watched him drive away.

"Where are you going, Mitch?" Sam said Thursday morning.

His son halted at the office door. "I've got a contract for Lottie Braun. We can't proceed until she signs it, so I thought I'd try to catch her at her office."

Sam held out a hand. "I'll do that."

Mitchell looked confused. "This is what you pay me for, Dad. It's fine."

Sam pulled the envelope from his son's hands. "I'd like to see the office remodel."

Mitchell threw up his hands. "All right. I'll put my feet up and drink coffee till you get back."

"You do that."

Twenty minutes later Sam knocked at Lottie's office door. She looked up from her desk and smiled. "What a surprise! Come in."

"I need you to sign your contract." He stepped inside. "I'd like to wait, if you don't mind."

She swept an arm around the small space. "Make yourself at home. Sorry there's no leg room."

She was right. When he sat on a piano bench, his outstretched legs nearly reached the door. The kids had done a nice job, though, especially with the finishing touches. He could tell from the framed oil painting above the desk that someone knew a fair amount about art.

Lottie proved to be the kind of customer who studied her contract. Sam didn't mind. He'd rather they didn't have surprises down the line. While he waited, a photo on her desk caught his eye. He picked it up to get a closer look. Lottie stood in the center, looking glamorous in a long evening gown. Two distinguished old men in tuxedos stood on either side of her. "When was this taken?"

She glanced up and her expression softened. "1969, the last time I ever saw Mr. Schultz. He died the next year."

Old Carl Schultz had been an ornery cuss, but he'd been a friend to Lottie. "So you did get to see him again."

"He came to my concerts whenever I played in New York."

"Who's the other guy?"

She shot him a glance full of amusement. "That's Vladimir Horowitz."

He felt his face go hot. Horowitz was a household name.

She didn't seem to notice his embarrassment. "That picture is a bit of a good-luck charm now. I put it on my desk wherever I go."

Sam set it gently on the desk. "I haven't thought about the old man in years."

"I have." She signed her name with the flourish of a professional autograph giver and handed the contract back. "You'd be surprised how often I think of those days."

♫

LOTTIE'S HOPE

The band was tuning up when Lottie pulled into her garage after work. She sat for a moment and watched them in her rearview mirror. The guitarist bent over his instrument, a picture of serious musicianship. The drummer fiddled with a drumstick, trying to spin and catch it with one hand, while the black-haired girl knelt in the front corner, stroking a large orange cat.

"Oh, dear," Lottie murmured. "Marmalade, you traitor."

As she emerged from the garage, Martha Williams called a greeting from the vegetable garden next door. "Would you like some zucchini?"

"Sure." Lottie crossed the lawn to admire her neighbor's handiwork. "Looks like you've got a bumper crop."

Martha wiped her forehead with the back of a gloved hand. "They're easy to grow, and hard to give away." She handed Lottie a pile of deep green squash and three perfect red tomatoes. "Say, Ed and I are grilling steaks tomorrow night. Would you like to join us?"

Lottie hesitated. "I don't want to intrude..."

"You're no intrusion. We'd love to have you. I'm baking a chocolate cake for dessert," Martha added persuasively.

Seeing no alternative, she gave in with a smile. "I'd love to come."

As she washed her plate and glass after dinner, she glimpsed Jessica taking sheets off the clothesline next door. The girl was a hard worker. Lottie thought about bringing her news of Marmalade's defection, but she went inside before Lottie could dry her hands.

Once again, she wondered how to help the girl next door. She'd thought about writing a check, of course. An offer of money was her standard response to any crisis. But Jessica hadn't come begging the other night, and Lottie didn't want to offend.

The thought of the awful brownies made her smile all over again. Martha's chocolate cake would certainly put them in the shade. Martha could teach anyone a thing or two about baking.

Now, there was a thought.

♫

Lottie hummed a little Mozart under her breath as she walked into the P.A.B. Friday morning. During the past few days, as the students moved in, the campus had slowly come alive. Upperclassmen greeted each other like long-lost siblings. Freshmen braved the dining hall by themselves or in pairs, having those first awkward conversations with new friends. Lottie had watched the same scenes on a dozen campuses. The squeaky-cleanness of a new school year never got old.

She breezed into the department office in a weekend frame of mind. "It's exciting out there," she said to Elaine Woodward as she checked her empty mailbox.

Elaine answered with the disdainful sniff Lottie had come to expect. The secretary didn't seem to like anyone.

Rhonda Kennedy hurried in, puffing hard. "I can tell the kids are back. I had to park a block away this morning."

Lottie nodded. "Parking is a constant problem on college campuses."

They smiled at one another with rare agreement. "I've got an idea to discuss with you," Lottie said, encouraged by the friendly exchange.

Rhonda raised her eyebrows. "Can we do it on the way to my office? I have an appointment."

"I've thought of a way to help the music department grow. What do you think about hosting an annual high school concerto competition?"

"Sounds like a lot of work."

"Yes." Lottie glanced at her colleague. "But the payoff would be huge, especially if we used nationally known judges."

"Judges that you would provide?"

"I do have a few contacts. Not only would it be great publicity for the school, we'd also meet some really talented young musicians."

Rhonda stopped at her office door. "Look, Lottie, you may be world-class, but we're just a regional school. We don't do high-profile stuff like that. I doubt if we could pull it off."

"I think we could."

The professor shook her head. "Count me out."

Before Lottie could draw breath to argue, Rhonda stepped into her office and closed the door. "Rhonda Kennedy is a big woman with a small mind," Lottie muttered under her breath as she walked away.

"This department won't get anywhere with thinking like that."

She'd barely dropped her book bag next to her desk when Cal stopped by the office. "I wanted to thank you for joining the jazz curriculum development committee."

"I don't mind working to support a good idea," Lottie said with a smile. "And speaking of good ideas, I've got one of my own."

"Let's hear it."

"What if Collison College sponsored an annual concerto competition for high school students?"

Cal's face lit up. "I love it. What do you need me to do?"

When Cal left a few minutes later, Lottie threw up her arms and spun her chair around with glee. She'd found an ally in this crazy place.

She came down to earth to find Elaine Woodward watching her from the doorway. "Human Resources called. They haven't received Form 624 from you yet." Her tone was accusing. "Here's a new one."

Lottie looked at the form in Elaine's outstretched hand. "I gave you that form on Monday, Elaine."

The secretary's lips tightened. "You did not. I'd remember if you had."

"I left it in the basket on your desk."

"Well, I didn't find it there."

"Never mind." Lottie snatched the form from the secretary's fingers. "Have a seat. I'll finish this in a jiffy."

But Elaine refused. "I have work to do. Bring it to my desk when you're finished."

Lottie filled out the three-page personnel form as quickly as possible and carried it downstairs to Elaine, who took it with an ungracious sniff. She returned more slowly, working out her irritation on the long flights of stairs. She didn't know which she hated more: Bureaucracies or the bureaucrats who ran them.

To top it all off, after all that running around, she returned to find her lucky picture face-down on the floor in front of her desk. The protective glass was cracked in half, and Schultz and Horowitz looked weirdly estranged.

With a sigh, she slipped the frame into her book bag to take home. Miranda would know what to do.

Miranda did not know what to do.

Jason pointed to the hole in the lattice under Lottie's back deck. "Something is living under there," he repeated. "It's probably a raccoon, but it could also be a possum or a skunk."

She took an involuntary step back. "What do you recommend?"

"Leave it alone. It'll probably move on when construction starts."

She swallowed. "Or?"

"If it were my house, I'd live-trap the animal and let it go in the country somewhere."

"That sounds good." The words came out in a relieved rush. She glanced at him. "I mean, would you be willing to do that for Lottie?"

He looked like he wanted to laugh. "I'll set something up tonight."

"Thanks."

She couldn't see what was so funny.

Lottie's spirits lifted as she locked her office door Friday evening. She'd put in a respectable week's work. Now it was time for a little weekend fun. She planned to have a nice time with Ed and Martha, and do Jessie McCall some good while she was at it.

Miranda was ready to leave when she got home. "You've got an animal living under your deck," she said on her way out the door. "Jason Harms is going to live-trap it and take it to the country."

"Good thinking. Did you reach Patti?"

"No luck."

Lottie pulled the broken picture frame out of her bag. "Can you have this repaired for me?"

"Absolutely." Miranda took the frame. "Have a nice weekend."

At six o'clock Lottie rang the Williams' doorbell, a small bouquet of flowers in her hands.

"Helen's roses!" Martha exclaimed when she opened the door. She buried her nose in the fragrant blooms. "I know exactly which rose-bush this is. Helen planted it one Mother's Day when Patti was little."

"That's a lovely memory." Another memory Lottie had missed. Her heart twisted at the thought.

As Martha bustled away to find a vase, Ed led the way to the living room. "Martha has me grilling tonight. How do you like your steak?"

"Medium-rare, please."

"I believe you've met our friend, Sam Harms."

Sam gave a sheepish wave from his spot by the fireplace. "Lottie."

Ed rubbed his hands together. "I'd better see if it's time to put the meat on the grill. I'll leave you two to talk."

"I hear you and Jason have come to terms over the sewing room," Sam said after Ed left.

She brightened. "He was so exactly right that what I wanted was the built-ins. I think he's rather brilliant for figuring me out."

"Didn't your little assistant tell you? It was her idea. Look out, or we'll be hiring her out from under your nose."

"You'd better not. I'd be lost without Miranda." Lottie looked around with an uncertain laugh. "Are Ed and Martha up to something here? Are we being set up?"

He looked taken aback. "I don't think so. At least, not that I know of."

"Oh okay. Forget I brought it up."

But the idea had obviously made Sam uncomfortable. He glanced toward the kitchen. "I'd better go see how Ed's doing with those steaks."

Left to herself, Lottie raised her eyes to the ceiling. "Helen? Can you give me a little help here? They're your friends."

Martha hurried into the living room a minute later, indignant that the men had left Lottie by herself. "You'd think they'd never been taught any manners."

Her fussy tone made Lottie smile. "Don't be too hard on them. I do very well by myself." She nodded at the painting that hung over the fireplace. The country market scene, while not masterful, showed promise. "Do you have an artist in the family?"

"Our daughter Carey painted that."

"She has talent."

"I've always thought so. She doesn't have much time for painting these days. With three little ones and another on the way, her time is filled with other matters."

Lottie glanced at her hostess. "Once an artist, always an artist, I think. Someday your daughter will have time to paint again."

"You're right, of course. Children grow up faster than you can blink." Martha sounded wistful. "One minute, Ed and I had five babies at home, and the next we were welcoming grandchildren."

"Sounds like you miss your kids."

"It seems silly when you put it like that," Martha said with a laugh. "Our kids all live nearby. They don't need me the way they used to, though. I guess that's what I miss."

"Steaks are ready," Ed called.

Martha smiled. "That's our cue."

She led Lottie into the dining room, where Sam and Ed waited. Lottie gazed with appreciation at the meal before her. "Steak, potatoes, and corn on the cob. What a feast."

Ed looked smug. "See, Martha? I told you she'd like it."

"How does the saying go?" Sam said. "You can take the girl out of Iowa, but you can't take Iowa out of the girl."

Lottie raised her water glass. "I'll drink to that!"

The dinner conversation began with Lottie's room addition. Ed and Martha wanted all the details, and Sam was more than happy to discuss his favorite subject. Lottie applied herself to the excellent food and waited for an opening. During a lull she set down her fork. "Speaking of home improvements, I understand Jessica McCall is trying to get her grandpa's house ready to sell."

Martha raised her eyebrows. "Is that what she's doing? What's taking so long?"

"She's a bit overwhelmed." Lottie warmed to her subject. "If it were only a matter of paint and deep cleaning, she'd be finished by now. But the house has plumbing and electrical problems that she can't fix."

Ed grunted. "Sounds to me like Jessie is freeloading on her grandpa."

"What makes you think so?"

"We've been watching that family for years," Martha said. "When-ever Jessie's mother ran out of money—"

"Or liquor."

"Or liquor, she'd show up at Joe's house and makes a scene till she got what she wanted." Martha shuddered. "You would not believe the things she's done over the years, right out in the open where the neigh-bors could watch. Screaming matches with different boyfriends, bro-ken bottles in the street. That woman was a nightmare."

"It stands to reason the girl would do the same thing. It's all she's been taught," Ed said.

Lottie's stomach began to churn. "Has Jessica brought the same kind of chaos? Drunken brawls and such?"

Ed and Martha exchanged a startled glance. "Not that we've seen." Martha said at last. "But I did see her with a beer in her hand once."

"One beer?" Lottie couldn't keep the disbelief out of her voice. "I'm not sure that makes her an alcoholic."

"She's the spitting image of her mother," Ed said with finality. "The apple doesn't fall far from the tree."

Throughout this exchange, Sam's head had bent lower and lower over his plate. Now he raised it and looked at his hostess. "Dinner was delicious," he said mildly. "What's for dessert?"

Martha shot him a grateful look. "I baked a chocolate cake just for you, Sam. I'll have it out here in a jiffy."

As Martha cleared the dishes, Lottie joined her in the kitchen. "I guess I put my foot in my mouth just now."

"It's not your fault. We can't expect you to know all the neighbor-hood dirty laundry." Martha smiled at her. "Let's change the subject. Have you had any luck reaching Patti?"

"No. Miranda and I have both tried, but nobody answers. I'm be-ginning to wonder if we've got her current phone number."

"You might track her down at work. She's a buyer for one of the department stores."

"Do you remember which one?"

"Let me see. It's not Marshall Fields, because I'd remember that." Martha frowned in thought. "Maybe Patti called it Carson's. Or was it Carter's? I always get those names mixed up."

"I'll ask Miranda to do some digging. She's good at research like that."

"Speaking of Miranda, the other day she said a neighbor gave you brownies? I didn't think anyone on the street had time to bake anymore."

"Jessica brought them over, to welcome me to the neighborhood."

Martha looked startled. "She did?"

"It was a lovely gesture, even though they tasted like sand." Lottie shrugged. "After everything you've said tonight, I guess I understand why she never learned to bake."

"Poor kid." Martha glanced at Lottie with a rueful smile. "Oh, don't look at me that way. Helen always stood up for the child. She said we shouldn't blame Jessie for her mom's faults."

Lottie smiled. "I agree."

"Of course you do. You're a lot like her."

The compliment warmed Lottie's heart.

Martha dried her hands and took the cover off the cake. "What kind of help do you think Jessie needs from us?" Her voice was casual. "Ed and I can't do plumbing or electrical work."

"She needs advice…Legal advice about her grandpa's finances. Practical advice about making that house look well-kept. A little motherly wisdom on life in general probably wouldn't be rejected, either."

Martha didn't reply, but Lottie could tell the wheels were turning. Time to move on. "That cake is gorgeous, by the way. I can't wait to taste it."

The cake lived up to its high promise. When every crumb was gone, and cups of coffee had been poured, Ed leaned back and patted his stomach. "Martha, you're an artist in the kitchen."

Martha smiled across the table at her husband. "I'm not the real artist in the family, though. Lottie noticed Carey's painting before dinner."

"She's got talent," Ed said proudly. "Painting doesn't pay the bills, though. Good thing she's got a husband to put food on the table."

"Art isn't always about making money," Lottie said. "Lots of wonderful artists don't make a living with their hands. Their gifts simply enhance their lives, much like Martha's baking enhances yours."

Sam chuckled. "She's got a point, Ed."

"Speaking of young artists, I once knew a boy who desperately wanted to be a premier concert pianist. We took lessons from the same teacher in New York."

"That's neat," Martha said.

"Not really. He wasn't a nice boy at all. He used to trip me every time we passed on the stairs."

Sam looked up from his coffee, a smile in his eyes. She glanced away.

"He sounds awful." Martha looked concerned.

Lottie pictured her tormentor's sullen face. "He was, at the time. But life has a way of evening things out. Ten years ago I arrived in New York for a performance and discovered a stain on my concert dress. I took it to a nearby dry cleaner and begged the clerk to take care of it right away. While she was writing up the ticket, I noticed a framed photo of the owner on the wall behind her, with the man's name printed below: Victor Gold. It was the name of my childhood enemy. The clerk told me he owned dry cleaners all over New York, just like his father before him." She chuckled. "Far from being a great concert pianist, my old nemesis had become the dry-cleaning king of New York. I couldn't hold back a thrill of vindication.

"I asked the clerk if she liked working for the company, and she nodded. 'Mr. Gold is a decent boss. He gives free piano lessons to anyone who wants to learn.' So you see, Ed, even though he didn't make his fortune through music, he found a way to fit his art into his life."

Ed chuckled. "The dry cleaning king of New York, eh? It almost sounds like you're making that up."

"She's not," Sam said. When everyone looked at him, he added, "At least, I believe her."

Lottie raised her right hand. "I'm telling the truth."

Martha rose from the table. "I know what we should do tonight. We should play bridge."

Lottie noticed with amusement that Sam looked as horrified as she felt. They both stood up at the same moment. "I should be going," she said.

He nodded. "Me too. I need to make an early night of it."

Ed joined the chorus. "Better get a good night's sleep."

Martha heaved a sigh. "Nobody likes to play cards anymore."

Lottie and Sam waved good-bye, and walked across the lawn toward Helen's house. "Well, that could have gone better," Lottie said. "I guess I've convinced Ed I'm some kind of bleeding heart softy."

"Don't worry about it," Sam said. "Ed's years of law practice have made him cynical. If you want, I can send one of my guys to take a look at Jessie's house. Maybe there's something we can do."

"Oh, would you do that? You can send all the bills to me."

"No need." Sam glanced at her. "So Victor Gold is the dry-cleaning king of New York?"

"I can't believe you remember him." She smiled back.

"How could I forget a punk like that?"

His disgusted tone filled her with unaccustomed warmth. Once, long ago, Sam had stood shoulder-to-shoulder with her against Victor. Tonight, she was pretty sure he still would.

"By the way, you were right," he said.

"Oh? About what?"

"That was definitely a set-up. Don't look now, but Martha's watching us from behind the curtains."

Lottie hummed under her breath as she let herself into the P.A.B. Saturday morning. Dinner with Ed and Martha had turned out okay. Even if she hadn't convinced them to help Jessica, at least she'd given them something to think about. And Sam's support meant a lot.

She took the stairs two at a time, in a hurry to get this chore over with. She was only stopping in to pick up a reference book. Then she was off to Riverfront Park for a brisk walk before the heat set in. She crossed the atrium, eager to grab the book and be gone.

Her office door was unlocked—careless of her. Or was it the cleaning staff that hadn't locked up? Not that it mattered in a town this small.

She flipped the light switch and froze. The room was in ruins.

Seven

Lottie stared in shock at the destruction. Every surface had been cleared, the contents dumped in heaps on the floor. Books lay every which way with sheet music cascading across them. Potting soil from a broken planter soaked the pages of a concerto.

Wrenched from the wall, the new shelves teetered at crazy angles. Leftover blue paint puddled on the desk and soft leather chair and splattered nearby piles. With a cry of pain, she snatched up a book and held it close. Aunt Eva's copy of *Treasure Island* would never be the same.

Tears clogged her throat. She could not imagine who would cause such damage. She had no enemies that she knew of. People thought her standoffish, not evil. Surely this was a random crime. But what kind of person would climb to the third floor to vandalize a professor's office? Why would a random stranger bypass the big offices near the atrium and hone in on hers?

What now? She slid to the floor and leaned her head against the door. If she called the police, reporters were sure to follow. She couldn't face that kind of publicity. If she dragged Katherine into this, on the weekend no less, she'd confirm her worst expectations of the Great Lottie Braun.

Long, miserable minutes passed. Finally, she reached under the desk for the phone and dialed the one number she had memorized. "Miranda?"

Half an hour later her assistant stared around the room, her hands clenched with rage. "What kind of creep would do something like this?"

Lottie shrugged. "I've been asking myself the same question."

"They've wrecked everything!"

"Everything but the pianos, thank goodness."

Miranda frowned. "Did you call the police?"

"No, and I don't intend to." Lottie made her tone forceful. "I don't want them involved, Miranda. That's why I called you."

"What do you want me to do?"

"Help me put everything back the way it was and pretend this never happened."

"Do you think that's wise?" The girl sounded worried.

Lottie hesitated. "It's my best option. Will you help me?"

Miranda looked around with a critical eye. "I'll need some help with the built-ins."

"I figured," Lottie said, relieved. "That's why I called in reinforcements."

Footsteps sounded in the hall. "I came as soon as I could—" Jason stopped short in the doorway. "Holy smokes! You weren't kidding."

Miranda couldn't help admiring Lottie's strength as they sorted through the mess. Though outwardly calm, she was pale, her mouth set in a grim line. They worked methodically to sort books and reassemble sheet music while Jason carted away the paint-soaked desk and chair. "I'll be back with replacements," he promised.

"Bring a carpet remnant or a rug if you can find one," Miranda told him. "We'll need something to cover the paint splatters on the floor."

"Got it."

"It's a good thing I came in this morning," Lottie said when he was gone. "I wouldn't want to face this mess Monday morning."

"That would be rough." Miranda frowned. "Do you think that's what this person wanted? To embarrass you like that?"

Lottie winced. "I thought of that, but I just don't think any of my colleagues is capable of this."

"What about Rhonda? You said she's been hard to deal with."

"Rhonda wants that big office all to herself. Why would she give me a reason to have to move in with her?"

"Good point." Miranda thought a moment. "What about Dean Snelling?"

"No."

"Nathan Bartholomew?"

"Definitely not."

"Cal Jefferson?"

"Why would he?" Lottie closed her eyes. "Why would any of them?"

"I don't know." Miranda put a tentative arm around her employer. "I can't imagine anyone wanting to hurt you this way."

Lottie's shoulders sagged. "I wish I believed you," she whispered.

"You know what?" Miranda sat back on her heels. "You should go home. Get away from here and do something nice for yourself. Jason and I can handle this mess."

To her surprise, Lottie didn't argue. Tucking a ruined book into her bag, she rose to her feet and slipped out the door.

Miranda finished sorting books and swept up the potting soil, her mind on her employer. Lottie was a thorough professional and a fierce competitor. She didn't suffer fools gladly, so why was she choosing to hush this up? Adding in the slashed tire and the broken picture frame, she could be in real danger.

She frowned. The broken frame was an accident. Wasn't it?

"Hey, Miranda?"

She jumped.

Jason stood in the doorway. "I brought up the new desk."

"That was fast." She followed him into the hall where a battered antique desk sat on a metal cart. "Where did you get that beautiful thing?" she gasped. "It's perfect."

"Mitch found it at an auction a while back. He's always buying stuff like this and putting it in the warehouse for later."

"Your brother's a smart guy."

He shrugged. "If you ask me, he just takes up a lot of room we could use for something else."

She laughed. "You sound like an older brother."

"That's what I am." He reached past the desk to grab a roll of carpet she hadn't noticed before. "I found this, too. Hope it works."

They rolled out the carpet and set the desk in place. "Perfect fit," Miranda said.

"I should have thought of this in the first place." He met her eyes in a look of understanding. "On the other hand, I'm glad I didn't."

"Oh, I nearly forgot." She reached into her purse for Lottie's re-framed photo. "This belongs on top."

"Is that Lottie?" Jason asked, looking over her shoulder. "She was gorgeous."

"Still is. There's something regal in the way she carries herself."

He pointed to the man on right. "Isn't that Vladimir Horowitz?"

She frowned. "How do you know his name?"

"My mom was a classical music fan." He frowned in thought. "The other man looks familiar, too. I wonder where I know him from?"

"Did your mom like him, too?"

"No, that's not it…" After a moment, he gave up. "Never mind."

She set the picture on the desk and looked around. "How are we going to protect this place? We can't let it be damaged again."

"Do you really think this could happen again?" He sounded doubtful.

"I think we should prepare for the worst."

"All right, then. Let's change the lock and give Lottie the only keys."

Just like that. He hadn't questioned her judgment. He'd simply come up with an answer. The thought made her smile. "Have you ever changed a lock before? Because I haven't."

He raised his eyebrows in mock surprise. "There's something you don't already know how to do?"

"What does that mean?"

"You're a pretty competent person. This week was challenging by any measure, and you proved yourself equal to every situation." He gave her a teasing look. "Except maybe the raccoon under Lottie's deck."

She wrinkled her nose. "I can deal with raccoons. You lost me when you said it might be a skunk."

"Well, it was a coon. I took care of it this morning."

"Thank you."

Their gazes caught and held for a long moment. Jason was the first to look away. "There's something you should know about Mitch," he said abruptly.

She blinked. "Oh?"

"He's been badly hurt. I don't want to see him get hurt again."

She stared at him in confusion. "Why—"

"Look, you don't need to stay. I'll change the lock and drop the keys off with Lottie on my way home."

For the first time, Lottie locked the Mercedes into the garage. Hands shaking, she unlocked the kitchen door, hurried inside, and locked it behind her, then stood still and listened for a long minute.

Silence filled the house.

She walked through the first floor, drawing drapes and pulling shades. The bolt on the front door, rusty from disuse, shot into place with a dreadful screech.

When she finally felt secure, she stepped into the sewing room, closed the door behind her, and sank onto the daybed. Reaching into her book bag, she pulled out the manila envelope she'd found in her mailbox on the way out of the P.A.B. Lifting the flap, she reached inside and pulled out a yellowed newspaper dated January 2, 1942. Her eyes widened as she read the headline.

MAN DIES IN NEW YEAR'S BARN FIRE.

She stared unseeing at the front-page account of Pop's death. She didn't need to read it to remember the details. He'd been working late in his machine shop, fixing small appliances and bicycles, when a spark from his tools was thought to have started the blaze. The newspaper didn't say Pop was desperate to pay off his debt for Lottie's fancy New York piano lessons. It didn't mention his heart condition, either. Nobody knew those details until later.

She read the yellow Post-It note stuck to the middle of the page. "Thought you might want a copy of this. The hard times are often the most meaningful, don't you think? Hope we can do business. - D.D."

This was an audacious move, even for Donna Davenport. Maybe she thought these little hints would intimidate Lottie into cooperating. But how far would the author go to intimidate her? Would she puncture a tire, for example? Or ransack an office? And how could she do any of that unless she lived right there in Collison?

She lay back on the daybed and stared at the ceiling. These nightmarish happenings felt far-fetched yet logical all at the same time. This exposure of her past—Pop's death, Charlotte Brown's existence—was the very thing she'd always feared about coming home. People would know who she really was and what she'd done. Maybe a flat tire and a demolished office were somebody's idea of justice: A little retribution for the damage she'd done.

She really couldn't argue with that.

Sunday morning she slept too late to go to church. Not that she minded. She didn't have the courage to leave the house just yet. Her problem looked better in the light of a new day, but she didn't want to push her luck.

She worked steadily at home until noon, when the phone rang. Sam sounded uncomfortable. "I thought I might catch you at church, but you weren't there." He cleared his throat. "Jason and I are going down to Westmont today to visit Aunt Cora and Aunt Eva at the nursing home. Thought you might like to come along."

"Don't you think I've taken up enough of Jason's weekend?"

Sam hesitated. "What do you mean?"

"Didn't he tell you what happened?"

He sounded puzzled. "No."

She felt rising respect for Jason. Few young men had that kind of discretion. "Never mind, Sam. I'd like to go."

He picked her up an hour later in an ancient and immaculately clean Plymouth Fury. As she settled into the front seat Sam said, "Jase is meeting us there. He won't ride in Bessie here."

She laughed. "Is there something I should know about her?"

A smile tugged at the corners of his mouth. "Oh, she's safe enough. My boy is a speed demon." His smile disappeared. "I got Jase to tell me what happened. I'd like to catch the jerk who did it."

She warmed to the determination in his voice. "Thanks, Sam. Me too."

"Is that why you weren't at church?"

She gave a reluctant nod. "I couldn't seem to leave the house this morning."

"You can't hide from a bully. That's how they win."

She felt a flash of irritation. "Staying in bed for one Sunday morning does not constitute running and hiding."

"Well, church is where you ought to be when you're scared."

She stared out the window. "I wouldn't know about that."

He started to say more, then seemed to change his mind. "All right. Sorry I stepped on your toes."

"Never mind." She glanced at him. "Why are you doing this, anyway?"

"I thought you should have a chance to see your relatives, if you want to."

"Well, I do. Thanks."

They reached the highway and Bessie picked up the pace a bit. Lottie settled back and watched the corn fields roll past. The road unfolded, familiar and unfamiliar, a cherished memory overlaid by progress. Here and there she recognized a farm or a crossroads, but most of the landmarks were new. Not until they reached the outskirts of Westmont did she begin to see things she knew for sure. They passed Uncle Harry's farm with its weather-beaten gray barn and little frame house. The old brick church still stood at the edge of the business district, though a new addition made it look more substantial. Most of the storefronts on Main Street were abandoned. She pointed to an empty lot. "What happened to the bank?"

"First National bought it a few years back, condemned the old building and tore it down. There's an ATM at the gas station, but folks have to go to Fort Madison to talk to a teller." He glanced at her. "You can't stop progress. At least, that's what they say."

She looked sadly out the window. "This feels mean-spirited somehow."

They reached the nursing home, a low, modern building with tidy landscaping. Sam parked the car and turned to her. "I should warn you before we go in. Cora doesn't track very well anymore. You can't expect her to recognize you. Eva may not know you, either, because you're an adult, and she remembers you as a little girl."

Her heart sank. "I'll try not to expect too much."

"There you are." Jason sounded impatient. "What took you so long?"

Sam shot Lottie a humorous look. "We didn't feel the need to break all the speed limits in the county, son."

Jason snorted. "That's good. Bessie couldn't go more than fifty-five if she tried."

They stopped at the nurse's station, where a young aide assured them the ladies were up from their nap. She smiled at Jason as if he were the only person in the room. "Do you know the way? I could take you down there."

"We know." Sam nudged his son none too gently. "Come on."

Lottie followed the Harms men down the hall, apprehension growing with every step. With all her heart she wanted her aunts to recognize her, to look at her as they had when she was a little girl, but she knew this was not possible. If they did not know her at all, as Sam had warned, she'd feel sad. But how would she feel if they did, and remembered the last time they'd met? Her stomach turned to jelly at the very thought.

They sat by the window in matching wheelchairs, garish polyester lap robes over their legs. Aunt Cora's hair, now wispy and white, was cut short, while Aunt Eva wore hers in a straggly bun. Their faces brightened when they saw their visitors.

"Well, this is a surprise," Aunt Cora repeated several times in a row. She peered up at Jason. "What are you doing here?"

Aunt Eva took possession of Sam's hand. "It's the boys, Cora. I told you they'd come."

Sam patted her gnarled fingers. "We had to see how you ladies are doing. Didn't we, Jase?"

Jason relaxed against the window sill, arms crossed over his chest. "Sure did."

Aunt Eva noticed Lottie, standing alone between the beds. "Why, it's…it's…" She trailed off. "Do I know you?"

Lottie stepped forward, smiling. "I'm Lottie. Lottie Braun, your niece."

"Wha-a-at?" Aunt Cora fiddled with the hearing aid in her ear. "Come over here. I can't understand a word you're saying." She swatted Eva's arm. "Who is that, Eva?"

Lottie faced her head-on and raised her voice. "It's Lottie. I'm home, Aunt Cora."

"Lottie!" Cora yanked the hearing aid out and dropped it in her lap. "Lottie's not here. She's at the conservatory."

Eva stared at her sister-in-law. "Not anymore, Cora. She's a famous pianist. Remember?"

Sam looked over their heads at Lottie. "See what I mean?"

She nodded. "It's all right."

"No, I know what happened," Cora said suddenly. "Lottie died."

Eva raised her voice. "Helen died, Cora. HELEN."

Aunt Cora's pink-rimmed eyes filled with tears. "I knew it."

Lottie stepped between the wheelchairs and sat next to Jason on the window sill. Reaching for Cora's hand she said, "Can I keep you company for a little bit?"

"What?" Cora said. "Say, you look familiar."

Eva rolled her eyes in disgust. "Don't mind Cora. She's having a bad day." She pointed at Lottie. "Now, who did you say you were?"

"I'm Lottie."

"Lottie. Oh, yes." Eva said nothing more, but her gaze didn't leave Lottie's face.

They stayed a half-hour, though it felt like a week. Sam kept the conversation going, while Jason did his part by looking young and handsome. Lottie did her best to follow Sam's lead as the truth about her aunts sank in. They were old, they were fragile, and they lived almost exclusively in the past.

Good-bye was much harder than hello at the nursing home. Aunt

Eva tightened her grip on Sam's hand as he rose to leave. He had to make many promises to return soon before she was willing to let go. Finally, Sam and Jason kissed each aunt's parchment cheek and headed for the safety of the hallway.

Lottie had an easier time with Aunt Cora, who had drifted off to sleep. She slipped her hand out of Cora's slackened hold and maneuvered carefully past the wheelchairs. "Bye, Aunt Eva," she said as she passed.

"Good bye, Lottie."

Startled, Lottie looked into the lucid eyes of the aunt she remembered. Eva nodded. "Come see us again, dear."

Lottie reached for Eva's hands. "I will," she said. "Oh, I certainly will."

As they emerged into the sunlight, Sam turned to Lottie. "Sorry about that. I was hoping to catch them on a good day."

Lottie smiled. "I'd say this was a very good day."

"Do you have time for a detour?" Lottie asked Sam on their way out of town.

"Where do you want to go?"

"I want to see my dad's farm. Turn right at the highway, then left on Cemetery Road, if that's still its name."

"I know the way," he said. "The first time I ever really noticed you was in that farmhouse kitchen."

"The night of the fire?" She forced herself not to think of the yellowed newspaper headline. "Whenever I think of the night Pop died, I see a big group of young men who walked in behind Helen, but I never see your faces." She glanced sidelong at Sam. "So you were there."

"At the time I wished I wasn't. Fourteen-year-old boys aren't good at handling that kind of stuff. It wasn't right, a bunch of strangers intruding right then."

Her smile was sad. "You all hightailed it out of there as fast as you could go. All except Parson." She paused, remembering the serious young man who had stopped to pray for her family. "He knew exactly what to do."

"He always did," Sam said. "Parson was a good man."

She nodded, her gaze on the passing farmland. "There it is! Slow down."

He pulled into the drive, and she drank in the sight of the old farmstead. The fire had taken the barn and Pop's workshop, so she did not recognize any of the outbuildings. But someone had taken good care of the house. It was white with black shutters, as she remembered, and a big patch of day lilies bloomed around the front porch. She closed her eyes and pictured the rhubarb patch, and the lilac bush by the back door, and Helen's rose garden.

Sam's voice broke into her thoughts. "They added on to the back a while ago. Must have doubled the square footage. I bet they wouldn't mind if we walked around and took a look."

Her eyes flew open. "No. I'm better off remembering how it used to be."

A smile lit his blue eyes as he threw the car into gear. "Fair enough."

As they left Westmont, Lottie turned thoughtful. "Sam, if you felt sorry for me when Pop died, why were you so mean when I joined the band?"

A grin stole across his face. "I wasn't mean. I was toughening you up."

"You were horrible."

"Well, how would you like to have a ten-year-old—"

"Eleven."

"Don't mess with the facts—a ten-year-old show you up every night? The way I saw it, I had a right to be mad."

"Being in the Neverland was like having a bunch of older brothers I never asked for," Lottie said.

"Yup. That's how it was. And the one brother who was mine by blood was the worst of the bunch."

"Did you ever see him again?"

He cracked a smile. "Oh, sure. Walt looked me up one Christmas, when he was feeling sentimental. He was a lounge singer in Las Vegas, and his third wife had just left him. Since she was the best part of the act, he didn't know what he was going to do. We invited him to our house for the holidays. After that, we always had a working address for him, anyway."

Lottie tried to picture dashing Walter Harms as a washed-up Vegas act. "Remember the night he left the band? I thought that woman's husband was going to murder him. I'll never forget the way you raced to the train station to get them out of town. You rescued Walter that night."

"Maybe so." He shook his head. "Too bad I couldn't help him the last time I saw him. One day out of the blue he showed up, dying of liver cancer. He passed away a few weeks later in Collison General, with Nancy holding his hand."

"That's so sad."

Sam shrugged. "Walt had a pretty good life—it was interesting, any-way—and he chose to go out on his own terms."

She dragged a tissue out of her purse and blew her nose. "I guess that's all anyone can ask for."

"I don't know about that. My brother refused the kind of hope that would have made it all worthwhile."

She looked out the window, mentally braced for a Sunday sermon. When he didn't continue, she breathed a sigh of relief.

Thanks to Sam's low-key presence on Sunday afternoon, Lottie felt equal to whatever Monday might bring. Her first challenge was a visit from Rhonda. Was it her imagination, or did the younger woman look around the office with extra-curious eyes?

Rhonda's gaze fell to the new rug. "You've added another touch since last week," she said. "So creative."

Lottie swiveled her chair toward her visitor. "What can I do for you?"

"We need to discuss this afternoon's new student reception. We'll have eight new students in total, with the addition of the two transfers from North Carolina. Have you studied the list I gave you?"

"Yes. They all seem very promising."

She rushed on. "So you know which are yours and which are mine?"

Lottie blinked. "I don't think—"

"It's important to get off on the right foot with your students." Her tone was bright as brass.

"Rhonda."

"Good communication at the reception can really set the expectations."

"Rhonda."

Her colleague pushed forward, determined to place a hands-off sign on her group of students. Lottie sat back and watched the plump white hands wave around in the air as they made each point. At last the storm of words blew itself out, and Rhonda waited expectantly for Lottie to agree.

Lottie got up and shut the door to the office, then indicated a piano bench. "Why don't you have a seat? I'd offer you a chair, but I don't have room for one. I know you understand." As her visitor perched on the edge of the bench, Lottie remained standing. "All right. You've told me how you want this year to go. Now I have something to say."

Rhonda crossed her arms under her ample chest and waited.

"I have no idea where you got this yours-mine-and-ours mentality, but I can't go along with it. I see no benefit in dividing the students up like intramural rugby teams. Certainly, when it comes to private lessons, we each will work with a certain number of students. But whether we meet them in the classroom or on the quad, we're both here to serve all the piano majors."

"It's a matter of work load," Rhonda said impatiently. "One person can't handle the whole department. That's why we divide them up."

Lottie raised her voice to make herself heard. "There are other ways to divide up the work without pitting students against each other."

Rhonda stood up. "I hear what you're saying, but we've always done things this way. Don't worry. You'll catch on." With that parting shot she swept out the door, her crepe-soled shoes squeaking all the way down the hall.

Lottie was left to shake her head at the conversation. She meant what she'd said. She was not going to treat half the piano majors as if they didn't exist.

A few minutes later, the scruffy young janitor put his head around the door. "Hey, I tried to unlock your room last night to empty the trash, but I couldn't get it open."

Lottie gave him what she hoped was a charming smile. "That's because I changed the lock."

"I can't do my job if I don't have a key."

"Don't worry about it. From now on I'll take out my own trash."

He shifted his weight uncertainly. "I'm gonna get in trouble for this."

She stared down her nose at him in her best Lottie-the-Great manner. "If your supervisor gives you trouble, send him to me."

He gave her a look filled with frustration, but he moved on down the hall.

Lottie felt a moment of pity for the young man. The maintenance staff supervisor must be a real drill sergeant to make him so fearful.

If Lottie thought she'd gotten rid of the janitor, she was mistaken. Soon he was back, this time in the shadow of Katherine Snelling. "What's this I hear about your lock being changed?" the dean asked.

Lottie raised her eyebrows. So Katherine was the drill sergeant who struck such fear into the janitor's heart. "I changed it over the weekend."

"Why?"

"For my own peace of mind."

Katherine's thick brows drew together over her long nose. "I know you're used to working in big cities, but extra security measures aren't really necessary around here. There's no crime in Collison."

Lottie would have liked to dispute that claim. "I'll do my own dusting and take out the trash," she said instead. "That way the janitor won't have any extra work."

"This is very irregular." Katherine shook her head. "Maintenance uses a skeleton key for all the offices. It's just easier that way. I'm afraid we're going to have to put your lock back the way it was."

The janitor whispered to someone in the hall. Lottie had the impression she was attracting a crowd. She clenched her fists and relaxed them, willing herself to stay calm. "I don't understand your reasoning, Katherine. I may be overly cautious, but I'm not hurting anyone."

"Please understand. I don't make the rules, but I do have to enforce them." Katherine looked decidedly unhappy. "I'll schedule someone to change your lock."

Lottie made a last effort to keep her dignity. "Could I simply give the extra key to the janitor? It would be simpler."

"That sounds reasonable." Katherine turned to the janitor who waited in the hall. "Did you hear that, Darryl? Miss Braun will give you a key to her office." She stuck her head into the hall. "As for the rest of you, don't you have work to do?"

Dean Snelling shooed the faceless group of people down the hall before her, and Lottie was alone again.

With a heavy heart, she headed across the atrium at lunch time. As she passed Rhonda's office, she steeled herself to look inside. "Want to go to lunch?" she asked. "We could discuss the reception."

"No thanks." The younger woman held up a glass full of brown sludge. "I'm having a SlimFast at my desk."

Lottie went on her way even more soberly. She caught up with Katherine Snelling on her way across the quad. Determined to take the high road, she asked, "May I join you for lunch?"

Katherine looked startled. "I'm on my way to the admin building, actually. I'll have lunch later, at my desk."

"Oh. Well, have a good afternoon."

As Lottie started past, Katherine stopped her. "How is everything going? Are you ready for your first classes tomorrow?"

"As ready as I'll ever be."

"And the student reception this afternoon?"

Lottie frowned. "I have some questions about that."

"That sounds serious." Katherine looked at her watch. "I'm late for a meeting right now, and won't be back until late this afternoon. Drop by my office sometime tomorrow, if you still want to talk."

She hurried off, leaving Lottie to stare after her. If that was the dean's typical way of dealing with questions, she didn't think much of it.

Suddenly the faculty dining room didn't seem so appealing. She needed a friendly face and some information. Maybe Alicia Maynard would be up for a visitor. She retraced her steps to the P.A.B. and stopped at Elaine's desk.

"May I borrow your faculty directory?"

Elaine did not look up from her typing. "Have you lost your own copy?"

Lottie gritted her teeth. "No. I'm on my way out, and I don't want to climb three flights of stairs to my office."

With a sigh, Elaine opened her desk drawer and withdrew the directory. "Here."

"Thank you."

"By the way, Miss Braun, have you ever met a pianist named Andrew Wood?"

"Andrew Wood?" The name sounded familiar. Lottie searched her memory as she wrote down Alicia's address. Handing back the directory, she said, "I don't think so. Why?"

"He was someone very dear to me. He said he met you once."

Lottie smiled. "Oh. Well, I wish I did remember him."

Elaine opened her drawer and dropped the directory back in place. As the drawer rolled shut, a framed photograph in the bottom caught Lottie's eye. "That's a nice-looking man. Is he a relative of yours?"

Elaine returned to her typing. "He was."

When she pulled up to Alicia's tidy bungalow, the first things she noticed was the "Danger: Oxygen in Use" sign on the door. A nurse answered her knock, and slipped outside to speak to her. "Miss Maynard isn't having a good day," she said. "She's asleep at the moment. Are you a friend or a relative?"

"An acquaintance," Lottie said. "I'll come back another time."

"There may not be another time. If it's important, you should wait."

Lottie hesitated. "This seems very sudden. Her retirement party was only two weeks ago."

"She was stubborn about keeping up appearances, but she knew this was coming. I've been caring for her off and on for six months."

Lottie's problems suddenly seemed very small. She'd have to crack the code on department politics without Alicia Maynard's help.

Mitchell was sitting on Miranda's desk again, leaning back on his arms, sure of himself. "Not even as friends?" he asked again, as if she hadn't answered him the same way a dozen times.

She stood by the window, as far away as she could get. "No, Mitchell. Not even as friends. Why do you keep trying with me?"

He treated her to the crooked smile that must have won a thousand hearts. "Because you're beautiful."

"You mean you're bored."

He clapped a hand to his chest. "How can you doubt me?"

"Huh." A movement in the yard outside caught her eye. Jason stood under her window, his head bent over a notepad, writing furiously. The intensity in every line of his body attracted her more than she wanted to admit. His brother's constant playfulness suffered in comparison.

Mitchell slid off the desk and joined her at the window. "I knew it." He hung his head in mock despair. "My own brother moved in on my territory."

He was so obviously not in pain, she had trouble keeping a straight face. "What a disgusting thing to say. I'm not anybody's territory."

He raised a hand to tap on the glass and she grabbed for it, twisting his wrist until he gave up. "Don't do that!"

"All right, all right." He held her at arm's length, laughing. "You've got some grip."

"I think you should go."

His face relaxed into the first genuine openness she'd seen all day. "You're serious about this, aren't you?"

"Yes."

"Does Jase know?"

She lowered her gaze. "He's not interested."

"I find that hard to believe. Did you know you have dimples when you smile?"

She glared at him. "Go home, Mitchell."

He laughed and dropped his hand. "Okay. If Jase is the man, I'm done here."

A panicky thought occurred to her. "You can't tell him."

Mitchell rolled his eyes. "Sheesh, you ask a lot. All right. I won't."

A minute later he was gone. A glance out the window proved Jason had left, too. With a sigh of relief, Miranda picked up her purse. She had errands to run.

She let herself out the back door and had to laugh. Across the lawn, Jessica McCall stood at the clothes line, hanging up her wash. Next to her stood Mitchell, crooked grin in place, chatting her up as if Miranda didn't exist.

He caught her eye and shrugged.

The new student reception turned out well. Lottie stationed herself next to the door and greeted each student by name. She'd prepared a little speech, assuring each of them she was always available, and she delivered it as she pressed a business card into each hand. Only after that did Rhonda succeed in rounding up her protégés.

Lottie talked at length with the remaining four students. She refused to think of them as hers, but she was interested in them. Two were from small Iowa towns where they were considered the brightest and best. They spoke of home with that combination of contempt and affection common to their breed. Her transfer students seemed less comfortable, but with time Lottie thought they would adjust.

When Rhonda called for attention, Lottie was ready. She jumped in as soon as the introductions were over. "I have a few things to say," she said with a winning smile.

Rhonda looked startled. "Oh…Of course."

Lottie looked around the little group. "As many of you know, this is my first semester teaching here at the college. For the freshmen in the group, I'll be learning just as you are. I want to get to know you, and to serve you any way I can." She nodded at Rhonda. "Professor Kennedy and I have discussed some exciting future plans. Stay tuned in the coming years for an expansion of the program. But for this year we'll concentrate on good teaching and accessibility. Now." She turned to her bug-eyed colleague. "That's all I have. Can we let these poor children go?"

Rhonda managed a faint smile. "We'll see you in class." The room emptied and she turned to Lottie, her face red with rage. "That was dirty pool. My students are just that. Mine."

"I will not follow such a destructive policy, Rhonda. We're not adversaries. We're a team, or we should be, anyway."

Rhonda looked skeptical. "Look, I don't know where you've been working, but around here it's every man for himself. Alicia taught me that."

"Well, Alicia was wrong," Lottie said gently. "I've spent the last ten years at the best conservatories in the nation. I've experienced great departments and weak ones, and all the great ones are team efforts. I don't know Alicia Maynard very well, but if she was as difficult as everyone says, I'm sorry for you. That doesn't mean you have to walk in her footsteps."

Throughout this speech Rhonda's gaze was trained on the carpet, but now it flew to Lottie's face. "I wouldn't follow Alicia anywhere."

Lottie raised her eyebrows. "Really?"

Rhonda hugged her arms to her body. "Look, this is my first job as a professor. They told me when I was hired that Alicia just needed to be jollied along until she retired. How was I to know she'd last another five years? And all that time, she made my life miserable. She chose only the classes she wanted, all the best students. She even showed off that corner office like some kind of status symbol."

"She's dying."

"No kidding." Rhonda gave a hollow laugh. "She's been dying for five years. That cough!"

Lottie broke in. "I mean I stopped by her house today. The hospice nurse said she could go any time."

The news silenced Rhonda. She swallowed hard. "You probably think I'm a horrible person."

"I do think you're trying to play out your grudge against Alicia at my expense."

A little of Rhonda's anger returned. "I'm just protecting my position. I didn't wait five long years just so you could come along and take Alicia's place.

"I don't want Alicia's place."

The younger woman rolled her eyes. "Sure you don't. You're Lottie Braun, for crying out loud. You're not some run-of-the-mill new hire. How on earth you chose Collison College I'll never know."

"I moved to Collison for personal reasons," Lottie said firmly. "The professorship is a bonus. Look, I don't want to be in charge, but I do want to be part of something constructive. So far, this isn't it."

Rhonda's gaze returned to the carpet. She was silent so long Lottie finally prepared to leave. "Think it over, anyway."

"Wait."

Lottie turned. "Yes?"

"You have a point about working as a team." Rhonda raised her head. "I'm willing to try things your way. But I'm keeping the office."

Miranda was beginning to wish this week would end. Now that classes had begun, her work load had slowed to a trickle. She rearranged Lottie's files for the fourteenth time and wondered what to do next. "Take a day off. Go shopping," Lottie had said when she mentioned how slow things were.

Shopping? In Collison? Miranda would rather work.

Having finished their planning phase, Harms and Sons were nowhere to be found. Even Mitchell stayed away, though she'd seen him from a distance in the yard next door.

At two o'clock she decided to take Lottie's advice and close up shop. A mid-week nap—such a luxury—would feel great.

The ring of the telephone woke her from her nap. Half-asleep, she rolled off the couch and stumbled to the kitchen to pick it up.

"My name is Donna Davenport," said the voice on the other end. "Is this Miranda Charles?"

"Yes." Miranda tried to gather her sleep-strewn thoughts.

"I wonder if you would be interested in a little business deal. I'm writing a biography of your employer, Lottie Braun. Now, as you may already know, I've been unable to reach her personally. It's a shame, because she is the best person to check the accuracy of my facts. I need source material for research purposes. Letters, photographs, official school transcripts. That sort of thing. Anything you can furnish would be worth a pretty penny."

Miranda was wide awake now. "I'm not interested." She hung up fast, while the woman was still speaking.

She sank onto the couch and shook her head to clear it. How many people had Donna Davenport approached with that offer? How many had accepted?

By the end of the first week of classes, Lottie felt good. Friday afternoon she double-checked the lock on her office door and walked away with a lighter heart. With any luck at all, this weekend would be uneventful. Lottie needed to put her feet up.

Marmalade wound around her ankles as she let herself into the house. "Wait a minute, big fella." She filled a bowl with cat food and set it outside the door. Maybe he only wanted her for her tuna-flavored nuggets, but he was still good company. A weekend alone wouldn't bother her, but the house did get quiet.

When the band began to tune, she steeled herself for the excruciating noise. Instead the unmistakable sound of a saxophone filled the air and added a surprising depth to the enterprise. It was not the squeak of a beginner, either: This sax player had chops.

Lottie was so intrigued she forgot to feel frustrated. She manufactured an errand to the garage and stood behind a little group of fans to see what was going on. The same three boys were making music, but the bass player had switched to sax. He had center stage, while the others backed him. She gave the band leader grudging respect for that. Not many men would share the spotlight. The sound they made as a group was a darn sight more original than Tommy singing bad '70s party songs.

Original it might be, but it still was not easy to sleep to, Lottie thought as she lay awake hours later. Where did young people get their stamina? The sax player's lip should be shot by now.

She sighed. At least she could sleep in on Saturday.

At eight o'clock Saturday morning, Sam took the stairs to the third floor of the P.A.B., skirted a janitor's cart and started across the atrium. Halfway across he passed a shaggy young man in coveralls, watering the plants. Sam said hello, but the kid didn't seem to hear him.

The back hall was dark and Lottie's door locked, as it should be. He pulled a flashlight from his pocket and shined it through the frosted glass window. As near as he could tell, nothing seemed out of place.

The whole process took seconds and he was on his way, this time to the freight elevator. He rounded a corner in time to see the elevator open and a man step in.

The man whipped around when he heard Sam's footsteps, and they stared at each other in surprise. "Dad?"

"Jason?"

They rode down in uncomfortable silence.

Eight

*I*f it weren't for Martha Williams, Lottie would not have returned to church. She didn't belong among that uncomplicated crowd of believers, singing innocent hymns of salvation and joy. But Martha had missed her last Sunday. She'd stopped by several times to say so, and her expressions of friendly concern felt so sweet that Lottie talked herself into going to church one more time, just to please her.

Now she walked up the sanctuary aisle, clutching a brand new Bible, and looked around. Martha and Ed were nowhere to be seen.

Jason Harms caught her eye and pointed at the seat beside him. Sam sat on his other side, nose buried in the church bulletin.

"Excuse me," Lottie said to the couple at the end of the pew. She eased past their knees and sank down next to Jason. "Thanks."

Sam reached across his son to hand Lottie the bulletin, open to a list of prayer concerns. She skimmed it without interest. The list looked to her like a polite way to spread gossip. "Mary Jorgensen will have her gall bladder out on Tuesday. Wisdom for the surgeon." "George Marshall flies out to visit his sister in Maryland on Thursday morning. Travel mercies." Trite.

She caught her breath at the third item on the list. "Carey Marks, daughter of Ed and Martha Williams, delivered a premature baby in Peoria on Thursday. Ed and Martha have gone to help out. Good health for the baby. Protection over the house while they're gone." Lottie stared at the words. She'd been so busy she hadn't even noticed they were gone.

The words to the first hymn were unfamiliar and strange, something about a mount and an Ebenezer, but the tune made her heart sing. She reached the phrase, "prone to wander, Lord, I feel it" and stopped singing to look around. Were any of these good people "prone to wander"? She doubted it.

The hymn came to an end, and Reverend Summers stood up. "Today's passage comes from the ninth chapter of Matthew."

The pages of Lottie's new Bible crackled as she scrambled to find her place. Once upon a time she'd memorized the books in order, but forty years of piano notes stood between her and that information. By the time she found the page, the minister was finishing up.

"When the Pharisees saw this, they asked his disciples, 'Why does your teacher eat with tax collectors and sinners?' On hearing this, Jesus said, 'It is not the healthy who need a doctor, but the sick. But go and learn what this means: 'I desire mercy, not sacrifice.' For I have not come to call the righteous, but sinners.'"

Reverend Summers looked up from the text with a smile. "Jesus spent time with some pretty shady characters."

Lottie found herself smiling back at the minister. She liked this man's Jesus.

"Are you doing anything for lunch?" Sam asked Lottie after the service. She took her time answering, which for some reason made his palms sweat. "Jase and I usually go down the highway to the Hawk's Nest. There's always room for one more."

Her smile was regretful. "I can't today. I have another engagement."

"Okay." He nodded, kept his voice relaxed. "We start demolition bright and early tomorrow morning. Did you clean out the sewing room?"

"Not yet." She pulled car keys out of her purse. "I'll have it done by tomorrow, though."

Jason joined them. "Are you ready to go, Dad?"

He gave his son a too-hearty clap on the shoulder. "Lead the way."

♪♩

Lottie kicked herself all the way home. "'I have another engage-ment.' Ugh. What am I, a New York debutante? He probably thinks I'm a first-class snob."

She'd reacted the way she always did when a man showed interest, warning him off before she hurt him. She wasn't trustworthy with the people she loved. But Sam was only being Iowa friendly. Surely she could trust herself to have a casual lunch with him. Couldn't she?

Sam's invitation and her response played in her mind until she pulled the Mercedes into the alley. Then, "It's no use beating myself up about it," she said firmly. "Next time, I'll give a different answer." If there was a next time.

Marmalade jumped onto the porch as she let herself into the kitch-en. She opened the door wider, and he marched inside.

Shortly after lunch Jessica stopped by. "I'm looking for the cat. I haven't seen him today."

"Come in," Lottie said. "He's taking up most of my couch."

"Tom, you bum. You know you belong outside." Jessica hurried to the couch and tried to lift the cat, but he would not budge. She turned her big eyes on Lottie. "I'm sorry about this."

"It's my fault. I feed him. By the way, I call him Marmalade."

"Marmalade." Jessica smiled. "I like that."

"Why don't you have a seat?"

She looked uncertain. "Well, if I'm not interrupting anything…"

"Not at all. I'm trying to avoid doing some heavy lifting, actually."

"Oh? Can I help?" When Lottie hesitated, she added, "I really don't mind. I need a break from painting the bedrooms in Grandpa's house."

"All right. But remember, you suggested this." Lottie led the way to the sewing room. "I have to move everything out of this room today. I've got builders coming tomorrow to start a new addition, and they're going to put a hole in this outer wall."

Jessica gazed around the tiny room. "This doesn't look hard."

"You don't know the half of it." Lottie opened the sewing cabinet and

113

an avalanche of remnants fell to the floor. "This is the real problem."

The girl's face lit up. "Look at all that fabric! I know a quilter in Iowa City who would give her right arm for this stash. Would you consider selling it?"

Lottie shook her head. "It all belongs to Patti. I'm holding on to it until she has time to come pick it up. We'll pack everything in boxes and store them in the garage."

Jessica proved to be a willing worker. She used all the space in each box, and listed the contents on each label. "You've done this before," Lottie said after a while.

She shrugged. "I'm an old pro at moving. My mom can't keep a place more than a few months before she drinks her rent money." Her lips turned up in a half-smile. "It's not like I'm all that stable, either. I'm always chasing better apartments or easier roommates." She glanced at Lottie, who was taping shut a box of patterns. "You're not so bad at this yourself."

Lottie nodded, her eyes on her work. "I left home at eleven years old. Since then I haven't lived anywhere more than a few years."

"Wow." Jessica shoved another box into the hall. "That sounds like me."

Lottie met the girl's sympathetic gaze with a smile. "It had its good side, you know. I always looked forward to the next new thing. If the shower in one apartment dripped cold water, at least the problem was temporary."

Jessica laughed. "I once had a roommate with a horrible temper. He was a painter, and whenever he got frustrated he'd fling his brushes at the wall. It made for a very Jackson Pollock-like living room."

Lottie chuckled. "When I was a student in Paris I roomed with an opera singer, a soprano, who liked to sing in the shower. Imagine waking up to that every morning."

Jessie looked at her curiously. "You studied in Paris? What was it like?"

"Wonderful. My teachers at the Paris Conservatory were exactly what I needed at that point in my career." She smiled, remembering. "For two years I did nothing but eat, sleep, and breathe music. It was heaven."

"Paris is so cool." Jessie sounded envious. "I've always wanted to sit at a sidewalk cafe and soak in the atmosphere. Was it as amazing as it looks in all those travel posters?"

Lottie opened another drawer and tried to remember what Paris looked like. Images of practice rooms sprang to mind. "I don't know," she said finally. "I was too involved in my work, I guess."

Jessie sighed. "I'll never get to Paris."

"Don't look so heartbroken. You can be just as lonely—or broke, or stuck—in Paris as you are right here in Iowa."

Jessie rolled her eyes. "You don't expect me to believe that, do you?" She brightened. "Y'know, when it comes to Grandpa's house, I've gotten a lot less stuck. Last week Mrs. Williams stopped by and offered to help me sort through his things. Then Mr. Harms brought me some cans of paint and took a look at the broken pipes. Mitchell's been helping me paint, too."

"That's good news."

"I'm pretty sure you had something to do with it," Jessie said with a smile. "Now it's my turn to do you a favor. Let's take some brownies to Tommy's band."

Lottie chuckled. "Are you sure that's a good idea?"

"Oh, they taste good. I promise. Mrs. Williams helped me bake them a couple of days ago. She was really sweet about it." Jessica got to her feet. "So how about it?"

"I'll pass," Lottie said. "If I give those kids brownies, they'll probably check them for pins, or staples, or whatever those creepy people put in apples on Halloween. You go ahead."

"Okay, but I'm going to say they're from you."

In the fading light of evening, Lottie turned on the sewing room light. A cool breeze from the window bathed her hot face. With Jessie's help, she had vanquished the sewing cabinet, but they hadn't touched the rest of the room.

The night was still as Lottie carried a box of fabric down the brick path. When she reached the garage, she glanced across the alley. Tommy sat alone in a pool of light, picking out a tune on an acoustic guitar.

His voice carried on the breeze, and she paused a moment to listen. He was singing "Dust in the Wind." She had to admit the boy could sing. She closed her eyes and let the music take hold.

The boy broke off in the middle of a word. Startled, she opened her eyes to find him looking straight at her. "Can I help you?"

His defensive posture reminded her of Sammy at that age, part anger, part bravado. "Go on," she said mildly. "I'm just putting something in the garage."

He stared at her as she opened the door and stepped inside, but when she returned with an empty box, he'd gone back to his song. The bleak words followed her up the walk: Nothing lasts forever.

Yesterday she'd have said that was certainly true. Nothing lasted forever. People, houses, even music served their allotted purpose and were gone. But today she'd sat in church with a whole lot of people who thought differently. She liked their ideas about a God who loved broken people. She only wished she could believe them.

She opened the screen door and dropped the box on the kitchen floor. "There, Helen. That should give me a good start."

She talked to Helen as though her sister could hear, as if she still existed somewhere. Foolishness.

She made short work of the bookcase by the sewing room door. Never a reader, she stowed the books without looking, shoved the full box into the hall, and moved on. The frames on the wall proved more difficult. Every garment was a work of art, from the choice of fabric to the tiny stitches in each hem. The pieces spoke of the woman who created them. Lottie touched the protective glass with reverent fingers as memories assailed her: Helen at Aunt Cora's sewing machine, learning to make buttonholes. Helen on endless trains, mending for the Neverland boys. Helen sewing tiny garments for the baby boy she loved.

After a while, Lottie wrapped most of the frames in paper and slid them carefully into a moving crate. The purple dress was the hardest to part with. Maybe it was like Sam said. Maybe Patti really wouldn't miss this if it was gone when she got here. Lottie traced the smocked bodice through the glass. For all she knew, the girl wasn't even coming.

In the end she wrapped the little dress and stored it with the others. At least she knew Helen had kept it all these years. A precious thought indeed.

Feeling efficient, she looked at her watch. Nine o'clock. The only thing left was the nightstand next to the bed. The narrow drawer was empty, except for Lottie's hand lotion and nail file. But when she yanked on the cupboard door below, dozens of photographs poured onto the floor.

She picked up the top one. Parson and Helen smiled at the camera, their arms around each other. Flipping it over, she found the date: May 25, 1956, written in Helen's sloping handwriting.

Easter 1958. A color picture showed Helen holding little Patti. The child arched away from her mama, her arms outstretched to the camera. December 1971. Teen-aged Patti stared out of the frame, her beautiful eyes rimmed with sooty black lashes. Lottie wondered what had happened to put the belligerent look on her face. June 1966. Thanksgiving 1974. The dates were jumbled. She frowned at the pile, dismayed by the mess. Here was a favor she could do for her sister. She slid to the floor and rested her back against the side of the bed. She had her work cut out for her.

It was slow going. Every picture told a story or filled in a detail of Helen's life. Lottie examined them, eager to understand the family she'd never known. Most precious were the details: Parson behind his black manual typewriter. Helen in a pillbox hat and white gloves, a la Jacqueline Kennedy. Gatherings of friends, including the Harmses and the Williamses. A child's birthday, with all the guests in paper party hats.

Some of the pictures were blurry, as though the camera had moved. Others were ruined by someone blinking or breaking their pose. She placed these in a "seconds" pile, so Patti could decide whether to keep or toss them.

Lottie didn't have enough snapshots of her life to fill a manila envelope. No pictures of family. Certainly no black-and-white photos of school chums, perhaps taken at a French cafe on the Left Bank. Her mementos were limited to plaques and awards and professional staff photos for the colleges she'd worked for.

A while later she stood and stretched, conscious of a job well done. The pictures, in order by date, filled three shoe boxes. She carried them to the hall and placed them with the others, all except the small pile of seconds. Against her better judgement, she stuck the seconds in an envelope and took them up to Miranda's office.

♪

When Miranda arrived at work Monday morning, she found her employer in the back yard with the Harms and Sons crew. Mitchell's face lit up when he saw her, but Jason never looked her way. She bit her lip and headed inside.

Coffee in hand, she started for the stairs, but a knock at the kitchen door stopped her. Jason stood on the porch, looking anywhere but at her. "Lottie says there's a bed to be moved before we get started."

She stepped aside to let him in. "She also wants the sewing machine removed from the built-in cupboard. It was the only thing she couldn't do herself. Do you need any help?"

"No thanks."

Before she could think of something else to say, he strode across the kitchen and into the hall. She hurried after him, but by the time she'd navigated a maze of moving boxes and reached the sewing room he'd already yanked off the bedding and dumped it on the floor.

She scooped the sheets and blankets into an untidy bundle. "I'll take these to the washer."

"Suit yourself."

The mattress hit the floor with a thud as she reached the basement door. He'd have his work cut out for him if he tried to carry that day bed alone.

She felt her way down the steps by the light from the kitchen and dropped her burden on the cool cement floor. Three steps forward, and she reached for the light bulb string she'd seen before, but found a spider web instead. "Ugh!" She wiped her arm on her skirt and peered around. What else might she find on her path to the washing machine? Path was the right word, too: a narrow walkway through piles of junk. A Schwinn two-wheeler with half a wicker basket. A faded green chair with reproduction claw and ball feet. She picked up a wooden tennis racket with no strings. Helen Parker must have had something against yard sales.

A chilling yowl tore through the air. With a startled scream, she whirled to meet the threat. A gigantic orange cat stalked toward her, its back arched. She crouched, racket out, and shouted, "Stay back!"

Jason's voice sounded from the top of the stairs. "Everything all right down there?"

"Yep." She shook her weapon at the hissing cat. "Scat!"

Jason's long legs appeared on the stairs, followed by the rest of him. He glanced from Miranda to the cat and started to grin. "Hey, big guy." The animal ran forward and rubbed its back against his work boots. He reached down and scratched it behind one scarred ear.

Miranda let the racket drop with a clatter. "You know him?"

He nodded. "I've seen him wandering the neighborhood." He pointed toward the back corner. "I'd say he got in through that window."

She peered through the gloom. Sure enough, a small, dirty window on the back wall stood ajar. "Well, don't I feel silly."

He looked at the racket. "What were you planning to do with that?"

"Protect myself." She lifted her chin. "I don't do *helpless female.*"

"I think we established that the other day." Was he laughing at her again? "I guess small animals just aren't your thing."

Above them, a pair of work boots tromped across the kitchen and stopped at the basement door. Mitchell called, "Jase? What're you doing down there?"

Jason threw an impatient glance over his shoulder. "A cat got in. I heard it yowling."

"Oh yeah?" Mitchell sounded interested. "The big orange one?"

He scooped the massive kitty into his arms. "I'll let him out for you," he murmured to Miranda. As he walked upstairs he said, "Come help me move that bed, Mitch."

With a sigh, she turned on the washing machine and threw in the sheets. Talks with Jason never went where she wanted them to.

The Harms brothers were making plenty of noise when she came upstairs. She stood in the front hall and waited while they carried the bed to the second floor, Mitchell in front, Jason bearing most of the load from behind. As they made the turn in the staircase, something fell to the floor with a crash of splintering glass. "Nice going, Jase," Mitchell said.

"There's too much china in this house," Jason muttered. "When is Patti coming to get her things?"

"How should I know?" Mitchell sounded defensive. "She doesn't exactly send me updates."

Miranda frowned. Everything depended on Patti coming home, but the wretch never answered her phone. Lottie said she worked at a department store with a name that probably started with C, but she wasn't sure what Patti did, or which location she worked in. After the fourth fruitless phone call to a suburban shopping mall, Miranda had given up in frustration.

A series of thumps in the room above her announced that the bed was now in place. When the brothers trooped downstairs a minute later, she stopped them. "I heard you talking about Patti. I've been calling her to find out when she's coming, but she never answers. If you know where she works, I can try calling her there."

Mitchell and Jason exchanged a look she couldn't read. "Last I knew, she bought shoes for Carson Pirie Scott," Mitchell said. "She worked at the headquarters downtown. Call the switchboard and ask for the purchasing department."

Miranda blinked. "Wow. I wish I'd asked you a week ago." She wanted to ask why he knew those particular details, but he'd already walked away.

Upstairs, she dialed the office phone. "Information? I need the number for the Carson Pirie Scott headquarters in Chicago."

After a few tries, she finally connected with the secretary in purchasing. "Patricia Parker is out of the office this week. May I leave a message?"

Of all the luck. "This is Lottie Braun's office, on a personal matter."

"Ma'am, I gave Patricia your last message. Please be patient. I'm sure she'll call you back."

Miranda sat up straight in her chair. "There must be some mistake. I didn't call you."

"Well, someone called about Lottie Braun. I remember the name because of Lottie Braun the famous pianist."

"Yes, that's who I work for."

"No kidding? Well, that changes everything." The woman sounded awed. "Patricia will be back in the office next Monday. I'd be happy to leave her a message."

Miranda left her name and number and hung up, her mind on the secretary's other caller. She was positive Lottie hadn't tried her niece at work. That left one other possibility: Donna Davenport.

Speaking of Ms. Davenport, Lottie had asked Miranda to find out everything she could about the woman. She'd started by checking out Davenport's Elvis biography from the library. The author's style was as lurid as her choice of title: *Burning Love*.

Miranda sighed. She'd finish the book today, or die trying.

Comfort was called for, so she slipped off her shoes, leaned her chair back, and propped her feet on the desk, ankles crossed. In a burst of inspiration, she remembered the bag of M&Ms in her top drawer. Perfect accompaniment to the schlock she was reading.

That's how Jason found her half an hour later, lounging with her feet up and her skirt well above her knees, her hand in an M&M bag. She sat up straight when he appeared in the doorway, but it was too late. He'd gotten an eyeful.

He raised an eyebrow. "This is what you do all day?"

Her face grew warm. "More or less. I throw in a little Danielle Steele now and then."

The reference passed over his head. "We need a decision on some rose bushes. Does Lottie want to transplant them?"

She reached for the phone, grateful for something sensible to do. "I'll have to call and ask. How many plants are we talking about?"

"Six or eight. Dad says they might be important to her."

A minute later, Miranda hung up the phone. "Keep the roses. She'll transplant them when she gets home."

"Okay." A smile crept into his eyes. "I'll let you get back to work. Those M&Ms won't eat themselves."

Before she could think of a comeback, he was downstairs.

Lottie's steps were light as she mounted the stairs to the third floor after lunch. The morning had been a productive one, and she'd even found someone to sit with in the dining hall. Since word had gotten out about the new lock on her door, Nathan Bartholomew had decided she was cool.

In deference to Rhonda's open office door, Lottie resisted the urge to hum as she crossed the atrium. Humming was a bad habit anyway, annoying to everyone but the hummer.

A surprise visitor waited for her in the back hall. Cal Jefferson leaned against her office door, a sober look on his face. "I need a word with you."

Her light mood drained away. "What's going on?"

"I had a phone call from a woman named Donna Davenport this morning. Do you know her?"

"I know of her."

Cal shook his head. "She interviewed me for her book about Elvis, so she pretends we're friends. She called to talk about you."

"May I ask what you told her?"

"I said I don't know anything more than the rest of your adoring public." He met her gaze squarely. "I believe we established that a few weeks ago."

She nodded, grateful. "Yes. Thank you."

He hesitated. "If it makes any difference—and for some reason, I think it might—she only asked about your celebrity connections. Sinatra, Leonard Bernstein, your Paris years. That, and some competition you judged in Philadelphia."

Lottie did her best to hide her relief. "All right."

He shrugged. "I thought you should know. When that woman sinks her teeth into a subject, she's like a hound with a cornered rabbit."

A rueful smile lifted the corners of Lottie's mouth. "Thanks, Cal."

As he sauntered down the hall, she unlocked her office with unsteady hands. A cornered rabbit, indeed.

After her last lesson Lottie packed her book bag and hurried downstairs, eager to get home and inspect the construction site. As she drove down the alley, she heard the commotion before she saw the backhoe digging beside her house. A pile of debris had collected in the yard, evidence of the day's work. This was exciting.

Jason met her in the yard. "Sorry for the mess. I'm afraid you'll be living with a lot of dust for a while."

She waved off his apology. "I appreciate how quickly you got down to business."

The young man's smile turned wry. "You've got my dad to thank for that. He should be here any minute. I guess he's decided to supervise this one himself." The back door banged and he looked past her, his eyes alight with interest.

"I thought that was you, Miss Braun." Miranda sounded a bit breathless as she joined them.

Lottie smiled at her pretty assistant. "I've been inspecting the construction site. Have you had a busy day?"

Miranda nodded. "Did you want to see those rose bushes? They're on the porch."

"Sure." Lottie started for the porch with Miranda, but stopped, hands on hips, as a black sedan rolled up the alley and stopped. "Another friend of Tommy's, no doubt," she said, disgusted. "Every night they crowd the alley until the rest of us can barely pass through."

"What are you going to do?" Miranda said.

"I'd like to give this one a piece of my mind. No one can get past that parking job."

But before she could move, the door opened and a slender, dark-haired woman stepped out. In one fluid move she opened the back door and released a small child from an infant seat. Lifting the baby onto her hip, she turned—and let out a shriek.

"What are you doing to my house?"

Nine

"Patti!" Lottie hurried down the brick path. "I'm so glad you've come."

"It's Patricia." The icy voice stopped Lottie in her tracks. "Who gave you the right to tear down my house?"

"Your mother did."

Patti's eyes shot sparks of anger. "Well, she didn't mean you could do all this." She jabbed a tense hand toward the construction site. "You've got a lot of nerve, you know that?"

"Welcome home, Patti." Jason moved to Lottie's side, an island of quiet reassurance.

Patti turned on him. "Jase. Make her stop."

He shrugged. "I can't. I'm the general contractor."

"I should have known you'd make a buck off this if you could."

A smile played around Jason's lips. "Same old Patti. You okay here, Miss Braun?"

"Sure, Jason. Knock off for the day." Lottie nodded toward Miranda, who had joined them. "Take my assistant with you. She works too hard." To Patti she said, "You'll be wanting to take care of your mother's things, of course. You can use your old bedroom while you're here."

Patti raised a sculpted eyebrow. "Where else?" She stepped past Lottie and started for the house.

Lottie made no move to follow.

Miranda kept her eyes on her shoes as she and Jason walked down the alley. "Well, that was interesting."

He snorted. "Patti's always been dramatic. It gets old pretty fast."

"She seemed to think you would come to her rescue."

"She has me confused with my brother. He's always been a soft touch." He stopped as they reached Miranda's car. "How is your running going? I haven't seen you on the square lately."

She chuckled. "I learned my lesson. I've been sticking to park paths."

"With your rape whistle, I assume."

She laughed. "Of course."

He stood there a moment longer, looking at her as though he wanted to say more. She smiled up at him and hoped she didn't look too eager.

"Well, see you around," he said, and ambled on down the alley, his hands in his pockets.

She couldn't decide whether to laugh or cry.

When Lottie reached the kitchen, all the cupboard doors were open. Patti stood in front of the open fridge with the baby on the floor at her feet. "There's no food in this house."

"I wasn't expecting company."

Her niece sighed. "We'll have to go out for dinner, I guess. Is Fresh Harvest still open on campus? It's the only decent place in town. I'm not raising Sarah on red meat and starch."

Lottie looked at the curly haired little girl who stared back with solemn blue eyes. "How old is Sarah?"

"Fifteen months." Patti reached for the phone book. "She was a preemie. That's why she's so small. Aha!" She jabbed a manicured fingernail at an ad in the Yellow Pages. "There it is."

Lottie nodded. "I'll see you after dinner, then."

Patti looked up, eyes narrowed. "Listen, you'd better come with us.

I'll fill you in on what I've decided."

An hour later they stared at one another across the remains of two aggressively healthy salads. The battle light still shone in Patti's eyes. "The estate company starts tomorrow. I assume that's okay."

Lottie's tongue found the remains of a walnut wedged between two molars. "Would you consider selling some things to me?"

Patti shook her head. "I need to get top dollar for everything. It won't do us any good to get into a haggling war over the china hutch."

There was more to this refusal than met the eye. "Fair enough. Have you scheduled a day for the auction?"

"This Saturday. I'm staying to supervise, of course. I can't afford to trust these people." Patti leaned in, her eyes trained on Lottie's face. "By the way, if you've stolen anything out of Mother's estate, I'll pursue legal action."

Lottie matched her glare for glare. "Why would I steal your stuff? I'm filthy rich, remember?" The accusation, leveled at her during the reading of Helen's will, had stung.

Patti lost the stare-down. Reaching for the baby she said, "We should get home. I've got a portable crib to set up before I can put Sarah to bed."

A crowd of Tommy's friends clogged the alley as they drove down it. Lottie gave an irritated snort at the noise they made. "Not this again."

Patti stared at the crowd. "I used to babysit Tommy after his dad left, when his mom was too depressed to move off the couch."

Lottie shot her a thoughtful glance. "So that's why everyone around here calls him 'poor Tommy.'"

"I always figured he'd turn out okay." Patti flipped her black hair back from her face. "Kids are pretty tough."

Lottie awoke to the sound of the shower running at the end of the hall. Patti was making an early start today.

She lay in bed for a moment, gazing at the ceiling. "She's here, Helen," she said under her breath. "Now what?"

The bathroom was warm and steamy after Patti's shower. Lottie washed her face and brushed her hair, then smoothed a stray wave with wet fingers. She'd shower at night while Patti was here. It would be no problem.

As she passed Patti's closed bedroom door, the sound of baby giggles made her smile. Whatever the young woman's faults, she obviously doted on her daughter.

Lottie was making scrambled eggs when her guests came downstairs. "I hope you like eggs," she said with a smile. "It's the only dish I've ever mastered."

Patti shook her head. "I bring my own cereal with me when I travel."

"And the little one?"

She relented a fraction. "Sarah can have some, I guess."

The three settled to their breakfast in silence. Patti munched on bran flakes in skim milk with grim determination, while Lottie sipped cream-laced coffee and read the paper. Sarah put away three helpings of eggs and a piece of toast before her mother took the plate.

"The estate company will be here any minute," Patti said. "You'll want to be out of the way."

Lottie looked up from the paper. "I wouldn't mind meeting them."

"No need." Patti's voice held a note of sarcasm. "I'll make sure they don't damage your house." She raised an eyebrow. "Any more than you already have."

Lottie ignored the jab. "I'd like to meet them anyway."

She was brushing her teeth when the estate company van pulled up. Their voices filtered through the window as they crossed the yard.

"How's it goin', Sam?" a woman's voice called.

"Hey, Tina," Sam called back. "Are you doing the estate sale for Patti?"

"Depends," Tina answered. "She wants a pretty short turnaround time. I gotta see what we're dealing with first."

When Lottie walked downstairs, Patti was in the kitchen with a wiry, gum-snapping ball of energy who turned out to be Tina. "We can be ready by Saturday," Tina was saying. "You and the baby can leave all the work to us."

Patti put up a hand. "I'm sticking around. I need to okay everything before you put it in the sale."

Tina looked up from the yellow pad of paper she was writing on. "You haven't taken what you want yet?"

Patti sounded defensive. "I live in Chicago."

"Okay." Tina began to write again. "I'll have my girls come get you when they finish each room."

"Fine." Patti's voice was forceful. "Tell them to call me right away if they find anything unusual."

Tina chuckled. "Everybody's got a different definition for unusual, honey. You'll have to be more specific."

"Anything out of place or very valuable. A diary hidden under a bed. A priceless antique. That sort of thing."

Lottie chose that moment to walk through the kitchen. "Hello," she said, and gave Patti an expectant smile.

"Tina, this is my aunt, Lottie Braun," Patti said impatiently. "Yes, she's *the* Lottie Braun."

Tina stopped chomping her gum. "Who?"

Lottie stifled a laugh, but Patti looked thunderstruck. "The famous concert pianist."

Tina's drawn-out "Ohhh" confirmed she had no idea who Lottie was. "Sorry, ma'am," she said to Lottie. "We mostly listen to country music. Kenny Rogers. Tammy Wynette. That sort of thing."

"Good for you," Lottie said with a twinkle in her eye. "I like a little Kenny Rogers myself, on occasion."

"You got to know when to hold 'em," Lottie crooned under her breath as she entered the P.A.B. She was glad to leave the chaos of the house and the tension that radiated from her niece. Tina from Treasure Box Estates had better be a miracle worker, or there would be fireworks.

She stopped in the department office to pick up some mail and have a word with Katherine. Elaine ignored her as usual, but Lottie had learned not to take offense.

When she reached the third floor, Rhonda stood in the atrium. "Did you hear?" she said. "Alicia died last night. The funeral is Thursday afternoon."

"I know. Katherine told me."

Rhonda followed her to the back hall. "The whole department will go, of course. We could ride together, if you want."

Lottie appreciated the thaw in their relationship over the past week. She smiled as she stuck her office key in the lock. "Thanks, but I think I'll take my own car."

"Okay. Let me know if you change your mind."

Lottie felt a little sorry for Rhonda as she waddled back to her own office, crepe-soled shoes at full squeak. "I'll think about it," she called.

Flipping on the light, she stepped into her office, and stopped dead. Something between a gasp and a scream escaped her as she took in the vandal's newest mess. Above the pianos, red-painted letters blasted a message:

Shame on you.

Squeaky shoes hurried down the corridor. "Lottie, are you all right?"

She stepped into the hall and pulled the door shut. "I'm fine. It's a spider, that's all." She shuddered. "I really hate spiders."

"Really? I don't mind them so much." Rhonda reached for the door handle, but Lottie stopped her. "I've already killed it. Thanks anyway. Next time I'll know where to turn for help."

"Okay." Rhonda gave her a searching look. "You're awfully pale. You should probably sit down."

Lottie nodded. "You're right. I'll do that." She opened the door a fraction and slipped inside. "Thanks again." The door closed with a click and she leaned against it. "What now, Helen?"

She forced herself to examine the message on the wall. The letters were thick and bold, with a few short drips of paint at the bottom. Fortunately, neither piano had been dripped on, which would have been hard to remove and harder to explain. The words spanned the length of both pianos, a difficult area to cover. Lottie sighed. She had a class to teach in fifteen minutes.

She reached for the phone. "Miranda?"

♩♩

Miranda skirted the beat-up truck with "Treasure Box Estate Sales" painted on the side and started up the walk. Between the construction site and Patti's activities, the alley was pretty crowded today. She couldn't help scanning the construction site for Jason. He was nowhere in sight.

Sam waved from the driver's seat of a skid steer. "There's a mess inside," he called, pointing at the house.

She waved back. "Thanks for the warning."

Sam was right. The house was in an uproar. A boom box on the kitchen counter blared the local country station, while a top-heavy girl in shorts and a Minnie Mouse T-shirt sorted dishes on the kitchen floor. "Step carefully," she said. "Mama will kill me if anything gets broke."

In the dining room, a pony-tailed lady in a pink ball cap was stacking the contents of the china cupboard onto the table. She gave Miranda a once-over glance. "The gal in charge is upstairs. You want me to show you?"

Miranda shook her head. "No thanks. I know the way." She picked her way around a big pile of empty boxes in the living room and headed upstairs, where she found Patti and a lady who might have been Mama working in the master bedroom.

Patti looked irritated at the sight of Miranda. "What're you doing here?"

"My office is in the house," Miranda said in a pleasant tone. "I'm here eight hours a day."

She bristled. "We're planning to go through that room next."

"Whenever you're ready, I can show you my inventory of the room. Everything belongs to Lottie, including the contents of the closet."

"I'm selling that light fixture."

The Treasure Box lady shot Patti a surprised look.

"Take it if you want it," Miranda said, and left.

When the office door was safely shut behind her, she indulged in a triumphant grin. Score one for meticulous record-keeping. The phone rang, and she sang into the receiver, "Miranda Charles speaking. Oh, hi, Lottie."

Moments later she picked up her car keys and hurried away.

♪♪

Miranda returned to the house, satisfied the bizarre message on Lottie's wall was hidden from prying eyes. Shame? What on earth would Lottie Braun be ashamed of? Luckily the college bookstore kept a healthy supply of posters for use as dorm decor. Four large travel posters now hung side-by-side above the pianos, hiding the odd graffiti from prying eyes. Nobody would be impressed with Lottie's taste, but they also wouldn't guess she was hiding something. Later she would go back and paint the words out.

Weirdly enough, the shaming message had somehow hit its mark. Lottie had been emphatic about telling no one. She sounded frightened, not angry, and that made Miranda furious on her behalf.

She paused on her way through the dining room. Treasure Box Estates did quick work. The china cupboard was now bare. A folding table under the window held stacks of dishes, each with a white tag attached by a thread. Lot numbers, she supposed. Efficient.

Patti was watching the Treasure Box lady unload bookcases in the living room. She threw Miranda a suspicious glare as she passed, and Miranda returned the favor. She didn't trust the arrogant girl.

The estate worker held up three record albums with Lottie's face on the covers. "Here are some more," she said. Patti snatched them from her hands and stuck them in the box she held.

Up to no good.

An hour later the sound of voices upstairs caught Miranda's attention. Patti was leading Tina down the hall to Lottie's bedroom. "This one's next," she said. "I'll help you figure out what belongs to my aunt and what goes in the sale."

"Let's get started," Tina said.

"Wait." Miranda's heels clicked on the hardwood floor as she hurried down the hall. "You can't invade Lottie's privacy that way. Why don't you wait until she comes home?"

Patti rounded on her. "This is none of your business. Unless you have an inventory for this room, too?"

Her sarcasm was irritating. "No, of course not. Like I said, this is her private bedroom."

"Okay, okay." The estate worker held up her hands. "Seems like there's some dispute over this room. I'm not touching it until you guys get it settled."

Patti crossed her arms. "You have no right to hold up this job. The furniture belongs to me, and I intend to sell it."

Miranda's fingernails dug into her palms. "Lottie left your mother's furniture alone rather than pile it into storage while she waited three months for you to show up. The least you can do is wait a couple of hours for her to get home from work before you go through her bedroom. You owe her that much."

Bright patches of red burned on Patti's pale cheeks. "I don't owe her anything."

Lottie's voice broke into the argument. "Miranda? Patricia? Is there a problem?"

Lottie looked from one hostile young woman to the other. She was glad she'd listened to Sam that morning when he advised her to check in at lunch time.

Miranda smoothed her skirt over her hips. "I'll be in the office if you need me, Miss Braun."

Lottie turned puzzled eyes to her niece. "What's going on?"

Patti held herself rigidly upright. "I brought Tina in here to price the sale items, and your secretary went ballistic."

Lottie hid her doubts about this version of events. "I have some time before going back to work. Why don't we go through the room together?"

"I hope you're aware I'm putting this furniture in the auction. It belongs to me, you know." Patti's eyes dared Lottie to disagree.

Lottie took her time answering. What next, Helen?

Patti filled the silence. "You didn't think I'd give you the furniture, did you?"

"Of course not," Lottie said. "I'll stop after work and buy a cot to sleep on until my bedroom set arrives next week."

Instead of calming down, the girl seemed angrier. "If you'd done that in the first place, we wouldn't be having this conversation."

Bile rose in Lottie's throat. She opened her mouth to put the spoiled child in her place, but something held her back. Down the hall the baby began to cry. Patti's gaze darted toward the sound. For a split second she looked exactly like Helen when Billy strayed too far from her side.

The fight went out of Lottie. "Go take care of the child," she said quietly. "It won't take a minute for me to gather my belongings. I'll lay them on the bed if you like, so you can see they're all mine."

Patti's shoulders relaxed a fraction of an inch. "Don't be silly. Mother didn't have anything you'd want, anyway." And she fled down the hall.

Years of nomadic living made moving out an easy task. Lottie pulled two suitcases from under the bed and filled them in the usual order. Her other belongings fit into two book boxes. When she finished, she carried them to the office, where Miranda stacked them against the wall.

Lottie brushed her hands together. "That's settled."

Miranda shook her head. "Shame on her, anyway."

Lottie winced.

Shame on you.

Activity continued in the front bedroom as Lottie walked downstairs. One of Tina's workers stopped her in the kitchen. "This was at the back of a silverware drawer," she said, holding out a man's onyx ring. "It looks valuable."

Lottie refused to touch it. "You'll have to ask Patti about everything here. I'm not involved in the estate sale."

The woman looked past her to Patti, who stood in the doorway with Sarah on her hip. "You want to keep this?"

"Yes." She slid the ring onto her thumb, her face a study in grief. "Excuse me." She brushed past the estate worker on her way out of the kitchen. A second later, the bathroom door slammed shut.

Lottie lowered her eyelids to hide sudden sympathetic tears.

The estate worker opened another kitchen drawer. "That one's a piece of work, if you ask me."

"That piece of work is my niece," Lottie answered frostily, "and she just lost her mother."

The woman threw her a respectful glance. "I'll remember that, ma'am."

Patti emerged from the bathroom a minute later, tear-stained but calm. "It would help to know where the rest of your moving boxes are, so we don't waste time opening them," she said.

Puzzled, Lottie said, "I told you. It's all in the office, with Miranda."

"So your furniture and household things are stored somewhere else?"

"No, dear. Everything I own is upstairs. In the office." Lottie turned away. "So don't burn my house down while I'm gone, or I won't have a feather to fly with."

Sam stopped Lottie on her way to the car. "How's it going in there?"

"All right. They're an efficient bunch."

His lips twitched. "If you can stand country music, they're the best in the business. Is Patti behaving herself?"

"Not really." She tried and failed to make light of the situation. "I think she's intent on creating maximum chaos in minimum time. She's even riled up Miranda, and that's hard to do."

He shook his head. "Patti can do that. Just ask my boys."

"How did it go out here this morning?" she asked.

"I've got these guys running like a well-oiled machine."

"What guys?" She looked around. "Have they all deserted you?"

He squinted at the sun overhead. "In case you haven't noticed, it's lunch time. Don't tell me you haven't eaten yet."

"There's a tuna fish sandwich waiting for me at my desk."

"That's not a lunch. What you need is a slice of Annie's pie."

"Who?"

"You haven't been to Annie's?" He stared at her in disbelief. "We're going to fix this problem right now."

Ten minutes later Lottie perched on a stool at the counter in Annie's

Cafe, looking over the finest display of pies she'd seen in decades. A middle-aged waitress in a flowered shirt sauntered over to take their order.

Sam tugged the menu out of Lottie's hands. "Two club sandwiches," he said to the waitress, "and two pieces of pie. Lemon cream for the lady and cherry for me."

"That was very high-handed," Lottie said when the waitress was gone. "What makes you think I like lemon cream pie?"

"In the old days, you used to order it every chance you got."

She was quiet, thinking this over. "We had some fun, didn't we, Sam?"

He nodded. "Seems like somebody else's life now."

"Do you ever talk about the Neverland with anyone else?"

"Nope. Nobody around here knows about it. Why?"

"There's a writer named Donna Davenport. Have you heard of her?"

"No."

"I'm not surprised. She makes the *National Enquirer* look like a Sunday school paper. She's researching a book about me."

He looked startled. "Why?"

She gave a helpless shrug. "I don't know. My career has been an open book."

"But your time with the Neverland is off-limits."

She nodded.

He studied her face with a puzzled frown. "Someday I hope you'll trust me enough to explain why."

The food came, and proved Sam right. Annie's pie could take its place alongside the great chefs of Europe. When Lottie had eaten every last crumb, she sighed. "Who is this Annie?"

Sam chuckled. "Meet her for yourself." He waved to a plump, orange-haired woman by the door, and she hurried over.

"Hey, Sam. How was everything?"

"Ask my friend here."

Lottie smiled. "It was very good. Are you the chef?"

The woman laughed. "Chef sounds pretty grand for what I do. I'm Annie Markham."

Sam looked from one to the other. "You two are related, you know."

Annie stared at her with dawning awe. "You must be Lottie."

She nodded.

Suddenly Lottie's hand was being fervently shaken. "I'm Cora's daughter. I heard you moved to Collison—gee, we all did—but I didn't think I'd be the first one to meet you."

Lottie placed her free hand over Annie's plump one. "I'd love to catch up with everyone. I've had my hands full since I moved, with the new job and everything. Oh, and Patti's back for a while, to sort out her parents' belongings."

"We had to do that for Mom and Dad this summer. I was a wreck about it, trying to decide what to keep and what to sell. It seemed so disrespectful, getting rid of the things it took my folks a lifetime to collect." Annie poked Sam's arm. "By the way, I didn't see you at the sale, mister."

"I sent Mitch." He sounded defensive. "He's the family favorite, anyway."

"Not true. Some of us aren't so fooled by charm and good looks."

"Most of you are."

Lottie had the uncomfortable feeling she was missing an inside joke. As the banter continued, she slid off the stool and reached for her purse. "Well, I'm due back at work. I'd better get going."

Annie flashed a big smile. "Don't be a stranger. Let me know when Patti goes home. I'll throw a party for you."

"I'll do that." She turned to Sam. "Thanks for lunch. I'll walk to campus from here."

She left without looking back, scared she'd see relief in his eyes.

Sam caught up with Lottie a block from the diner. "Hey, lady, was it something I said?"

"No." Her expression was guarded. "It looked like you and Annie had some catching up to do, that's all."

"It wasn't anything important." A new idea occurred to him. "Or was that your way of telling me you don't want to go back to campus in a pickup truck?"

She stopped short, her eyes shooting sparks. "How could you even think that? You ought to know I'm not ashamed of any pickup truck."

"All right then, what happened?"

"I...I just didn't want to be a fifth wheel, that's all. You and Annie belong here. I don't. Maybe I never will."

He took off his cap and scratched his forehead. "That's hogwash. Of course, you belong here. You just have to give it time."

She didn't look convinced. "We'll have to agree to disagree about that. Meanwhile, you can walk me back to my office to pay for that crack about your pickup truck."

He fell into step beside her. "From where I sit it was a logical conclusion. I've seen that fancy machine you drive."

"I like to drive fast."

"Just like Jase. No time to look at the scenery." He shook his head in mock disgust.

At the entrance to the Performing Arts Building, Lottie stopped. "Thanks for lunch, Sam. The pie was delicious."

"I have a few more minutes. I can walk you upstairs."

She hesitated. "Well...all right."

Lottie's manner changed as soon as they walked through the doors of the P.A.B. Her shoulders tensed, and she walked upstairs without any of the easy conversation Sam had enjoyed during lunch. Maybe he'd been right the first time. She didn't want to be seen with a guy who drove a pickup.

"Here we are," she said, unlocking the office door. "Jason and Miranda did wonders with the place."

He gave the office a cursory once-over. "It's better than ever."

"Sure is." She darted a nervous glance toward the pianos. "Thanks again for lunch. I'm afraid I have to go teach a class."

He followed her gaze to the travel posters on the wall. Unframed and so new the edges still curled, they seemed out of place with the rest of the room. "New York, Chicago, Los Angeles, and Miami?" He gave her a quizzical smile. "Are those places you've been or a wish list?"

"Places I've been." Her words were clipped. She made an impatient gesture toward the hall. "Now, if you don't mind, I really have to ask you to leave."

"Okay, okay. Sorry." He stepped into the hall and she followed, pulling the door shut behind them and turning the key.

She gave him a distracted half-smile as she hurried past, "I'll see you later."

He raised a hand in acknowledgment. "All right."

He watched her rush away down the hall and cursed himself for being a fool. Lottie was very good at giving the brush-off.

Halfway across the atrium, he stopped in his tracks. What if embarrassment wasn't the reason for Lottie's jumpy behavior?

He found the janitor wringing out a mop in the cleaning closet. "I left my wallet in Miss Braun's office. Could you let me in to get it?"

"Sure, man."

The janitor unlocked Lottie's door and headed back down the hall without even turning down his Walkman.

Sam made sure the door was closed before he lifted the first poster off the wall. The rest peeled away easily. His mouth dropped open at the garish red letters underneath.

Shame on you.

All afternoon the steady beat of Tina's country station thrummed through the house. Miranda did her best to concentrate on work, but the noise finally got the best of her. Close to quitting time she slipped out the front door to the shaded porch swing, her aching head in her hands.

Mitchell came around the side of the house and joined her on the porch. "You're just the person I came to see."

"Why me?" She smiled at him. "Is Jessica busy today?"

He laughed. "Believe it or not, I've been working over there. Ed Williams cashed in a bunch of favors to help her get her grandpa's house on the market, and my dad offered to fix some of the more obvious issues. Martha's been over there every day, too, helping her clean. If everything goes okay, the For Sale sign should go up in a week or two."

"And then pretty Jessica will move away. Doesn't that make you sad?"

"Not really." He laughed. "Don't look at me like that. She knows I'm not serious. Look, I didn't come here to talk about Jessie. I have papers for Lottie to sign."

She took the file folder from his outstretched hand. "Thanks. I'll take care of that."

"Great." He hesitated. "I heard Patti came home."

She looked up, her attention caught by the change in his voice. "She got here last night. I think she's in the kitchen, if you want to see her."

He shrugged. "Whatever."

"Come on, then." She slipped off her shoes. "We'll go through the yard. After all day with the auction crew, the house is a disaster area."

Mitchell matched his long strides with Miranda's short steps as they walked through the cool grass toward the kitchen. He pointed at her feet, still encased in businesslike nylons.

"You could go barefoot, you know. We're not fancy around here."

"Yes, but I'm fancy," she said. "I like the way I dress."

"I like it too. I still can't understand why you like Jase better than me."

She opened her mouth to answer, but stopped short as they reached the back yard. "What in the world?"

Mitchell gave a low whistle. "How'd they get the drum set up there?"

Patti came out as they reached the porch. "Those crazy kids."

Tommy's band stood on his garage roof, dark outlines against the summer sky.

Ten

Lottie could not believe her eyes. Tommy and his friends were about to fall off a roof, and nobody had the good sense to stop them. The squeal of electric guitars pounded in her ears as she jumped out of the car. Running to the alley, she screamed to be heard over the noise. "Hey! Get down!"

She knew they couldn't hear her, but she couldn't help herself. Tommy's shoes hung over the gutter. The roof might only be nine feet off the ground, but he could still be killed if he fell. She marched through the long grass to the back of his garage. The door stood open, a row of extension cords hanging across it. Pushing them aside, she rushed to the outlet and unplugged them one by one.

The bass died first, then the keyboard. Next came Tommy's guitar. The drummer played a few more licks before breaking off.

Lottie savored a moment of triumph before the guitarist appeared in the doorway. "You're trespassing," he said.

She planted her feet in front of the outlet, cords clutched in her hand. "It isn't safe up there. You kids need to come down."

He stepped toward her. "It's none of your business what we do. Get out of the way."

She folded her arms, nervous but determined. "Not until you all come down. I can't turn my back and let one of you get hurt."

"Yeah, because you're such a big fan of my band."

She took a deep breath. "No. I think you're wasting your talent, but it's not worth killing yourselves. Now, get out there and tell your friends to come down."

He shifted his weight. "Who's gonna make me?"

"Do as the lady says, Thomas."

They both turned to the doorway, where Sam stood. "She's right." His mild voice defused the tension. "You guys need to get down. It's about to rain."

This seemed to knock him off-balance. "It is?"

Sam nodded. "I've already seen a drop or two on the backhoe."

Lottie stepped forward and dropped the cords into Sam's hand. This was her cue to make an exit. She swept past him and through the doorway, relief and triumph crowding her head. When she reached her yard, she glanced over her shoulder. Tommy was back on the roof, talking with his band mates, while Sam crossed the alley with long strides. When he caught up, she said, "Do you think he'll get down?"

His lips twitched. "One thing's for sure. They don't want those guitars to get wet."

She chuckled. "That was brilliant. Imagine how fast Johnny would have made us move to keep his equipment out of the rain."

A slow grin spread across his face. "What do you know about it? All you ever had to do was stack a few chairs."

"Stack a few—" She put her hands on her hips. "Why, Sammy Harms! That's a big fat lie."

He threw back his head and laughed.

A reluctant smile tugged at her lips as she watched him enjoy the joke.

When he came to himself, she pointed at his face. "You've got something on your cheek." She leaned closer. "Is that paint?"

"What? No." He swiped at his cheek, but the silvery-gray smudge remained.

"Everyone all right?" Miranda called from the porch. Mitchell and Patti, on either side of her, looked equally interested.

Sam's grin disappeared as Lottie took a step away. "We're fine. Sam's just here to…" She frowned at him. "Why are you here?"

He looked insulted. "I'm supervising your project. Remember?"

"Well, go supervise it, then."

"I will." He stomped away, then stomped back. "Later, we're going to have it out about that red paint in your office." He left before she could respond, striding across the lawn like an avenging angel.

Her heart sank. He'd seen it.

"Did you enjoy the show?" Lottie asked drily as she joined the trio on the porch.

Mitchell looked thoughtful. "I sure did. I haven't seen my dad move that fast in years."

Lottie felt her cheeks grow warm. "I was talking about Thomas and friends. Or do rock bands play on rooftops every day of the week around here?"

Patti pursed her lips. "They were just being kids."

Lottie stared at her in rising irritation. "Sometimes 'just being a kid' can be dangerous." She glanced toward the open bedroom windows. "Sarah's crying."

Patti narrowed her eyes. "I know." She looked like she wanted to add something else, but the wails drifting down from above proved too much for her. Turning on her heel, she stalked inside.

Lottie looked at Mitchell. "What can I do for you?"

"You'll have to ask Miranda. I placed the matter in her efficient hands."

"Smart move." She looked from one to the other. "May I ask a favor?" She beckoned them closer and continued in an undertone. "I have a great deal of work to do tonight. Would it be too much to ask you to invite my niece out for dinner? I don't have much food in the house, anyway."

Mitchell and Miranda exchanged unenthusiastic glances. "I'm game if you are," he said. When she didn't reply, he added, "I'll make Jase go too, to sweeten the pot."

Miranda glared at him. "Sure. Yes. I'll go if it will help you out, Miss Braun. Would you like to go over these papers before we leave?"

Lottie finished her business with Miranda and shooed the young people out the door. As soon as they were gone, she grabbed her car keys. She needed to get to the store before it closed.

It was time to buy a cot, and avoid Sam.

♪♪

Miranda sat in the window of Giovanni's pizza parlor and watched the local traffic wind its way around the courthouse square. She hated being the first to arrive. Was she in the right restaurant? Had the others changed their plans and forgotten to tell her? The old familiar fears plagued her. Ironically, she almost always ran early, so this happened all the time.

She breathed a sigh of relief when Jason's red car passed the restaurant and turned left to go around the square. He and Mitchell joined her a few minutes later. Jason was handsome in a polo shirt and jeans, his hair slicked back as if it were still damp from a shower. Mitchell looked the same as he always did—cute, friendly and eager to please. "Sorry we're late," he said. "Jase took forever to shower."

Jason shot his brother an irritated look. "Wow, Mitch. Thanks for that."

Mitchell ignored him. "Patti's not here yet?"

"No." Miranda smiled at the tentative note in his voice.

"Let's order garlic bread while we're waiting," Jason said.

They were munching on bread and listening to Mitchell talk about the Cubs when Patti crossed the dining room with Sarah on her hip, her silky brown hair bouncing on her shoulders. She looked cool and collected, the modern woman who had everything together. A waitress followed with a wooden high chair, which she placed next to the table. "Hi, guys," Patti said as she buckled Sarah's safety belt. "Boy, this place has gone downhill."

Mitchell raised his eyebrows. "It's the same as always, Patti."

"It's Patricia." Her mouth quirked up in a superior smile. "And you're probably right. The place is the same. I've changed."

"Not for the better," Jason muttered under his breath.

Miranda stifled a smile. "What should we order?" she asked the table at large. "Does this place have a specialty?"

Jason set down his menu. "I like their pepperoni."

"I'll just have a salad," Patti said. "I don't eat processed meats."

Mitchell stared at her in amazement. "Since when?"

"Since I learned what they do to your body."

He looked disgusted. "Pepperoni's fine with me. Miranda? What looks good to you?"

"I'll take a page out of both books—a slice of pizza and a side salad."

Her conciliatory gesture earned a look of dislike from Patti.

The waitress took their order and left, and Jason said, "How did it go with Tina's crew today, Patti?"

"Fine," she said. "And I said it's Patricia now."

"I heard you." Jason held up a hand in self-defense. "But I'm never going to remember. You can get on your high horse about it or move on with life."

The light of battle flashed in Patti's eyes, but Mitchell jumped in before she could unload. "Miranda, how was work today?"

She admired his determination to keep the conversation afloat. "To be honest, it was a bit hard to concentrate with all the noise."

"You need a Walkman," Mitchell said cheerfully. "You can listen to tapes to block out the noise."

"You could charge the Walkman as a business expense." Sarcasm laced Patti's voice. "Let your boss pay for it." The other three turned to stare at her. "What? She's loaded. She told me so herself."

Miranda frowned. "That doesn't sound like Lottie."

"Are you saying it's not true?"

Jason threw Patti an irritated glance. "Can't you be nice for once in your life?"

"I don't see why I should," she shot back. "Lottie wasn't nice to me."

"All right, all right." Mitchell waved his hands in a time-out signal. "Let's try this again." He turned to Patti with an exaggerated simper. "Ms. Parker, your baby is adorable. Where did she get those gorgeous yellow curls?"

The simple question took the light out of Patti's face. There was an uncomfortable pause. "Eric is Norwegian," she said finally.

Mitchell's smile froze in place, and his eyes went curiously blank. For once the life of the party had nothing to say.

Jason stepped into the breach. Addressing Miranda directly for the first time. "I ran into a problem with another remodel that might interest you."

She tore her fascinated gaze from the drama playing out in front of her and read the plea in Jason's eyes. "I'd love to hear about it."

"It's a pretty common problem. The homeowner doesn't have enough space for everything on his wish list."

♫

Lottie folded the last hospital corner under the mattress of her new, De-Luxe hideaway bed. The furniture store sold cheaper models, but she couldn't imagine sleeping on them. This wheeled model with its twin-size mattress looked like the only trustworthy one in the place.

She gave the bed a final pat and headed downstairs, glad to be alone. Dinner was simple as always, a can of tomato soup and half a sandwich. Afterward, she puttered around the garden, Marmalade at her side, grateful for the quiet evening. Apparently the afternoon jam session had taken the place of nighttime practice for the band across the alley.

When twilight fell, she put her gardening gloves in the garage, and saw a stranger walking toward her across the alley. She was a faded woman in a nursing uniform, her hair pulled back in a tidy clip. "I'm Mary Allen, Thomas's mom," she said when she reached Lottie. "I hear you've been interfering in his business."

"I stopped him from doing something dangerous."

Mary Allen hugged her arms against her body. "Says you. He might be playing music you don't approve of, but that doesn't make it dangerous."

"That wasn't the dangerous part." Lottie drew a steadying breath. "Did your son tell you his band was practicing on the roof of your garage?"

Mary's mouth tightened at the corners. "He said he was being care-ful, and I believe him." Pulling a scrap of paper from her pocket she said, "This is my phone number at work. From now on, if you see him doing anything you don't approve of, you call me. I don't let my boy get away with anything bad." She looked straight into Lottie's eyes. "But kids are kids, Miss Braun. They're going to pull some pranks."

Before Lottie could respond, Mary Allen turned and marched away, head high, back straight. Lottie stared at the scrap of paper in her hand. Was she so wrong to be concerned?

Sam could probably shed some light on the Allens. He seemed to know Tommy quite well. He had the boy's respect, too, but Lottie didn't want to talk to Sam right now. She started for the house, resolved to ignore the whole situation.

Her resolve lasted until the first screaming chord tore across the lawn. Then she picked up the phone.

Sam listened carefully as she poured out her story. When she finished, he was quiet for a minute. "I can see both sides of the situation," he said. "Mary's been through a lot, and somehow she's managed to raise a good kid. I guess she's a little touchy about other people disciplining her son when she's not around."

Lottie sucked in her breath. "You think she was right to call me out for making her son get down from the roof?"

"I didn't say that. I said I see her point of view." Sam continued in his calm voice. "The fact remains that Thomas's band keeps you up at night. I'm just not sure you want to start a war with Mary over it, especially since you're the new kid on the block."

"Start a war!" Lottie couldn't believe her ears. "I'm not the one who's picking a fight here. All I want is a good night's sleep."

"I think the problem will resolve itself soon." Sam's reasonable tone was beginning to irritate her. "Tommy will get caught up in school work and won't have as much time for the band. And when cold weather comes, he'll keep that garage door shut to stay warm. Meanwhile…"

"Meanwhile?"

"I've got an idea," he said. "Tomorrow I'll bring you something to help the situation."

"I've already tried earplugs," she said doubtfully. "They don't work."

A note of amusement entered his voice. "Something better than earplugs."

"All right. Whatever it is, it's worth a try. Thanks, Sam."

"Don't mention it," he said. "And now that we've got that squared away, I've got a thing or two to say about that red mess in your office."

Her heart sank. "How did you know it was there?"

"You should have picked your posters more carefully." He sounded scornful. "Everyone knows you hate Los Angeles."

She felt a small thrill of satisfaction. "You're a fan!"

He ignored her. "Did you call the police?"

She sobered. "No. I'm handling it myself."

"So you know who's behind it?"

"Not exactly."

"You have no idea?" He sounded impatient.

"Well…Not really. No."

She could feel Sam's frustration coming through the silence on the wire.

"Don't you want to ask me what the message means?" she said in a small voice.

"What it means?" His voice rose. "I know what it means. It means there's a crazy person who wants to hurt you." He continued more quietly. "Look, I understand you might not want a guy in uniform showing up at work, but they won't necessarily do that."

She closed her eyes. "In a town this size, the uniform won't matter, will it? Everyone knows who the police officers are."

"So stop by the police station and make a statement. It'd be a start, anyway."

"I'll think it over."

"Have you considered a Murphy bed for your client?" Miranda asked as she helped herself to another slice of pizza.

Jason frowned. "Murphy beds are never very comfortable."

"You could build it yourself, and make it comfortable."

"Well…" He thought this over.

The discussion had gone on much longer than the topic merited, but Miranda and Jason trundled on, debating the merits of one type of layout over another. Across the table, Mitchell shoveled pizza into his mouth with dogged determination, while Patti helped her daughter finish her banana bites and canned green beans.

The race to finish ended in a tie. "That does it for me," Mitchell said, pushing back his chair. He nodded at the check, which sat next to Jason's plate. "Can I pay you back later, Jase?"

"Sure, buddy."

Patti wiped the baby clean with a wet wipe and released her from the high chair. "I have to go." She reached into her purse, but Jason stopped her.

"This one's on me."

"Thanks."

Miranda looked around for her bag. "I should go, too."

Jason set a hand on her arm. "Let them get out of here," he said in a low voice.

Mitchell and Patti crossed the restaurant without looking at each other. When they were out of sight, Jason lifted his hand.

Miranda looked at him. "Wait a minute. You and Mitchell rode together. I saw you."

Jason took a drink of beer. "Patti doesn't know that."

"So she's the one who broke his heart."

He looked at her curiously. "You don't sound too upset."

"I feel terrible for him." She met his eyes. "Do you mind telling me what happened?"

He shrugged. "Mitch and Patti were always close growing up. Sometime during college, friendship turned to dating, as natural as breathing." He tapped his fork against the edge of his plate. "Patti wanted out of Iowa, and Mitchell was happy to go along. He started law school while she finished up her bachelor's degree in Iowa City. He had a year to go when she graduated and took a job in Chicago."

"And absence didn't make the heart grow fonder?"

"Right." He closed his eyes for a moment. "Things were already headed south for Mitch and Patti when my mom was diagnosed with cancer. Mom died a week after Mitch finished his law degree, and Patti broke up with him a few days later." Jason shrugged. "That was three years ago, and my brother is still stuck. He never took the bar exam. He doesn't have any ambition. He's just stuck."

"And Patti?"

"By September, Patti was married to this big, blond guy. An artist of some kind."

"Eric."

He nodded. "It didn't last. The way I heard it, Eric split when Patti got pregnant. He said he wasn't ready for the responsibility."

"Poor Patti."

"Huh." Jason reached for his billfold. "Save your sympathy for my brother."

"Why did he even come tonight?" she asked, almost to herself. "Why would he put himself in her path like that?"

He shot her an unreadable look. "I assume it's because you wanted him to."

"That's not it," she said, her mind on the problem. "He volunteered before I could refuse."

♫

Lottie set one last shoe box on Patti's bed and pulled paper and pen out of her bathrobe pocket. "I found these when I cleaned out the sewing room," she wrote. "Thought you'd want to save them. They're organized by date. – Lottie" She paused, pen in the air, thinking.

A floorboard squeaked, and Patti walked in. "What are you doing in here?" she whispered as she lowered her sleeping daughter into the portable crib.

Lottie pointed at the shoe boxes. "I wanted to give these to you," she whispered back. "Your mom kept all these pictures in the sewing room, so I had to clean them out before construction started."

Patti gave the boxes a blank stare. "Thanks."

"Well, good night." Lottie stepped into the hall, pulling the door shut behind her. Pausing a moment to listen, she caught the soft whoosh of a lid coming off a shoe box.

Eleven

Lottie was eating breakfast Wednesday morning when Sam stuck his head around the door. "You got a minute?" At her nod, he stepped inside, followed by one of his workers, who held a large box. "It's a window air conditioner. If we install it in your bedroom, you'll sleep through anything."

Her eyes lit up. "That's just the thing! What do I owe you, Sam?"

He pressed a business card into her palm. "Think of it as a reminder to run that errand we talked about. Here's the name of the guy you should talk to. You can trust him."

"Will you take away my noise blocker if I don't do as you say?" she said dryly.

His eyes crinkled in a smile. "Something like that. I'd like to install it now, if that's okay."

"Go on up. It's the front bedroom."

Sam threaded his way through the piles left by the auction workers. "Morning, Patti."

"Good morning." Patti brushed past Lottie and made straight for the coffee pot. She looked younger this morning in sweat pants and T-shirt, her hair pulled back in a ponytail. Blue shadows under her eyes accentuated her ivory skin.

"Late night?" Lottie said.

"I went through those photos you gave me. I couldn't stop looking."

"There's another envelope around here somewhere. I thought I put

151

it in the office closet, but it wasn't there when I checked last night."

Patti froze for a moment, her mug raised halfway to her mouth. Then she took a sip and set the mug down. "I was thinking. Maybe tonight we should go through those pictures together. You can probably tell me who some of the second and third cousins are, and I'll tell you whatever you want to know."

Lottie felt a tiny flame of hope rise in her heart. "I'd like that."

"Okay then." Patti took another gulp of coffee. "I'd better go get Sarah dressed."

She hurried away as Miranda walked in from the yard. "What's that banging noise?"

"Sam's installing an air conditioner in my room for noise control."

"Good plan," Miranda said. "While I've got you, I wanted to mention something."

Lottie raised her eyebrows. "Go on."

She lowered her voice. "I overheard Patti asking Tina to give her anything to do with you. Tina gave her a bunch of your records and some magazines with you on the cover."

"A lot of people collect that kind of memorabilia."

"Does Patti strike you as someone like that?" Miranda took a mug out of the cupboard. "I forgot to tell you, on Monday I called the place where she works. Her secretary said someone else had called Patti asking about you. I think that sounds kind of suspicious."

The flame of hope flickered, but Lottie refused to let it go out. "I'll take that under advisement."

With all the activity at home, Lottie ran late for work. To save time she skipped the police department, but promised herself she'd pay them a visit at lunch time. Her private lessons started at 8:30, so she sped through the department office, grabbed her mail on the run, and hurried upstairs.

She walked in to find her first student standing on a piano bench, a roll of masking tape in his hand. He nodded at the poster of Los Angeles. "This thing was on the floor. I'm taping it up for you." He jumped off the bench while she stood stock still in the doorway, her face numb with shock. "This is just my opinion, but I like the painting on the wall better than the posters."

The painting on the wall? Was he mocking her? She turned her suspicious gaze to his face, and he gave her a tentative smile. "I mean, it looks like something that belongs here, since it's music-related."

Suddenly Lottie could move again. "Let's see what you mean, Brian."

She resisted the urge to squeeze her eyes closed as he climbed back up and removed the posters. But when they were gone, she breathed a sigh of relief.

In place of the horrible red scrawl, a long rectangle of black formed the background for a staff of metallic silver. Musical notes marched along in orderly fashion for five measures, playing a jaunty tune. Not one drop of red bled through.

"See?" he said. "It's perfect for your office."

She smiled. "You are so right. I'll take the posters home."

While Brian began his warm-up exercises, Lottie stared at the measures on her wall. She'd seen that silver paint before, on the cheek of a man who was always looking out for her.

Brian finished his lesson and left, and she turned her attention to the mail on her desk. Once again she found the familiar envelope addressed in block letters. She held it in her hands for a long minute, debating whether to open it here or take it home. In the end she broke the seal. Out fell two photos: The first, an old black-and-white snapshot of Aunt Cora's house in all its gingerbread glory; the second, a current-day photo of Helen's house. No, she corrected herself, make that Lottie's house. An accompanying note said:

Once you talk to me, you won't stay in that old house. - D.D.

A shiver went down her spine. Donna Davenport had been to her house.

Miranda rested her head in her hands and listened to the rhythmic bang of a hammer down below. This was the least productive work week ever. Even with the window closed, she could hear the crew shouting to one another. She had to stop herself from picking Jason's voice out of the crowd. Last night they'd parted ways on a friendly enough note. He seemed to see her as a fellow construction engineer. It was nice in a way, but not what she wanted.

If she didn't find a new project, she'd go crazy. She couldn't spend the whole day rehashing what happened last night. Her desk was clean, her files in perfect order. Maybe the estate company could find her something to do.

Tina looked her over critically. "You're not dressed for this."

"She could catalog things, couldn't she, Ma?" said one of Tina's daughters.

Miranda's face lit up. "I sure could."

Tina installed her at the dining room table with a ledger and a pen. In a few staccato phrases she explained her system, and left Miranda to fend for herself. It was detailed work, which she liked, and some of the household items interested her. Helen had drawers full of mysterious kitchen gadgets she'd never seen before. Tina's crew helped her identify everything, and she recorded lot numbers and suggested starting prices.

From where she sat, she could see Patti in the kitchen, going through boxes of toys from her childhood. Once in a while she exclaimed over a forgotten treasure, but she didn't set anything aside to keep. Everything was cataloged to sell, even an original Barbie doll with an exquisitely hand-stitched wardrobe. Some lucky collector was about to make the discovery of a lifetime.

Close to lunch time, Tina came up from the basement with the biggest find of the morning. "Here's a set of original house plans," she told Patti, unfurling a big roll of paper. "And this next one is a map that shows the boundaries of the farm before it was sectioned out for houses."

"Put it in the sale," Patti said. "It'll make some map collector very happy."

Tina sounded surprised. "Are you sure you don't want to leave it with the house? That's where stuff like this belongs."

"I said sell it." There was an edge to Patti's voice.

Tina rolled her eyes and handed the maps to Miranda. "She's really something, isn't she?" she muttered under her breath.

Miranda didn't answer. She wasn't sure what to make of this ultra-disciplined house-cleaning. Until last night she would have said Patti was the most cold-blooded person she'd ever met, but today she seemed soft, even vulnerable, as she parted with her childhood memories.

Miranda cataloged the map and went to stand in the kitchen doorway. "Why are you doing this?" she asked softly.

Patti looked up. "Doing what?"

"Getting rid of your past so religiously. Do you need money that badly?"

Patti went back to sorting puzzles. "I'm a single mom. Money troubles come with the territory." She looked up, her face set. "Sarah's birth didn't come cheap."

"And there's no other way to pay for it?"

"Nothing legal." She rose from the floor. "And now I'm leaving before you suggest I ask dear Aunt Lottie for a loan."

"She's a good person, you know," Miranda said. "The best, actually."

Patti's eyes narrowed. "Why are you so convinced she's an angel? Because she signs your paychecks?"

Miranda swallowed hard. "Let's just say she saved my life once."

They looked warily at each other for a moment. Then Patti sat back down and pointed at the place next to her on the floor. "Have a seat. You can tell me the story while we sort toys." She waved an arm across the pile in front of them. "This is going to take a while. I'm pretty sure my mother kept everything I ever touched."

Miranda slipped off her shoes and knelt beside Patti on the kitchen floor. They worked in silence for a little while, until Patti finally said, "Well, are you going to tell your story or not?"

Miranda placed a box of marbles in the "sell" box, and looked at her companion. "I'm not sure if I should."

"You don't trust me?" Patti wrinkled her nose. "Well, maybe you shouldn't at that. Have you ever heard of Donna Davenport?"

Miranda stared at her in surprise. "What do you know about Donna Davenport?"

"She called me a few weeks ago. Asked me to—"

"Spy on Lottie," Miranda finished for her. "She called me, too, but I hung up on her. Is that what you're doing here?"

Patti hesitated. "Maybe." She glanced sideways at Miranda. "I'm trying to make up my mind. To be honest, two days ago, I was planning to sell her out completely. But now I don't know."

Miranda reached for a child-size weaving loom and began to untangle the yarn. "All right. I'll tell you my story. Maybe it will help." She shifted her weight to a cross-legged position. "After high school, I got a full ride scholarship to a college in Seattle, to pursue interior design."

"That sounds promising."

Miranda's lips tipped up in a sad smile. "It was, for a while. I got accepted into the school of design as a junior, and the most respected professor in the department was assigned to be my adviser." She set the yarn in her lap, remembering. "Everything was great for a while. He got me a student job, and made himself available any time I needed help with an assignment. Then…"

Patti looked up with a knowing frown. "Let me guess. He made a move on you."

Miranda nodded. "When I refused to sleep with him, things went downhill fast. He was teaching two of my major classes, and he flunked me in both." She punched the air. "Boom went the scholarship. Boom went the design degree."

"Ouch. What did your parents say?"

She gave a small shake of the head. "My parents washed their hands of me when I took the college scholarship. Girls from my neighborhood weren't supposed to go out on their own like that."

Patti stared at her. "So what happened?"

"I was sitting in the student union on the last day of finals, wondering what to do next. For the first time in my life, I had no plan, and when the dorms closed, I'd also have no place to live. I noticed a tall, regal lady with white hair sitting at a table nearby. Someone stopped to talk to her, and she said she was looking for a new personal assistant to help her move to Kansas City.

"I knew nothing about Kansas City, except that it was far away from Seattle. When the other person walked away, I went over and talked Lottie into hiring me as her personal assistant."

"And that's how she saved your life?" Patti sounded unimpressed.

"That's not everything." Miranda picked up another hank of yarn to untangle. "That night, Lottie asked me why I was leaving school. I gave her the general facts, but she guessed the rest. Several months later we were having lunch together in Kansas City, and she said, 'Oh, Miranda, the other day I heard that a professor at your college lost his job.' She named my former adviser." Miranda's eyes glowed at the memory. "I don't know how she put it all together, but I'm sure she got him fired."

"Good for Aunt Lottie! No wonder you're loyal."

Miranda smiled. "I'd risk a lot for her."

"I can respect that." Patti was quiet for a moment. "Do you have any idea why Donna Davenport wants to write about Lottie?"

"She used to be glamorous. She had the perfect figure for couture, so fashion designers lined up to dress her. Rumor has it she even spent a weekend with Frank Sinatra."

"Sinatra?" Patti rolled her eyes. "There's no accounting for tastes, I guess."

Miranda secretly agreed, but she was too loyal to say so. "Still, I think that's the stuff Donna Davenport wants to hear about."

"So why does she want those tax returns?"

Miranda's head came up. "Tax returns?"

Patti clapped a hand over her mouth. "You really did hang up on her. Well, it doesn't matter. I've decided not to give her anything."

Tina walked into the kitchen just then, carrying an olive-green suitcase in her arms. "You're going to want to see this," she said to Patti. "It looks like your mother's wedding things."

Patti set the case on the floor in front of her. "Where did you find this? I've never seen it before."

"I almost missed it myself," Tina said. "It was hidden behind a board in the corner of the attic. It's a good suitcase, though. Kept the mice out." She pivoted on her heel. "Well, gals, I'll get back to work."

Together they unlatched the rusted clasps and lay the suitcase open.

Patti gently picked up the faded blue dress hidden inside the case. "This isn't my mother's wedding dress. She wore a long white gown with a train." Patti handed the dress to Miranda with careful fingers. The silk was worn in spots, and fragile. Under the dress lay a formal photo and a bouquet of flowers pressed in waxed paper. The bride in the picture looked young, beautiful, and radiantly in love. "That's Mother, all right," Patti said.

Miranda pointed at the broad-shouldered, crew-cut young groom. "Your dad was gorgeous."

"No, he wasn't," Patti said, her voice strained. "My dad was kind and funny and good, but he wasn't gorgeous."

"I don't understand."

She pointed at the bridegroom. "That man isn't my dad."

The flat denial left Miranda speechless.

Patti scrambled to her feet and kicked the suitcase aside. "I have to get out of here."

Miranda winced as the door slammed shut, but she couldn't blame Patti for being upset. She herself couldn't imagine her parents hiding such a big secret from their children.

A few seconds later the door opened again—more gently this time—and Mitchell walked in. "What's with Patti?"

Miranda draped the blue silk dress over the wedding picture. "She's upset about something she found." She raised her gaze to Mitchell's. "A memory." Or lack of one, in this case.

He looked toward the alley with a frown of concern. "Shouldn't you follow her? She might need a shoulder to cry on."

The anxious cries of a child floated down from upstairs. Miranda pointed at the ceiling. "I'll take care of Sarah. Why don't you find Patti?"

The look he gave her was half-fear, half-hope. "Me?"

"You've known her longer."

She left him to his thoughts and headed upstairs.

When she reached the bedroom, Sarah stopped crying and gave her an owlish stare. Miranda stared back, unsure of her next move.

Sarah raised her arms. "Up."

"Okay, kid." Miranda gripped her around the ribcage and lifted, surprised at how light she was. "Now what?"

Sarah stuck her finger in her mouth and smiled.

Miranda drew her brows together. "You seem to think I know what I'm doing." She wrinkled her nose. "Oh, no."

The baby's smile grew wider, as if she were laughing at a private joke.

Ten minutes and three botched diapers later, Miranda carried Sarah down to the empty kitchen. With no relief in sight from childcare duty, she scooped a set of building blocks off the floor and headed outside. "We can play in the sunshine," she told her charge.

Sarah looked enchanted with the idea.

They settled in a deck chair with a few building blocks for the little girl to examine. Sarah dropped a red one and crowed happily when Miranda picked it up.

They were playing this exciting game when Jason left the job site and joined them on the porch. "How did you get stuck with the kid?"

To Miranda's surprise she didn't feel stuck at all. "Patti needed a break."

Just then Mitchell and Patti appeared around the end of the garage. His hands were in his pockets, his head bent toward her. She was absorbed in what she was saying, oblivious to the observers on the porch. Miranda felt the satisfaction of a job well-done.

Jason glanced at her with a quick frown. "This isn't good."

"I say it's very good."

"You really don't mind?"

Something in his voice made her look up. Their gazes caught and held. "I don't mind," she said firmly.

After a moment he looked away. "Good."

That one word held a wealth of conviction.

Lottie drove up the alley at a snail's pace. Between them, Treasure Box Estates and Harms and Sons had turned it into a gravel-covered obstacle course. She breathed a sigh of relief when she reached her garage, but the sigh turned to a groan as the door rose. Boxes filled every square inch. Her Mercedes would have to sleep outdoors tonight.

With a mental shrug, she backed onto the lawn and popped the trunk. She might as well unload groceries before she moved the car.

Sam met her halfway up the walk and took the bags that dangled from her hands. "Did you call the police?" he asked in an undertone.

She spoke through clenched teeth. "How could I, when someone painted over the evidence?"

"Oh." He shot her a sidelong glance. "Do you know who it was?"

"Someone with a working knowledge of Glenn Miller, apparently." She chuckled. "Sam, only you would think the opening bars of 'In the Mood' were appropriate for my office."

"It was the first thing that came to mind," he said with a sheepish smile. "I have to admit, I didn't think about evidence when I painted over those words. I just wanted them gone."

She placed a hand on his arm. "Police or no police, you saved me a lot of embarrassment."

He flushed. "I wanted that red garbage covered up."

His words warmed her as she took the groceries inside.

"What's all this?" Miranda said as she helped put away groceries.

Lottie gave a determined nod. "It's time I learned to cook."

"Do you know what to do with this stuff?"

"No." Lottie held up a large red and white checkered cookbook. "That's what this is for."

Miranda looked like she wanted to laugh. "Okay."

Lottie shot her a defiant glance. "You're laughing at me, but that's all right. How did everything go today?"

"It was pretty quiet. I helped catalog items for the auction." Miranda paused, a bag of macaroni in her hand. "I learned something about your niece today."

Lottie looked up. "Oh?"

"Apparently, she has some pretty big medical debts from Sarah's birth."

"She does?" Lottie's voice was sharp with concern.

Jason stuck his head inside the door. "Miranda? Are you ready?"

"Yes." She reached for her purse. "I have to get going. Jason asked me to stop by his office for something."

Lottie smiled at her self-conscious tone. "Before you go, can you tell me where Patti is?"

"I think she's in her room."

"Oh, good," she said happily. "Maybe I'll have time to make dinner before she comes downstairs." She flipped open the cookbook. "Beef Stroganoff. One pound ground beef. Check. One can cream of mushroom soup. Check."

Half an hour later, she looked at the mess in her new pan and sighed. It did not look like anything she'd ever eaten. She hoped it would taste all right.

Patti walked in with the baby on her hip and sniffed the air. "Something smells funny. What did you make?"

"It's beef Stroganoff. But it didn't turn out right." Lottie's heart sank.

Patti grabbed a spoon and dipped into the soupy mixture. She took a taste and wrinkled her nose. "Did you pour the fat off the ground beef?"

"I don't think so. Is that bad?"

Patti nodded, distracted by the taste in her mouth. "There's something else in here I can't quite name. Something sour."

Lottie shrugged. "I didn't have sour cream, so I substituted milk with a little lemon juice."

"That's a substitute for buttermilk." Patti looked at her aunt. "You don't know how to cook?"

Lottie's gaze fell to the mess on the stove. "Not really."

"Mom had a great recipe for this stuff." Patti smiled at her aunt. "We'll need to go back to the grocery."

Lottie took her first bite of Stroganoff and closed her eyes. "Did your mom cook like this all the time?"

Patti nodded. "Pot roast, fried chicken. She was a great cook."

"If tonight is any indication, I'd say you followed in her footsteps." Lottie raised her glass. "Here's to your mother."

"Hear, hear." Their glasses clinked, and Sarah clapped with delight at the sound.

Lottie chuckled at the little girl. "She's such a ray of sunshine. Didn't you say she was a preemie?"

"Yes. She was six weeks early. She had to stay in the hospital until she could breathe on her own."

"That sounds terrible. How did you manage?"

"Mom was a rock. She and I took turns at the hospital, staying with Sarah as much as they would let us." She reached out and flicked the little girl's cheek. "It's been hard, putting her in day care, but nothing is as bad as those first few weeks of her life."

"Forgive me for asking, but where was her father?"

"Eric? He left before she was born. Last I knew, he'd joined some kind of artists' commune in Maine."

Lottie winced. "I'm sorry I brought him up."

"He happened, he's over," she gave a dismissive wave, "and I got to keep the prize. Now, let's change the subject."

"How was your day today?"

Patti's fork stopped halfway to her mouth. "Better than I expected," she said in a funny voice.

Lottie raised her eyebrows. "How so?"

"Miranda pitched in and helped sort my mom's junk, for one thing. She was kind of sweet about it."

"That sounds like her." Lottie reached for a plastic container on the counter. "How do you feel about oatmeal raisin cookies for dessert?"

Patti wrinkled her nose. "I'd rather have chocolate chip. Mrs. Williams must have made those."

"Yes, with Jessie McCall's help."

"Really? That's an odd combination. The Williamses don't approve of the McCalls."

"So I've been told, though no one will tell me why."

"I'm not totally sure myself," Patti said. "When Jessie visited, she always seemed a little neglected. Her clothes were too big or too small, and her hair smelled dirty." She shrugged. "I guess Mrs. Williams thought she'd be a bad influence on the rest of us kids."

"The other day, Jessica said your mom always made you play with her."

"That was a mistake." Patti crumbled a cookie onto Sarah's tray. "I wasn't a compassionate kid. Plus, Mitchell was nice to her, and that always made me mad."

The way she said Mitchell's name caught Lottie's attention. "Mitchell?"

Patti glanced up. "We were…best friends, as kids. Allies."

"I see." Lottie glanced toward the alley. Outside, the garage band started to tune.

Patti looked at her curiously. "You know, your whole body gets tense when they start up." She reached for the radio on the counter behind her. "Would it help to play some music? There's a good oldies station out of Muscatine."

Lottie smiled. "By all means, let's drown out the heavy metal with a dose of Buddy Holly."

This surprised a laugh out of Patti. "You know Buddy Holly? I always imagined you living in a bubble of classical music."

She shrugged. "My downfall is the car. I'll listen to practically anything when I'm driving long distances."

"You couldn't just drive in silence?"

Lottie shook her head. "Music is companionship."

"You could always take a friend along."

A friend. Lottie stood up and began to stack the supper dishes. After she finished rinsing them, she turned to her niece. "You cooked. I'll clean up."

Patti reached for a dish towel. "You wash. I'll dry."

While Lottie ran hot water in the sink, Patti hummed along to the radio. "The Beach Boys remind me of middle school, when I had a gigantic crush on one of Mitchell's friends."

Mitchell again. "Was he cute?"

"Oh, very. He had green eyes and the best smile." She dried a plate and put it away. "He got married right after high school graduation. I hear he owns an auto body shop in Bettendorf now."

"And you're left with the Beach Boys and some memories."

Patti laughed. "I think I got the better end of the deal." She sang a few bars of "Surfer Girl."

Lottie set a plate in the drainer. "You sing like your mother."

"No I don't." The words burst out of her.

Lottie turned to her with a questioning look.

"Mother only sang hymns." She sounded defensive. "You know the operatic tone people have when they sing in church? Well, that was Mom. The rock revolution happened without her."

Helen as a stodgy old church lady? Lottie had to smile. "She wasn't that way when we were young. She kept up on all the Big Band hits." Lived with them. Traveled with them. Lottie closed her mind against the memories. "Our mother was a gifted singer, too, you know."

Patti nodded. "Great-Aunt Eva likes to talk about her."

"She always did."

"Do you sing?"

Lottie wiggled her soapy fingers. "All my talent is in here."

"Do you play anything but classical?"

"Not if I can avoid it."

They were silent a moment, each lost in their own thoughts. Patti said, "What were they like? My grandma and grandpa, I mean."

Lottie pulled the plug and watched the suds flow down the drain. "Pop was a farmer through and through. Lean and tough and weather-beaten. Mother died when I was a baby." She glanced at Patti. "Your mom raised me, of course. But Pop loved us, and provided well for us." She busied herself with the hand towel. "And then he died."

Patti stared at her. "I didn't know Mom raised you."

Lottie frowned. "You didn't?"

"No." Impulsively she said, "There's something I'd like to show you. Wait here."

Scooping Sarah into her arms, she hurried upstairs. When she returned, Lottie had settled on the living room couch. Patti plopped down next to her and held out a picture. "Who is this man?"

A jolt of surprise went through Lottie. "You don't know?"

"No."

Lottie pretended to examine the old familiar photo while she scrambled for an answer. *Now what, Helen? Where did you draw the boundary lines around your life?*

She closed her eyes, drew a breath, and said, "They look so young and carefree. If only they'd known what was coming next."

Patti gave an impatient bounce on the couch cushion. "For Pete's sake, who are you talking about?"

"Helen and Bill." She looked at her niece. "Your mother was married briefly, during the war."

Patti's eyes grew round. "Tell me everything."

How much, Helen? How much do I say? "His name was Bill Turner," Lottie began.

Sometime later, Patti leaned back with a satisfied sigh. "I can't believe Mother was a war bride. It's so romantic, and sad. But why didn't she ever mention it?"

"I don't know." *That, at least, was the unvarnished truth.* "Maybe she put it behind her out of respect for your dad."

"For Dad?" Patti sounded surprised. "Believe me, Dad was not the jealous type."

Lottie smiled at her niece. "Most people have trouble seeing their parents' marriages clearly."

"Hey, wouldn't it be something if Mom had gotten pregnant before Bill went to war? I always wanted sisters and brothers."

For a moment, Lottie stopped breathing. Then, "That would have been a lot of work for your mom, don't you think?"

Patti waved a dismissive hand. "She had all the aunts to help her." She looked at Lottie. "And you. You'd have helped with a baby, wouldn't you?"

Lottie's throat went dry.

But her mother's hidden tragedy had energized Patti. "I have an idea," she said suddenly. "Let's go get those shoe boxes and look at more pictures."

Lottie let out the breath she'd been holding. "That sounds wonderful."

The next few hours were ones she would treasure all her life. Through family pictures, Patti opened up about her childhood and her parents, giving Lottie a guided tour through Helen and Parson's years together. The girl relaxed as they talked and laughed, and even cried a little bit together.

It was midnight when they went to bed, but Lottie had trouble sleeping. Tonight she'd had a chance to tell all—to give Billy a voice in the world once more—and she'd blown it. The weight of that knowledge sat on her chest like a malevolent cat with accusing eyes.

She'd held her peace out loyalty to Helen—hadn't she?

The cat blinked.

She turned on her side and bunched the pillow up under her head. "Helen, I held the boundary," she murmured to the darkness. "Now what?"

This time, oddly, an answer came.

Helen is safe, someone seemed to say. The truth can't hurt her now.

Twelve

ottie washed her cereal bowl with one eye on Patti, who didn't look up from her coffee. The girl seemed moody and preoccupied, not at all the way she'd acted last night. Lottie couldn't blame her. She didn't feel too happy herself.

Sarah was oblivious to her mother's bad mood. She grabbed cereal and banana slices off her tray and pushed them into her mouth with a toddler's disregard for neatness, and broke into a sunny smile when she caught Lottie's eye.

Lottie tugged at a yellow baby curl. "I think Sarah likes it here."

"What? Oh, yes." Patti lapsed back into silence.

Miranda hurried in from the yard and made straight for the coffee pot. Lottie brightened. "How was your evening?"

"Fine." She zipped through the kitchen and soon could be heard climbing the stairs.

"What on earth?" Lottie stared after her in confusion. Picking up her book bag, she followed her assistant upstairs. "Are you all right?"

"I'm fine." Miranda didn't quite meet her eyes. "What do you want me to work on today?"

"I need your help with a special project."

Miranda listened with interest as Lottie explained her idea. "It's risky," she said finally, "but I can give it a try."

"Good." Lottie pulled a folder out of her bag. "I also need revisions on this packet, and fifteen copies by this afternoon. Sorry about the rush job."

Miranda looked through the packet. "I'll drop off the copies after lunch."

Lottie's heart felt a little bit lighter as she left for the office. The plan she'd hatched in the night would require help from many people. She could count on Miranda to do her part. Outside, the construction crew was starting work. Sam detached himself from the group and crossed the lawn to talk to Lottie. "How's that air conditioner working out for you?"

She smiled. "I can't hear the band anymore. Now I just have to get used to the racket from the air conditioner."

His eyes lit with amusement. "You're downright hard to please, lady."

"I know." Her smile flickered, then died.

He gave her a searching look. "Is everything all right?"

She took a deep breath. "Sam," she said. "Do you think Helen can hear us, where she is?"

He gave the question serious consideration. "I have no idea if she can hear us," he said finally, "but I don't think she's listening. I'm pretty sure heaven is so amazing that she's no longer interested in what's happening here on earth. Why do you ask?"

"You'll think I'm crazy."

"Try me."

"Lately I've been talking to Helen, asking her advice about certain situations." She peeked up at him. "I told you this was crazy. Anyway, last night, I asked her a question." She swallowed hard. "And it felt like someone answered. Not an audible voice," she hastened to add, "but in my thoughts."

Far from being repelled by this lunacy, Sam smiled. "That's often the way it feels when God answers prayer." He leaned a little closer. "I do know one thing. Helen may not be able to hear you now, but God definitely can. And you can be sure He'll help you when you ask."

She gave him a grateful smile. "I don't know what to think about all that theological stuff, but somehow I'm glad you believe it."

Cal met Lottie as she unlocked her office. "How's the sale prep going?"

"They've made a lot of headway. We should be all cleaned out by supper time tomorrow. Will you be there?"

"Yep. Teresa and I love a good auction."

"The same goes for me," Lottie said. "I wonder if the two of you would do me a favor."

He listened closely as she outlined her idea. When she finished he said, "Sure. What are friends for? Say, did you have time to read the article I sent you on the jazz department at the University of Michigan?"

"I did. It was very informative." She pulled a music journal from her book bag. "I also read your article about the history of jazz in Chicago. Your writing is fantastic."

Cal's face lit with pleasure. "I get a lot of advice from my wife. Well, have a good morning." He went on his way, whistling.

Lottie turned on her office light and dropped her purse in the bottom desk drawer. Before she could sit down, Katherine knocked on the open door. "Got a minute?"

"Pull up a bench."

Katherine paused to examine Sam's artwork before she sat down. "What composition is that?"

Lottie smiled. "Why don't you work it out for yourself?"

The dean placed her hands on a piano keyboard and played the first few measures. "It's not classical," she said, clearly puzzled. She played it over again, then turned to Lottie. "'In the Mood'? That's a strange choice."

Lottie chuckled. "The artist chose it without my knowledge."

"I see." Katherine lost interest in the wall painting. "I wanted to ask if you ever take private students. I have a young friend, a twelve-year-old, with tremendous talent."

"I've never been asked before," Lottie said. "I'll have to think it over and get back to you."

"All right. Well, that was it. I'll see you at Alicia's funeral this afternoon."

"I'll be there. Before you go, I'd like to ask a personal favor."

Tina and her girls arrived and set to work in the basement, which nicely muffled their radio station. Grateful for the relative quiet, Miranda spent the morning revising Lottie's packet. When she finished, she reached for the phone. She'd learned that the guys at the copy shop worked faster with a little advance notice.

She picked up the receiver only to find the line already in use. The woman on the other end spoke in a strong Southern drawl. "That's a hundred for the tax return, and twenty-five apiece for family photos, but only if I use them."

Patti responded, "I'll see you Saturday, then." The line went dead.

Miranda sat with the phone to her ear and let the truth wash over her. Patti Parker had a colder heart than she'd ever imagined.

She made her call to the copy shop, then sat back and examined her options. Part of her wanted to run downstairs, grab Patti by the collar and shake her until she promised to behave, but her calmer self said that would be counter-productive. She could call right now and tell Lottie what her niece was up to, but why ruin her day? In the end she decided to wait and talk to Lottie after work. In the meantime, she stayed upstairs with the office door closed.

She was on her way out to pick up the copies when Lottie called, sounding panicked. "I spilled chili down my front at lunch. I need a clean blouse to go to Alicia's funeral."

"Which one do you want?"

"There's a pink rayon blouse with a ruffle at the neck in my big suitcase. Bring me that one."

Miranda pulled a suitcase off the pile. "Give me half an hour."

"Hurry!"

She grabbed the blouse from the suitcase and hurried away. After a swift stop at the copy store, she made it to the P.A.B. in twenty minutes flat.

"Thank goodness you're here!" Lottie pulled her into the office and shut the door. Her white top was indeed covered with an ugly red-brown stain. "Did you find the blouse?"

"In here." Miranda gave her a shopping bag. "These are your copies."

"You're a life saver." Lottie was already unbuttoning her blouse. "By the way," she said, "were you able to help Jason with his project last night?"

"What? Oh." Miranda nodded. "He just wanted an opinion on something he's building."

Lottie gave her a quizzical glance. "That's all?"

"That's all." She tried to keep the disappointment out of her voice. She'd spent two hours alone with him, and all they'd talked about was how to build a Murphy bed. As nice as it was that he took her seriously, she could have strangled him.

Lottie finished changing clothes and reached for her purse. "I've got to fly. The funeral starts in fifteen minutes."

Miranda followed more slowly, not really wanting to go back to work. The department office was empty when she walked through, except for Elaine, who was filing her nails. "Not going to the funeral?" Miranda asked.

"Katherine said I didn't have to." Elaine blew on her nail. "Professor Maynard retired before I got this job."

Alicia's funeral was a quiet affair. Her home health aide sat on the front row in place of family. The rest of the crowd, Lottie guessed, was made up of students and faculty. The eulogy could have fit any number of people, as if perhaps the minister didn't know her very well.

Nathan made no pretense of staying awake. His chin dipped onto his chest and he emitted a low snore as the minister spoke. Katherine nudged him none-too-gently, then pretended not to notice when he opened his eyes and glared at her.

Only Rhonda seemed upset. She sat beside Lottie and sniffled into a used tissue through the last half of the service. When she could stand it no longer, Lottie extracted a new one from her purse and tucked it into Rhonda's hand. "Blow," she said firmly.

"It was all so sad," Rhonda said afterward. "Alicia didn't have one friend outside work. Did you notice that? And here I am, with a husband and kids—a real life—and I never once reached out to her."

Nathan gave her a disgusted look. "Why would you? She was horrible to you."

171

Rhonda's blue eyes widened to saucers. "Maybe she'd have been nicer if she felt more loved."

Nathan snorted. "Hogwash."

Lottie smiled at her colleague. "How old are your kids, Rhonda?"

"I saw what you did there," Katherine said on the way to the parking lot. "Pouring oil on troubled water like that. Rhonda's kids are brats, but she loves to talk about them."

Lottie chuckled. "Everyone likes to talk about their kids. Did you know Alicia had no family?"

"Not really. She never talked about her personal life." Katherine shrugged. "Her whole identity was wrapped up in being the first female professor at Collison College. She was all Katherine Hepburn and Dorothy Parker, using caustic wit to show she belonged in the old boys' club. She didn't want to compromise her ground-breaking status by having a softer side."

"I've met women like that."

Katherine glanced at her. "From what I'd heard before you came, I thought you'd be a lot like Alicia. You have a reputation for being unapproachable. No offense."

"None taken." Lottie knew what people thought of her. "And now?"

"There's a big difference. Alicia pushed people away. You're very good at pulling people together." The dean pulled her keys out of her purse. "I must say I'm glad that's over. Funerals always make me think about how brief our lives are." She smiled. "I'll probably go home after work and call my mother."

"I know what you mean," Lottie said. "I have two great-aunts in the nursing home at Westmont. They may not last much longer."

Katherine gave her a sympathetic glance. "Visit them while you can. You'll regret it if you don't."

Tina's crew was gone when Miranda got back from Lottie's office. The house was quiet, no sign of Patti or Sarah. With a sigh of relief, she climbed the stairs, her mind on Lottie's special project. How could she help when she didn't agree with the objective?

Yet another problem with no solution. She'd have to sleep on it.

Lottie's big suitcase lay open on the floor, where Miranda had left it. She knelt to put the clothes back in and flip the latches into place. In the process, a pile of envelopes slid from between the clothing and fell on the floor. As she picked them up, the return address on the top one caught her attention. "D.D?" she said softly. She stared at the envelope for a moment, then reached a decision. Leaning back against the wall, she stretched out her legs, crossed her ankles, and opened each letter.

Long minutes later she set them aside, thinking hard. Donna Davenport had written two letters to Lottie directly, and signed her name. Why would she also send anonymous, vaguely threatening notes like these? Miranda found the letters in her file drawer and set them next to the newspaper clippings on the floor. Too bad she'd thrown away the envelopes. She closed her eyes and tried to reconstruct them. Did they too have that strange return address?

Something about the mysterious letters made her want to reexamine the pocket knife blade that had wrecked Lottie's tire. She pulled it out of its file folder and set it on the floor with the letters. Next, she grabbed some three-by-five cards and a marker. "Office vandalized," went on one. "Picture frame broken," went on another.

She frowned. What had Donna Davenport said this morning? Something about a tax return and family photos. Did they belong in this puzzle?

Slipping off her shoes, she tiptoed to the room next door. The house still felt empty, but she had to be careful. Patti's door swung open without a sound, and she breathed a sigh of relief. Nobody was there.

Taking a lesson from the past twenty-four hours, Patti's suitcase was the first place she searched. Sure enough, she found Lottie's tax return and two black-and-white pictures at the bottom of the clothing stack. Lottie's family needed to think of other hiding places.

A minute later she was back in her office, adding new clues to her layout. The tax return would take time to figure out, so she turned her attention to the pictures. One showed a pretty, dark-haired young woman in a dress with a sailor collar, holding hands with a little girl. Lottie and Helen? Probably. The other, an old studio portrait of a little boy, was puzzling. Did they have a little brother? She couldn't remember. The name on the back, written in neat, looping cursive, didn't enlighten her.

Who in the world was Billy Turner?

When Lottie got home after work, Sam waved from across the yard. "Would you like to see the progress we've made?"

She crossed the lawn and joined him next to a big, shallow rectangle cut into the ground. "Tell me what I'm looking at."

That was all the invitation he needed to talk about his area of expertise. Lottie listened carefully, trying to comprehend the moving of pipes and cables and methods for pouring a sound slab on which to set her music room. She didn't mind the unfamiliar jargon. Sam was fun to listen to when he got into his favorite subject. In the end she understood enough to know her construction project was in capable hands. "Thanks for the update," she said when he finished.

"I got a little carried away." He gave her a sheepish smile. "Sorry about that."

"No apology necessary." As they strolled back across the lawn she added, "Thanks again for answering my oddball question this morning."

"I'm glad you felt you could ask me. Say, I'm meeting my boys at Annie's for supper tonight. Would you like to come?"

She felt a little glow of pleasure at the invitation. "I'd love to. What time should I be there?"

"Would six o'clock work? I've got to get cleaned up first."

"I'll be there."

As they reached the edge of the deck, Miranda burst out the door with her arms full. Taking the steps at full speed, she tripped and seemed to fall in slow motion, flying through the air to land spread-eagled at their feet. Sam lunged forward to stop her fall, while Lottie ran around the lawn picking up the papers that had spilled from Miranda's arms.

"Are you all right?" Sam asked with concern in his voice.

"I think so." She sat up and examined her palms. "My hands and knees took the brunt of the fall."

"Your knee's bleeding," Sam said. "Lottie? Do you have a Band-Aid?"

Lottie was too preoccupied to answer. She held up her old tax return. "Miranda? What is the meaning of this?"

Miranda's eyes widened. "I can explain. I'm taking those things home to keep them from Patti."

Lottie's blood began to boil. "From Patti?"

"Yes. She was going to sell your personal papers to Donna Davenport."

Lottie shook an envelope in her face. "These letters were all in my suitcase. The only way Patti could have gotten them is if she had your help. Looks to me like you're the guilty one, Miranda." She dealt the final blow. "Don't bother to come in tomorrow. You're fired."

Crying too hard to speak, Miranda picked up her book bag and limped away. A minute later her car puttered down the alley.

Lottie turned to Sam, her thoughts in a jumble. "I don't think I'll go with you tonight. I wouldn't be very good company."

"Well, it won't do you any good to sit alone and brood."

Her temper rose at his impatient tone. "I'm staying home, Sam. Go have your dinner."

"Fine." He bent to pick up an envelope that slid from her fingers. Handing it back, he frowned. "That thing in the corner looks familiar."

Lottie snatched the envelope and hid it against her stomach. "Don't start, Sam. It's none of your business."

As hard as she was crying, Miranda wasn't sure how she made it home alive. Shoes in hand, she limped up the walk between townhouses with swollen eyes and torn nylons, heartbroken. All she wanted was to hide inside in the dark and nurse her wounds.

Lottie had fired her. Tears threatened all over again.

Mrs. Carlson stood on her porch as usual, sweeping the spotless concrete slab. "Hello, honey."

"Hi, Mrs. Carlson."

The orange-haired lady cupped a hand around her mouth and stage-whispered, "I see you've got a visitor."

Miranda's head came up. Sure enough, Jason leaned against her door, his hands in his pockets.

And she'd thought this day couldn't get any worse.

He pushed off the wall as she approached. "What happened to you?"

She heard the concern in his voice, but she just didn't care. Shoving her key in the lock, she said, "Look, I'm not in the mood to talk shop tonight. Whatever you want will have to wait."

"What's wrong?"

She rounded on him. "Lottie fired me, all right? She fired me for something I didn't even do. So I don't want to chitchat with you right now, or help you with some construction plan, or pretend I just want to be your friend, because it's not true. Go stand on some other girl's porch. I want to be alone."

He went still. "I don't want to stand on any other girl's porch."

She stared at him. "Why not?"

"Because I love you, Miranda."

Tears spilled down her cheeks. "You do?"

He nodded.

"Well, you have a funny way of showing it."

"Oh, Miranda." He opened his arms and she stepped into them, grateful for his enfolding strength. "For the longest time, I thought Mitch was the one for you. It ate me up inside."

"But he loves Patti."

He nodded against her hair. "I know that now."

She tipped her head back to look at him. "Besides, Mitchell's too much of a party boy. Give me a workaholic businessman any day."

He laughed and lowered his face to hers. Their kiss felt exactly right, like coming home after a long time away.

Across the walk, Mrs. Carlson gave a gusty sigh. "So sweet."

Miranda smiled at Jason through her tears. "We should take this inside."

♪♪

Lottie sprinkled scouring powder around the porcelain sink and scrubbed like her life depended on it. The rest of the kitchen already gleamed from her adrenaline-charged efforts. If she owned a piano, she would have poured her worries into the keyboard, but tonight she'd had to make do with a cleaning spree.

After Sam left, she'd locked the disputed letters in the trunk of her car and marched inside to nurse her anger. Everyone was against her: Patti, Miranda, even Sam had ticked her off with his blunt words. She'd been a fool to let down her guard and trust them. Her years of isolation might have been lonely, but at least she'd never been hurt this way.

She hugged her injuries to herself, building a case for bitterness, but it wasn't long before doubt crept in. Had she done the right thing with Miranda? The girl was loyal to a fault. Had she really sold out to a woman like Donna Davenport?

But Miranda couldn't have seen those letters unless she was snooping in Lottie's suitcase. There was no excuse for it.

And yet Lottie would have sworn the girl was genuinely upset.

Back and forth she went, debating the case until she thought she'd go crazy. That's when she'd decided to scour the kitchen.

She rinsed the sink one final time and wrung out her sponge. Outside, shadows covered the back yard. The band started warming up, heavy on the saxophone. She didn't mind so much tonight, but Marmalade seemed to object. He set up a fuss under the window until she opened the door to shoo him off the porch. Instead of leaving, he stalked past her with his tail up, leaped onto a chair, and fixed her with a knowing stare.

She threw him one exasperated look and stepped onto the porch.

She started across the lawn with half-formed intentions. The cool night air sent a chill down her back, a reminder that fall was around the corner. When she reached the alley, Thomas and his band mates were alone. No audience tonight.

The guitarist stopped playing when she stepped into the light. "What do you want?"

She nodded at the electric keyboard in the corner. "May I?"

He shrugged.

She pulled a round stool away from the wall and settled behind the keys. Bending her head, she picked up the melody of a song she'd been humming a lot lately. These kids wouldn't recognize "I'll Be Seeing You," but it didn't matter. She funneled all her fear and sadness into her fingers, and trusted her audience to pick up the emotion.

The song ended, and nobody spoke. Lottie glanced around and found every face turned to her. "Can you do that again?" the sax player said. "I want to try something."

She started again, and he joined her a few bars in, showing off a flair for improvisation. Not to be outdone, the drummer added a muted beat. They followed easily when she picked up the pace, and for a split second she felt like a Neverland member again.

Only Thomas stayed out of the game. When the music ended he said, "What was that?"

She lifted her chin. "That was a song I used to play when I was your age. I was in a band called the Neverland Orchestra."

The drummer's jaw dropped. "No way."

"I was eleven when they hired me. My sister Helen—" she pointed at Helen's house—"Mrs. Parker, you know, went along as my chaperone."

Thomas's eyes narrowed. "Why are you telling us this?"

The question took her aback. "I don't know," she said. "Since I moved in I've noticed how dedicated you are to your music. I guess you remind me of myself at your age. That band was my life back in the '40s."

The waif looked disgusted. "It's not the same."

"Oh? Why not?"

"Life is so much harder now," Thomas said. "Darker."

Lottie felt her eyebrows shoot up into her bangs. "Darker than a world at war?"

The boy slouched over his guitar. "We have to worry about nuclear war, right? The communists have their finger on the button, and so do we. And then there's AIDS, and drugs, and divorce, and stuff."

Thomas's friends nodded agreement. "Tell me something," Lottie said. "What are you trying to say when you play your music?"

The question seemed to stump Thomas, but the saxophonist spoke up. "We're saying, 'Life's pretty messed up, so we might as well party.'"

Lottie's fingers found the keys once more, and "String of Pearls" took shape beneath her hands. "That's not far from what we were saying back in 1942. When we played songs like this one, we were saying, 'Good-bye, my friends. Tomorrow a troop train will take me to the front. I may not come back, so let's dance and sing and be happy tonight.' That's what we were saying."

"My grandpa fought in World War II," the drummer said. "I guess he's lucky he came back alive." His eyes grew big. "I guess I'm lucky he came back alive."

Lottie played the opening bars of "In the Mood." "One more song and I'll leave you kids alone. Thomas, if you want to join in, you could switch to the bass guitar." She turned to the sax player. "Pick it up as soon as you can. This song loves the saxophone."

He nodded. "No problem. I play this in the school jazz band."

Thomas switched instruments, and Lottie counted them in. Out of the corner of her eye, she saw the waif's toes tapping.

This time the music ended on a big note, and Lottie stood up. "I won't keep you any longer. Thank you for letting me join in for a while."

For the first time since she'd met him, Thomas smiled. "Any time, Ms. Braun."

A thought occurred to her. "By the way, there's going to be an auction at my house on Saturday. You'd be welcome to come check it out."

Lottie felt lighter as she walked back across the alley. If she could patch things up with the band, maybe there was hope for the rest of her messes.

She had to admit she loved playing the well-remembered music from those early days. She wondered what Helen would say about the impromptu performance.

According to Sam, Helen never talked about the Neverland Orchestra. Had Lottie crossed the line? Was the line important anymore?

Eva would know. She and Cora had invented the line when they swore each other to silence on the journey home to Iowa. Eva would know many things, if Lottie caught her in a good moment.

What had Katherine said after the funeral? "Visit them while you can. You'll regret it if you don't." It was time to pay the aunts a visit.

"Lottie." A figure stepped out of the shadows, startling her from her thoughts.

Fright made her voice sharp. "Sam, you scared the life out of me. What are you doing here?"

He held up a white paper bag. "I thought a piece of pie would cheer you up."

Pie and sympathy. Not a bad combination. "You might as well come in." She stepped past him and opened the door.

"Hope you like banana cream." He set the bag on the table. "That was quite a performance back there. Are you joining the band?"

"Oh, you heard that?"

"Johnny'd be proud."

She glanced at him. "What about you? Do you think it's okay for me to play songs from those days?"

"I never understood why we couldn't."

"Then why'd you keep quiet?"

"Parson asked me to."

Lottie turned to stare at him. "You trusted him that much?"

"He never steered me wrong." Sam pulled two slices of pie out of the bag. "Are we going to eat or what?"

When every crumb of pie was gone, Lottie leaned back with a satisfied sigh. "I could eat that every day."

"Annie only makes banana cream on Thursdays." Sam flashed a grin. "That's why the boys and I eat there every week."

"I'm sorry I missed it tonight."

He shrugged. "Actually, I was the only one who remembered. Mitch and Jase stood me up."

"Oh, Sam! Now I feel even worse. Where were they?"

"I don't know where Jase was, but Annie said Mitch and Patti stopped in for supper. They left before I got there."

"Patti and Mitchell? How do you feel about that?"

"I hope they work things out." He set his napkin on the table. "They always did belong together."

She smiled. "I had a feeling that was how it was."

Thirteen

Friday morning Sam caught his oldest son at the office. "Hey, Jase. Missed you last night."

Jason slapped his forehead. "Thursday night at Annie's. I completely forgot."

"You must have been somewhere interesting."

The boy's half-smile gave nothing away.

Mitchell breezed in with a fast-food egg sandwich in his hand. "Hi, guys. Sorry I missed you last night at Annie's."

Jason gave his dad a startled look. "Did you eat alone?"

"Not exactly." Sam concentrated on pouring a cup of coffee. "Lottie was with me."

Now he had their attention.

"I hear she fired Miranda," Jason's voice held a note of disapproval.

Sam looked up. "How in the world did you hear that?"

Mitchell grinned. "I can guess how."

Sam turned to his younger son. "Did you and Patti have a good time last night, Mitch?"

Jason gave a snort of laughter.

Sam blew on his coffee. "Next time you boys want to duck out on me I'd appreciate a heads-up."

"Yes, sir."

Jason brought up Miranda again on the way to the job site. "Lottie got the situation wrong, Dad. Miranda really was trying to protect her."

Sam glanced at him. "I know you like the girl. Are you sure that's not clouding your judgment?"

"Positive. Miranda loves Lottie. She'd never betray her like that."

Sam thought this over. "Do you think Patti would?"

"If she got mad enough."

He had to admit the boy made sense.

Lottie sipped a cup of strong coffee and willed it to work its magic. Her eyes felt heavy from lack of sleep. She'd woken up at midnight when Patti came upstairs, and couldn't get back to sleep. At three a.m. she'd turned on the light, pulled Miranda's file folder out from under her cot, and examined every single piece of evidence. She had to admit the girl was thorough. She'd even penciled in dates where she knew them.

The three-by-five cards convinced her that Miranda was telling the truth. She wasn't a traitor. She was an amateur detective. Lottie went to bed with a lighter heart, then lay awake trying to figure out how to rehire her assistant.

Today she would call and beg Miranda to take her job back. Right after she got home from Westmont.

Patti came downstairs and settled Sarah in the high chair.

"You two were out late last night," Lottie said.

Patti barely acknowledged her.

Lottie gave an inward sigh. Last night she'd spent a long time gazing at Billy's portrait. She'd loved him so. His name on the back in Helen's handwriting came as a blow. If Patti had found his picture, then she'd probably guessed Lottie had lied to her. The past two days of cold silences made perfect sense.

Jessie McCall caught up with Lottie on her way to the car. "I've got good news." She sounded breathless. "My grandpa's house is ready to go on the market. We're putting up the For Sale sign today."

"That's wonderful!"

"It's all because of you."

"I think you mean it's all because of Martha Williams."

"You're the one who got her to help me." Jessie gave her an impulsive hug. "Thank you."

Lottie pulled away as soon as she could. "What will happen to Marmalade?"

The red-head laughed. "He's your problem now."

Across the lawn, Lottie caught Sam's eye and gave a little wave. "Well, I hope the house sells fast. Are you coming to the auction tomorrow?"

"I guess so."

"Can I ask a favor?"

♫

Miranda rolled down the alley at nine-thirty in jeans and a neon T-shirt, determined to win her job back. As arranged, Jason waited by the garage to give the all-clear signal. "Be careful," he said. "Patti's home."

Her stomach did a flip. "Is your dad here?"

He nodded. "I talked to him, though. He's willing to give you the benefit of the doubt."

"Wish me luck." Taking hold of her courage, Miranda marched across the yard and into the kitchen.

Patti looked up from the table as she walked in. "What's with the jeans?" she asked without much interest.

So Lottie hadn't told her about Miranda being fired. Her spirits rose a smidgen. "I'm taking a casual day. Where's Tina's crew?"

"They're done until tomorrow morning."

"I see." Miranda peeked into the crowded dining room. "I can't resist an auction. Would you give me a preview?"

Patti shrugged. "What do you want to see?"

Miranda pretended to think about this. "Anything valuable," she said finally. "You know, the things you'd keep, if you could."

Patti looked up. "Those are two different categories."

"Show me what you mean."

"Okay. Let's start in the dining room. See this?" Patti picked up a piece of sterling silver flatware. "This is my mother's silver pattern. Tina says it's worth a lot of money, but see how ornate it is?" She wrinkled her nose. "Give me something sleek and modern any day." She moved on to a stack of dinner plates. "This is Homer Laughlin china, a wedding gift to my parents. Mother didn't care for it. She started collecting that stuff over there,"—she pointed at a set of dishes covered in pink roses—"but I adore it. When I picture it gathering dust in some shoddy antique store on the highway, I feel sick, but there's nothing I can do about it."

They moved on to the living room. "What about the furniture in here?" Miranda asked. "Did your mom buy quality pieces?"

Patti snorted. "Quality? Yes. Tasteful? It depends on who you ask. I'm not a fan of flowers and lace."

Miranda smiled. "My mother has the same kind of taste, and she puts clear plastic slipcovers over everything so it won't get damaged."

Patti returned the smile. "Then you know what I mean."

Miranda was beginning to enjoy herself. "What about that desk in the corner? It fits this room perfectly. Will you be glad to see it go?"

"No. I love it. I can still picture my dad sitting there, paying bills or grading papers." She hesitated. "But it would look pretty silly in my little apartment."

Miranda shot her a sympathetic look. "You're doing something brave, you know."

Patti looked sad. "I wish it didn't hurt so much. Do you want to see the stuff they brought up from the basement? There's a late Victorian bedroom set that'll knock your socks off."

"Sure."

The front hall was full of miscellaneous items. Patti climbed around a floor lamp and a steamer trunk and beckoned Miranda to follow. "This stuff will be spread out on the lawn come Saturday. Here's the headboard. It kind of goes with Mom's silver pattern."

"I see what you mean." Miranda ran a finger around one carved bedpost. "It's a bit of a dust catcher."

"If you think that's bad, you should see the hat rack. I think it's over here somewhere. Ouch!" Patti tripped over a long black case on the floor.

"What's that?"

"That's my dad's saxophone. He played it in college."

"Must be hard, getting rid of a memento like that."

Patti shrugged. "I never saw him play it. I hope it goes to a good home." She reached behind the hat rack and pulled out a framed purple dress. "Now this darling little dress is one of my favorite things. It always hung in Mom's sewing room, and I dreamed about wearing it." She traced the collar with her finger. "The color has faded over the years, though. It used to be royal purple."

"Couldn't you keep that one thing?"

"No." She set the dress down and turned away. "If I keep one thing, I won't be able to stop. One thing will lead to another and I'll end up keeping everything. Besides, I really do need all the money I can raise."

Miranda hated feeling sympathetic toward this girl. "I hope you meet your goal."

For a moment, Patti looked like she was going to cry. Then, "Want to see the stuff in the garage?" she said with forced cheer.

"Lead the way."

As they left the kitchen and walked across the yard, she caught Jason's eye and smiled. He gave her a discreet thumbs-up in return.

The tour of the garage was fast and efficient, but it accomplished Miranda's purpose. "You stand to make a good profit," she said when they finished.

A glimmer of gratitude shone in Patti's eyes. "Thanks."

Miranda took a deep breath. "It was nice of you to show me all your treasures," she said quickly, before she lost her nerve. "Now I've got something to show you."

"Cora and Eva?" The receptionist smiled. "They're in the activity room, having their morning exercise. I'll take you down there." She led Lottie to a sunny room full of people in wheelchairs. "I've got a visitor for Cora and Eva," she sang out.

Cora didn't move, but Eva turned to see who had come. "That's my niece, Lottie Braun," she told her neighbor, "the famous pianist." She released the brake on her wheelchair and maneuvered herself toward the door. "You'll have to push Cora's wheelchair," she said to Lottie. "She doesn't do much for herself anymore."

Lottie did as she was told and soon was pushing Cora's wheelchair down the hall next to Eva. "Let's go to the lounge," Eva said. "No one will bother us there."

They parked in a sunny corner of the deserted lounge, and Eva patted her sister-in-law's hand. "Lottie is here to see us, Cora. LOTTIE."

Cora opened her eyes, blinked a few times, and closed them again.

"She's having one of her sleepy mornings." Eva sounded sad. "They happen a lot lately."

Lottie cast about for words of comfort. "That's a shame."

"When she goes, I'll be the last Hoffman sibling. Oh, I know Cora isn't my sister by blood, but she's still one of us."

Lottie nodded. "She was so good to me when I was a little girl. Cora always had the gift of mothering."

"Except once."

Eva's flat statement took Lottie by surprise. "What do you mean?"

"Neither one of us was much use to you in California." At Lottie's murmured protest she added, "That's what you've come about, isn't it?"

Lottie gave a reluctant nod. "Do you mind talking about it?"

Eva opened her eyes wide. "It's the least I can do. I've always been sorry for putting you on that train, but Cora said you'd be safe in Ohio. Helen wanted to kill you."

Lottie swallowed hard. "I deserved it."

"No, you didn't. Helen should have looked after that baby better. I knew it, and Cora did, too."

"Then why…?"

Eva nodded toward the big television set. "What does Walter Cronkite call it? Damage control. We'd already lost that little baby. We weren't going to lose either of you, if we could help it. We knew we had to separate you. You could go to the conservatory, but Helen had to come home." She shrugged. "So that's what we did."

Lottie leaned toward her aunt. "Nobody around here seems to remember about Billy. Why didn't you ever talk about what happened?"

"Least said, soonest mended," Eva said simply. "That's what we were always taught. We figured Helen would heal faster if nobody knew. It worked, too. Pretty soon it was like he'd never existed."

Lottie's heart twisted. At the very least, Billy deserved to be remembered.

Lottie took her aunt's gnarled hand. "Aunt Eva, it's time for me to talk about Billy's death. Patti needs to know. Is it okay with you if I do that?"

Eva looked shocked. "You don't need my permission, child. Tell whoever you want."

Lottie drew a breath. "Do you mind if I tell Sam?"

Tears gathered in the red-rimmed eyes. "Do you have to?"

"I think so. The Neverland Orchestra was a chapter in his life, too. All these years he's kept silent about it for your sake, and he doesn't even know why. I think that kind of loyalty deserves an explanation."

Eva plucked at the edge of her lap robe. "I hate for him to know the hurt I caused."

Lottie wiped a tear from her aunt's cheek. "He'll understand."

Miranda pulled a legal pad out of her book bag and set it on the kitchen table. "I heard you on the phone yesterday, talking to Donna Davenport. Why did you change your mind about her?"

Patti narrowed her eyes. "That's none of your business."

Miranda crossed her arms and waited.

"Lottie lied to me," Patti said finally. "She told me something about my mom that wasn't true."

"Was it about a little boy named Billy?"

The question earned her a swift glance of surprise. "How did you know that?"

"His picture's not in your suitcase anymore." Miranda held up her hand for silence. "I took the tax return, too. You'll be happy to know

Lottie fired me for having them in my possession."

"Good."

Miranda pushed the legal pad across the table. "Last night I wrote an account of all the things that have happened since Lottie moved to Collison a month ago. You need to read it."

"Why should I?"

Patti's suspicious tone made Miranda sit up straighter. "I think it'll change your mind. And if it doesn't—" She shrugged. "At least you'll have a good story to tell your friend Donna."

As Patti pulled the legal pad close and began to read, Miranda ticked off the events in her mind. Punctured tire. Broken picture frame. Vandalized office. Threatening notes from D.D.

Patti finished the last page and looked up. "How do I know this is true?"

Without a word, Miranda went to the porch and waved to Jason. He walked over to speak to his dad, and the two of them crossed the lawn together.

The kitchen felt crowded with all four of them in it. Patti looked from one face to the next. "What's going on?"

"Miranda says you need convincing," Jason said calmly. "I don't expect you to believe me, but ask my dad what's been happening to Lottie."

Patti looked from one face to the next as they stood shoulder to shoulder across from her. "All right, I believe you." she said finally. "Why didn't Lottie tell me all this herself?"

They looked at each other. "She doesn't want to make a big deal out of it," Sam said.

"But it is a big deal. She's obviously in danger." Patti's eyes grew round. "Oh, my gosh. I invited Donna Davenport to come to the auction. What am I going to do?"

"Uninvite her," Jason said.

Patti shook her head. "I can't. I don't know where she's staying."

They looked at one another in silence. Finally, "We'll handle her when she gets here," Jason said. "I'd be happy to escort her off the premises."

Lottie sat in the lounge with her aunts for another half-hour, before a nurse's aide came looking for them. "Time for your hair appointments," she said with an apologetic smile. "The hairdresser only comes one day a week, so we have to keep to a schedule."

"Don't be a stranger," Eva said as she unlatched her parking brake.

Lottie kissed her parchment cheek. "Don't worry. Now that I'm back, I won't lose touch with you again."

As the group moved into the hall, they met Reverend Summers coming in the front doors. His face lit up when he saw the aunts. "How are my two favorite ladies today?" He held first Cora's hand and then Eva's, and they beamed at each other. "Are you coming to chapel service this morning?"

Eva's smile dimmed. "We have to get our hair done."

He didn't miss a beat. "I'll look for you afterward, then." He spotted Lottie, hanging back behind them. "Miss Braun! This is an unexpected treat."

"I was visiting my aunts."

"Oh, yes. Excellent ladies, your aunts. Helen took after them in many ways." He shot her an apologetic look. "But of course, you would know that."

"I didn't know my sister as an adult. Won't you tell me what she was like?"

Reverend Summers' eyes filled with compassion. "I'd love to. Let's sit down for a moment." He indicated the lounge she had just vacated.

She glanced toward the chapel at the end of the hall. "I don't want to keep you."

"I have a few minutes." He smiled. "In a place like this, it doesn't matter if the service starts a little late."

"Does this place ever make you sad?" she asked. "All these people, imprisoned in their failing bodies, living on a schedule they don't control."

"Prison comes in many forms, Miss Braun. Lots of people spend their lives chained up by anger or greed or guilt."

She felt the truth of this deep in her gut. "I know that kind of prison. Someone set me free from it a few months back."

"Was it Helen?"

She nodded. "When I was thirteen, I did a terrible thing that hurt her very much. I thought she could never forgive me, but I was wrong. She forgave me a long time ago. I just wouldn't let her close enough to tell me."

His eyes were bright. "Helen always struck me as somebody who had come through deep suffering by the grace of God. She exuded the kind of peace and loving-kindness that only come from walking through the fire with Jesus."

Lottie sighed. "In some ways I feel worse than ever, knowing I have only myself to blame for staying away so long."

He looked at her for a long moment. "Miss Braun, if Helen set you free from your prison, why do you suppose you're still standing inside?"

"Because I don't deserve it." The words rushed out of her. "I've tried, Reverend. I've been a good neighbor, and I've done a good job at work, but it isn't enough. If people knew what I did, they'd hate me for it. I don't deserve to be forgiven."

"Ah. Now I understand." He sat back, hands folded across his belly, and regarded her with a thoughtful stare. "Miss Braun, what do you know about the apostle Paul?"

"Nothing," she said simply.

He nodded. "After Jesus died, his followers began to preach that he had been resurrected. They claimed if people believed in Jesus, he would forgive all their sins and give them new life. Now, the Jewish leaders were enraged by this message, and felt the need to stamp it out by killing the men who preached it. A man named Saul headed up the campaign to stamp out the Jesus-preachers. He stood by and watched while men were stoned to death. Saul went from house to house, rooting out Christians and carting them off to prison. One day, he traveled from Jerusalem to Damascus—This doesn't sound familiar?"

"Vaguely. Go on."

"Well, on the way to Damascus, a bright light flashed out of the sky and knocked Saul off his horse. A voice said to him, 'Saul, Saul, why do you persecute me?'

"Saul said, 'Who are you, Lord?'

"'I am Jesus, whom you are persecuting,' said the voice. 'Now get up and go into the city and I will tell you what you must do.'

"To make a long story short, Miss Braun, Saul believed from that point on that Jesus was the Son of God. As soon as he recovered from his experience on the road, he started preaching Christ to all who would listen. He was a changed man, and Jesus changed his name to Paul to mark that fact."

Reverend Summers fell silent for a moment.

"What does that story have to do with me?" Lottie said.

"Paul stood in awe of the way Jesus had forgiven his sins. Later in his life he wrote to his friend Timothy, 'Christ Jesus came into the world to save sinners—of whom I am the very worst.' By that time, he'd helped thousands of people receive the forgiveness of Christ. Now, what do you suppose would have happened if young Saul had rejected Christ's forgiveness?"

She frowned. "I can't even picture that. If Jesus forgave him in person, he'd be pretty arrogant not to accept it."

Reverend Summers broke into a delighted smile. "Well, in that case, have I ever got good news for you." He set a gentle hand on Lottie's arm. "My dear, Jesus died to forgive you, too. The Bible says, 'As far as the east is from the west, so far has he removed our transgressions from us.'"

She looked at him with dawning hope. "Is that true?"

"It's the truest thing I've ever known."

"Reverend," she said. "Show me what I have to do."

Sam had to hand it to the kids. They'd really gotten through to Patti. Right now, she and Miranda had their heads together, forming a plan to protect Lottie from that Davenport woman.

Jason had gone back to work as soon as Patti made up her mind, but Sam needed a minute to gather his thoughts. He poured himself a cup of coffee and went to sit on the porch steps.

The Williams clan—and Mitch, too—had done a good job cleaning up the McCall property. He wished young Jessie luck settling her grandfather's affairs.

With a leap and a yowl, the big orange cat joined him on the porch.

"Hey, fella." Sam bent and scratched the animal between the ears. Lottie must be feeding him, the way he hung around this door.

He drained his coffee cup as a Cadillac pulled up in front of the McCall house. Now, this was interesting. A buyer already? A woman stepped out of the car and waved. When he realized who she was, he ducked, but it was too late. She'd spotted him.

"Yoo-hoo, Sam," the woman called. "I see you there. I've listed this house for sale. Isn't that great?"

He watched Diana Deering hustle across the yard with a For Sale sign under her arm, her brassy yellow bangs fluffed up above her forehead. "That little Jessie McCall is just the sweetest thing," she said when she reached him. "I'm tickled pink she's asked me to sell this little gem."

"Congratulations, Diana." Sam looked past her. "There's Jessie now."

Cousin Diana leaned close. "I'll be over to see Lottie after our meeting. When she decides to sell this old place, I plan to be first in line." She hurried away, calling, "Yoo-hoo, Jessica. Let's sell this house."

When she planted her sign in Jessie's yard, Sam did a double-take.

He should have thought of that before.

Fourteen

Lottie checked her watch as she left the nursing home. Reverend Summers had invited her to stay for the chapel service and play hymns for the residents, but she had a few things to do before her afternoon class. "Remember," he said as they parted ways. "'If the Son therefore has set you free, you shall be free indeed.' The past belongs to Him now. Don't try to take it back."

She drove home in high spirits, with freedom and joy running in her veins. When she reached the alley, she schooled herself to drive slowly, but she wanted to get out of the car and skip and jump and run.

She waved at Sam as she passed the work crew, and he started across the yard to meet her. "There's something you have to see." He grabbed her hand and began to pull her across the yard.

She hurried to keep up. "Wait, Sam. I have to tell you something." She stumbled, and he steadied her, but didn't slow his pace. "What's this all about?"

"You'll see." He propelled her into Jessica's front yard and stopped in front of a realtor's For Sale sign. "Notice anything?"

She looked at the sign. "Jessica said the house was on the market. Good for her." She shot him a dubious glance. "But I don't get why you're acting this way."

He dropped her hand and pointed. "Look at the name of the real estate company."

The logo on the sign looked eerily familiar. Her jaw dropped. "D.D!

What in the world?"

"Diana Deering is the most successful real estate agent in the county." His smile was tinged with satisfaction. "She's also your cousin."

Lottie stared at him in disbelief. "My cousin Diana is 'that Deering woman'?" She imitated Nathan Bartholomew's grumpy voice.

"Yes. What's more, she thinks you're going to be her next customer." "Wha-a-a-at?"

He nodded toward Jessica's house. "Here she comes now. Be strong."

Diana rushed toward them, arms outstretched. "Lottie, I heard you'd moved back. You haven't changed a bit." She swept in for a hug. "Ooh, I could just eat you up. Have you gotten my letters?"

Lottie gently extricated herself from the hug. "Your letters? I don't think so."

Diana looked coy. "Well, I made a little game out of them. I knew you'd appreciate a puzzle. But the clues I left pointed directly to me."

Lottie was beginning to feel dizzy. "You sent the newspaper clippings?"

"That's right." Diana gave a pleased little laugh. "I knew you'd figure it out. You were always so smart. Now, I don't think for one minute a person of your standing will want to stay in this neighborhood. It's nice enough in its own way, but not truly distinguished. I have several beautiful properties with river views just waiting for you to claim them."

Lottie finally found her voice. "Oh no, Diana. You have the situation all wrong. I plan to stay in this house for the rest of my life. No ifs, ands, or buts."

Undeterred, Diana Deering pressed a business card into her hands. "I give you till spring to change your mind. The heating bills in that place are going to eat you alive." With a wave she headed for her car. "Call me."

Lottie and Sam stood rooted to the spot until Diana was out of sight. Then she caught his bemused expression and burst out laughing. When her giggles subsided she said, "That woman is the spitting image of her mama. Did you ever meet Aunt Eloise?"

A reluctant grin tugged at the edges of his mouth. "Diana should pay for scaring you that way."

"Let it go," Lottie said. "She wouldn't understand, even if you told her. Sam, there's so much I want to tell you when I have more time."

"We've got a number of things to tell you, too."

"Can it wait? I'm late for class."

"Better hurry." He stepped aside.

She started to leave, then turned back. "Could you call Miranda for me? Ask her to come to the house. I need to rehire her."

His face relaxed in a grin. "I'm way ahead of you. She'll be here when you get home."

Lottie parked in the faculty lot and raced toward the P.A.B. at top speed. Her heart felt light inside her chest, minus the burdens she'd carried so long. Gone were the habitual guilt and unnamed dread she had come to accept as normal. Now that Diana had shown her cards, the sinister letters would stop. She even felt equal to defeating Donna Davenport, though she had no idea how she'd do it.

She hurried through the department office, waved to Katherine, ran down the hall, and burst through the classroom door as the clock struck two. "I'm here," she called out. "Don't even think of leaving."

At the front of the room, Nathan Bartholomew turned his wheelchair. "To what do we owe the pleasure, Miss Braun?"

She was in the wrong classroom. "Sorry, Nathan."

"Pull yourself together, girl," she murmured as she walked next door. She felt the familiar adrenaline rush that came with the possibility of failure. At the door to the correct classroom she stopped, patted her hair and straightened her shoulders. So what if she was a few minutes late? She was the Great Lottie Braun, for goodness sake. She was worth waiting for.

She opened the door and marched inside. "Good afternoon, students. Give me ten facts about the Baroque era."

By the time class ended, Lottie knew what to do about Donna Davenport. When the last student left, she marched upstairs to call her lawyer. Aunt Eva had given her the courage to say what she should have said long ago: She owned the rights to her story, and nobody was going to tell it without her permission. She sailed through the atrium, head high, borne along by righteous anger.

An uproar met her in the back hall. Katherine, Cal, and Nathan filled the hallway, all intent on the scene inside the office. Lottie skirted a janitor's cart and touched Katherine on the shoulder. "What's going on?"

Katherine moved aside to let her see. "Rhonda caught the janitor destroying your personal property."

Inside the office, Rhonda jabbered away at top speed to a blue-uniformed policeman, while a second officer took notes. Next to him, in handcuffs, stood the scruffy young man in coveralls.

"I've been suspicious of him from the beginning," Rhonda said. "He was hired this summer while I was in Europe—"

Nathan groaned. "She had to mention Europe."

"—and he didn't look trustworthy. I know a good face when I see one, you know. It comes from years of working with students—"

"This office belongs to me," Lottie said as she stepped into the room. "What seems to be the problem?"

The officer turned to her with obvious relief. "Mrs. Kennedy says she caught this man in the act of destroying your property. The item in question is right over there." He pointed at the floor behind Rhonda.

There lay the picture of Mr. Schultz. His frame and glass were smashed to bits, and the picture itself blotted with white splotches. The white splotches continued onto the rug underneath.

Lottie's shoulders slumped, all her bravado gone. She turned to the man in handcuffs. "Why?" He ignored her question, so she stepped forward and asked again. "Out of this entire room, why that? Why?" She wanted to shake him.

The police officer looked apologetic. "He hasn't said a word since I got here, ma'am. I don't think he's all there upstairs."

"I see."

He turned to his partner. "Go ahead and take him to the station. I'll need a statement from Ms. Braun and Mrs. Kennedy, but unless you know something about this mess, the rest of you are free to leave."

"I'm the dean of this department. I'd like to stay," Katherine said.

"Fair enough." He turned to Rhonda. "Mrs. Kennedy, I'm going to read the information you gave me. If it's accurate, you're going to sign your name to it, and you'll be free to go."

Rhonda nodded. "I'm sure it will be, Chief Holt. I watched you take lots of notes—"

"Here we go, then. You came down the hall at five minutes past two, looking for Miss Braun. A janitor's cart was parked in the doorway to her office, and the suspect was inside, bent over something on the floor. He stood up, and you saw a bottle of bleach in his hands and the mess on the floor exactly as it appears right now."

"That's right. —"

He held up a hand for quiet. "The suspect saw you, stood up, and threw the open bottle of bleach at you. In defense, you rammed the cart into him. He fell backwards, hitting his head on a bookshelf bracket, and fell to the floor, unconscious. You called the police, then Dean Snelling, and stayed outside the door until the police arrived." He looked up. "Is that how it all happened, Mrs. Kennedy?"

"Yes, sir."

"Great." He pushed his note pad toward her. "Sign your name there at the bottom, and you are free to go."

Rhonda signed the statement, then patted Lottie's shoulder. "I'm sorry this happened."

Lottie smiled at her. "You did a brave thing, Rhonda. I'm in your debt."

Rhonda's face softened. "I think that makes us even."

Lottie felt grateful for Katherine's presence as she faced Chief Holt. "You wanted a statement?"

"We may as well have a seat." He pulled out a piano bench for himself. "Jason Harms called me last night. He and my son played basketball together in high school. He says there's been a pattern of criminal mischief in your office since you arrived. Would you care to tell me about it in your own words?"

Katherine shot her a look of confusion. "What on earth is he talking about, Lottie?"

Lottie sank into her office chair. "Have a seat, Katherine. This could take a while."

Her statement took an hour, with Chief Holt stopping her to clarify different points along the way. By the time it was over, Katherine looked permanently stunned. "I just don't understand why you kept all this to yourself."

Chief Holt looked up. "I'm confused about that, too."

Lottie spread her arms wide. "There's an expectation about people like me, that we'll be hard to get along with because we're well-known."

"She means she's famous." Katherine looked at the police chief. "In classical music circles, Lottie is world-famous."

He raised his eyebrows. "I'm aware of that."

Lottie went on. "Here I was, a newcomer in a fairly unwelcoming department—sorry Katherine, but it's true. The last thing I needed was to whine about some damage to my office."

"But this kind of damage?" Katherine sounded outraged. "That man has been harassing you regularly. That's the kind of thing you're supposed to speak up about."

"It's over now," Lottie said quietly. "Can't we just forget about it?"

The construction site buzzed with activity when Lottie crossed the lawn in the late afternoon. She was emotionally exhausted by this roller coaster day, but she wasn't unhappy. Her office harasser had been caught, her sinister pen pal was an overzealous real estate agent, and her assistant's car was in the alley, where it belonged. For the first time in weeks she felt a modicum of control over her life.

She stepped into the kitchen and looked around with delight. "Well, if it isn't my two favorite career women."

Miranda and Patti looked up from the kitchen table, uncertainty in both their faces. Miranda spoke first. "Sam said you wanted to see me?"

"I do." Lottie crossed the kitchen and put a hand on her assistant's shoulder. "I'm so sorry I yelled at you like that. You've been the most loyal employee anyone could ask for. And I never should have fired you. Will you forgive me?"

Miranda covered Lottie's hand with her own. "I'm sorry, too. I should have told you what I was doing, instead of hiding it that way."

"Will you take your job back?"

Miranda smiled into Lottie's eyes. "I never really gave it up."

Patti cleared her throat. "This is very touching. Can we get to my apology now?"

Lottie sat down and faced her niece. "Shoot."

Patti opened her mouth, then shut it, all bravado gone. "This is hard."

"Take your time."

Nervously she said, "I think I should start with Mom's will." She glanced up and away. "Wow, it made me mad when Mom gave you this house." She shrugged. "But it didn't feel right to blame her, so I blamed you instead."

"That's understandable," Lottie murmured.

"I've been stewing about it ever since," Patti continued. "So when Donna Davenport called me a few weeks ago, it felt like I finally had a way to get back at you." She squeezed her eyes shut. "Sorry. That's the first time I've said that out loud. Anyway, I came home to get the auction rolling and to track down information about you that I could sell to her. Then I totally changed my mind the other day when Miranda told me how good you'd been to her, and we spent the evening talking about Mom." She sighed. "But when I went up to my room afterward, I found that baby picture in the lining of Mom's suitcase, and all the anger came back stronger than ever." Her lips tightened. "I was furious, thinking you lied to me, so I called Donna Davenport and told her I had the things she wanted. She's coming to the auction tomorrow, to buy them from me."

"Are you going to sell?"

"I can't." Patti's lips twisted in a wry smile. "Miranda stole them out of my room, and now she says you've got them." She looked up, her eyes shining with regret. "But I wouldn't anyway. I'm ashamed I ever thought I could sell you out like that."

Lottie reached for her niece's hand. "I forgive you. Oh, my dear, I forgive you completely."

They gazed at each other with eyes full of tears, their hearts too full for words. Then Lottie reached for Miranda's hand. "Thank you for this."

Miranda squeezed her fingers. "You did it. Not me."

A moment later, Jason walked into the kitchen, took one look at three tearful women, and turned around to leave. "I'll wait outside," he said over his shoulder.

Miranda looked toward the door with a lovely, self-conscious smile. "I should go. We've got a date tonight." She scooted back her chair and reached for her purse. At the door she paused. "Lottie, I left something for you in the top drawer of my desk. Be sure to look at it tonight."

Patti got to her feet as the screen door slammed. "I have to get going, too. Sarah and I are meeting Mitchell at Riverside Park."

Lottie raised her eyebrows. "You and Mitchell are spending a lot of time together."

"Yes, we are." Patti's self-conscious smile was every bit as bright as Miranda's. "You're not the only person who's forgiven me in the past day and a half."

As Patti ran upstairs to wake Sarah from her nap, Lottie sighed. The rest of their conversation would have to wait until later.

She sat at the kitchen table for a while after Patti left, listening to the buzz of the saw blade outside and making little plans in her head. Now that they'd cleared the air, she and Patti had a real chance of forging a relationship. Lottie's head filled with dreams of holiday dinners in Helen's dining room and watching Sarah grow up.

Billy was the only cloud left on her horizon.

She was setting the table for one when Sam stepped into the kitchen. "I've wrapped things up out here. I guess I'll see you tomorrow."

"Wait." She turned to face him. "Sam, they caught the man who's been messing with my office."

"They did?" He paused with his hand on the door latch. "Who was it?"

"The janitor. Rhonda Kennedy walked in on him in my office, destroying my picture of Mr. Schultz."

"Your lucky picture?" He rubbed a hand along his jaw. "That's a crazy thing to do."

She shrugged. "I guess he's not all there, mentally."

"Are you all right?"

She nodded. "By the time I walked in, Police Chief Holt had everything well in hand. The suspect was in handcuffs, and Rhonda had given her statement. There wasn't anything to be afraid of."

Frown lines deepened between his eyes. "I meant, are you all right about losing that picture?"

The concern in his gruff voice warmed her heart. "It hurts, Sam. I won't say otherwise. Mr. Schultz is a part of my past that I can't get back. But I'll live."

"Will you be okay until Patti gets home?"

"I think so. She said they wouldn't be out late." She nodded at the oven. "I made tuna casserole. There's plenty, if you want to stay."

Her invitation seemed to throw him off-balance. "I'd have to wash up first."

"Go ahead." She waved him toward the hall. "I'll set another place at the table."

A few minutes later he emerged from the bathroom with his face and hands scrubbed clean. "Sorry about the rest of this mess." He indicated his work clothes and boots. "Nancy used to make me shower before she even kissed me hello."

Lottie shrugged. "I don't mind."

He gave the air an appreciative sniff. "Smells good in here. Where did you learn to cook?"

"I didn't." She held up the cookbook. "This is my first tuna casserole ever, so you're taking your life in your hands, eating it."

He chuckled. "How bad can it be?"

"Pretty bad." She told him about the Stroganoff disaster. "Patti did a good job of saving that meal."

Sam laughed. "That brings back memories of when Nancy and I were first married. We ate our share of burned or undercooked food before she got the hang of things."

"That surprises me."

"Why? People aren't born with all their life skills in place. We all have to learn on the job."

Lottie pulled the casserole out of the oven and set it on the table. "Have a seat and let's give this thing a try." She looked at Sam. "Will you say grace?"

This time when they bowed their heads she didn't feel awkward at all. She felt grateful, and joyful, and alive.

Sam said amen, and she passed him the dish. "I went down to Westmont to see the aunts this morning, and had a wonderful conversation with Reverend Summers."

He took a scoop of casserole. "Tell me about it."

"He helped me understand that I really am forgiven. Not just by Helen, but by God, too. He told me God is a God of second chances. Isn't that amazing?"

"It changed my life when I learned that truth."

After supper Lottie shooed him out the door. "Go home and get some rest. Tomorrow's going to be a long day."

He picked up his hat. "I'll see you around seven."

"No, you won't."

"I won't ?"

"I won't be here." She smiled. "Before you go, I need to ask a favor."

After Sam's pickup truck drove away, Lottie went upstairs to take a shower. She stood under the hot spray and let the cares of the day wash down the drain. As her mind cleared, Miranda's parting words came back with sudden clarity. She'd left something in her desk for Lottie.

She found it in the top desk drawer: The cornerstone to her plan. After a search for stationery and envelopes, she sat down to take the next step.

Around nine o'clock a car door slammed, and Patti walked in, with Sarah asleep on her shoulder. Lottie had finished her work by then and was reading a music history textbook at the table.

"You don't look comfortable," Patti whispered.

"There's nowhere else to sit," Lottie whispered back.

"True." Patti pointed at her daughter. "I'll be right back."

She came downstairs a few minutes later and joined Lottie at the table. "Sarah didn't even wake up when I put her pajamas on. Mitchell ran her wheels off at the park tonight."

Lottie smiled at the quiet pride in her niece's voice. "I'll bet he's good with her."

Patti's eyes were dreamy. "He'll make the best dad."

Lottie raised her eyebrows. "Is there something you'd like to tell me?"

"Nothing big." The girl couldn't keep from smiling. "But we've come a long way in the past few days."

"I'm so glad."

"Enough about me," Patti said. "How was your evening?"

"Fine…Patti, there's one more thing we need to talk about."

"What's that?"

She braced herself. "The little boy in the photo you found was your half-brother."

The blaze of anger she expected didn't materialize. Instead, Patti nodded. "I figured."

"Billy was born in August 1942. He died just shy of his second birthday."

"How did he die?"

Lottie closed her eyes. "He choked on a sourball I brought home from the candy store in Santa Monica, California. I was supposed to be babysitting that night, while Helen was out." She turned her gaze to Patti's pale face. "But instead of watching Billy, I snuck out to meet a boy. While I was gone, Billy woke up and got the candy out of the dresser." She raised her hands in a futile gesture. "By the time I got back, it was too late to save him."

"Oh, Lottie."

The compassion in her niece's voice nearly undid her. "Aunt Cora and Aunt Eva arrived that night by train, in time to keep your mother from outright killing me. They shipped me off to a music conservatory in Ohio, dealt with the baby's burial, and took Helen home with them." She swallowed hard. "That's why I stayed away, Patti. I was sure your mother could never forgive me. I certainly never forgave myself." She pulled Helen's letter from her bathrobe pocket and handed it to her niece. "Ed Williams gave me this the day the will was read. It's the reason I moved to Collison."

Patti opened the letter and began to read. When she finished she looked up, but didn't speak.

When the silence became unbearable Lottie said, "Are you all right?"

"This explains so much about my mother." Her voice was sad. "She was so overprotective. I hated her for it as a teenager, but she was only trying to keep me safe." She smoothed out the letter. "I wish I'd known what she went through. I might have been a little easier on her."

"Maybe, maybe not. Teenage girls are unpredictable creatures."

"That's fair." Patti reached for Lottie's hand. "I hope this goes without saying, but I don't blame you for what happened. My mother was incredibly irresponsible with this Johnny guy. Who was he, anyway? And what was this band she talked about?"

Lottie sat back and looked at her niece. "You're not going to believe this."

Lottie could have talked all night about life with the Neverland Orchestra. In fact, she very nearly did. Patti kept asking questions, which led to more stories, and even more amazing facts. She was awed to find out her dad played saxophone in a traveling band, and dumbfounded to learn that Sam Harms had been the drummer. "Not really!" she kept saying.

But it was all true.

The little hand on the kitchen clock pointed to the two when they finally dragged themselves up to bed. Patti reached out to hug her aunt. "Thanks for the history lesson."

Lottie held her close. "You are so welcome, dear heart."

Her only regret, as she settled into bed, was that Patti would not let her help financially. She'd offered, and been gently rejected.

"This is my mess," Patti said. "I'll get myself out of it."

Fifteen

The last thing Lottie wanted to do at 5:30 the next morning was get out of bed. More than anything, she longed to burrow back under the covers, but she reached for her robe and headed down the hall instead.

The auction crew filed into the kitchen while she was buttering her toast. Tina made brief introductions, and the men of the family tromped back out the door. Tina turned to Lottie. "Where's Patti? We need her okay on some stuff."

"She'll be down soon. We had a late night."

Tina's husband stuck his head around the back door. "We gotta have some decisions here."

"Keep your pants on. I'm coming." Gum a-snapping, Tina followed him outside.

Alone in the quiet kitchen, Lottie took a bite of toast and a sip of coffee.

Patti came downstairs, yawning hugely. "I'm letting Sarah sleep a little longer. No need to start her day just yet."

"Good thinking." Lottie set her empty plate in the sink. "I'll see you at supper time. Hope it all goes well today."

"Are you sure you won't stick around?"

"You need a chance to finish what you started without me around to be a distraction. Miranda will call me at the office when it's over, and I'll come right home to help you celebrate."

"Well, if I can't change your mind, then I'll see you tonight." With one

207

last glance at her aunt, Patti hurried outside to help set up for the auction.

Lottie picked up her book bag and slipped out the front door. Time to put the plan in motion.

When she pulled up to the townhouse, Miranda was waiting "Is this everything?" she asked, looking through the stack of envelopes.

"Yes. Call me at the office if anything goes wrong."

A sleepy kind of quiet enveloped the Performing Arts Building so early in the morning. Later, the halls would come alive with students practicing their various arts, but for now the halls were silent. Lottie's footsteps echoed in the stairwell, and she crossed the atrium with a spooky sense that someone might be following her.

She unlocked her door and flipped the light switch with a thrill of foreboding, but the office was just as she'd left it. Her fears were groundless.

Throughout the long morning Lottie filled the air with music, practicing for an upcoming performance. After an early lunch she turned her attention to her lesson plans, until the silence became oppressive.

She had much more silence in her future, she supposed. After today, her big old house would be empty. She would miss Sarah's baby sounds and the gum-snapping verve of Tina's crew as they went about their business. She'd especially miss Patti.

"What now, Helen? The crisis is over. What should I do next?"

A new and joyful thought occurred to her. Raising her eyes to the ceiling she said, "Lord, I guess I should ask You these questions now. What do You want me to do?"

She lowered her eyes with a self-conscious chuckle. Her first made-up prayer. Well, she would just have to wait and see what happened.

Half an hour later, she yawned. This would be the perfect day for an after-lunch nap. Maybe she should talk to Jason about wedging a sofa between the two pianos. The thought made her chuckle.

Come to think of it, there was a nice little love seat in the atrium. It stood against one wall, nicely hidden by palm plants and a ficus tree. Lottie would bet money she'd find at least one amorous young couple there before the semester ended. For today, it would make a lovely napping spot.

♪

Miranda parked on campus to save the close parking spots for Patti's paying customers. She wouldn't be taking home anything she bought, so it didn't matter that her car was several blocks from the house.

Jason joined her at the edge of the neighborhood. "Hello, beautiful."

"Hello, yourself. Are you ready for this?"

"Yep." He took her hand as they walked. "I'm here to work hard and follow Patti's orders."

"That's the spirit."

Mitchell met them at the next street corner. "I don't know about you guys," he said, "but I can't wait to get this day over with."

Jason raised his eyebrows. "Why?"

"I've got things to do, Jase." Mitchell rubbed his hands together in anticipation. "First thing Monday morning I'm going up to Iowa City to register for the bar review course. It starts next week. I'm a little rusty, so studying will be more than a full-time job, but I can do it. I figure if I take the exam in February, I can find a job with a Chicago law firm by April, and move up there in May at the latest."

Jason raised an eyebrow. "What do you want to do that for, Mitch?"

Mitchell didn't take the bait. "I'm going to need a real job to support my family. That's why." He stared his brother down. "So there."

"I can respect that."

They reached the alley and joined a group of people walking to the sale. "It's kind of early for customers, isn't it?" Jason said.

Miranda disagreed. "They want a look at the merchandise and a place near the front of the crowd. We're only going to get busier from here."

Cal and Teresa Jefferson caught up with them. "Lottie said you had something for me," Cal said to Miranda.

She pulled an envelope from her purse. "Here you go."

Cal thanked her, and the couple moved past.

Mitchell looked at her curiously. "What was that all about?"

She snapped her purse shut. "Lottie won't be here today. I'm running errands for her."

"On a Saturday? Do you get overtime?"

"It doesn't work that way. Lottie is my friend, not just my boss."

They reached the yard, and Jason stopped to talk to his dad. Miranda slipped Sam an envelope and joined Patti on the porch. "What can I do to help?"

"We need someone to hand out sale fliers and keep people from going upstairs. Do you mind?"

"I can handle that."

Miranda took the stack of fliers and departed, glad to be out of the way. She stood in the front entry, where people lined up to see the tables full of smaller items. At the stroke of eight, the crowd surged forward and filled the house. She had her hands full giving out fliers and keeping people from climbing the stairs. "There are no sale items on the second floor," she repeated, though a large sign on the first step said the same thing.

When the rush ended, things settled into a slower rhythm. Miranda entertained herself by people-watching and listening to snatches of conversation.

Katherine stopped to chat. "I haven't seen Lottie. Is she around?"

Miranda pulled an envelope out of her pocket. "She can't be here today, but she asked me to give you this."

Katherine read the brief note. "That's what I needed."

She had an identical conversation with Ed Williams, who stuck the envelope in his pocket, unread. "I know what to do," he said with a big grin. "Your boss is something special, you know that?"

She smiled. "I know."

Rhonda Kennedy walked in, holding a small child by the hand. "Did you hear about all the excitement yesterday?"

"I sure did," Miranda said. "You're quite a hero."

The professor puffed up like a peacock. "I did what anyone would do."

"Well, I know Lottie is grateful."

"She's a good person. I hope she'll stay in Collison for a long time."

The house emptied out as the auction began. Miranda gave her remaining fliers to Tina's daughter, and hurried to join in the fun. Down the front steps and around the house, she stopped only to buy a brownie from Jessie's bake sale. "How's business?" she asked.

"Great." Jessie glowed with happiness. "We're nearly sold out. Martha's inside getting our last dozen."

Miranda reached into her purse. "Lottie asked me to give this to you."

Jessie took the envelope. "I'm happy to help."

The loudspeaker squawked, and Miranda hurried away to find Jason.

She squeezed through the crowd to the back deck, where he waited by the rail. "What did I miss?"

"Dad just got in a bidding war for a bedroom set."

"Did he win?"

"Yep, but the other guy didn't make it easy."

"I'm glad he kept going." She pointed. "Look. The dining room set is next."

The auctioneer began his chant, and three or four people raised their cards. When the price rose to a reasonable level, Ed Williams entered the fray. One by one the other bidders dropped out, until Ed carried the bid. "Going…going…gone," said the auctioneer. "Sold to number twenty-eight."

Jason laughed. "For a guy who just won a contest, Ed looks pretty unhappy. The man doesn't like to part with his money."

"His wife is proud of him, anyway." Martha stood at Ed's side, beaming her approval.

The auction continued at a steady pace. Tommy's band mate won the saxophone, and all his friends slapped him on the back. A baseball card collection went for top dollar, but an old John Deere mower sold cheap. When a set of fishing tackle went for a few dollars, Jason swore under his breath.

Miranda glanced at him. "Catching auction fever?"

He looked disgusted. "Well, that just wasn't right."

"You could have bid on it."

"I would have, but I don't fish." He leaned his elbows on the rail. "Now here's a useful item. A circular saw."

Miranda didn't answer. Her mind was on Patti, who stood in the shade of the garage, shoulders slumped, her face full of defeat. For all her bravado, she was suffering. When Mitchell stepped from the crowd and put his arms out, Patti walked into them and hid her face against his shoulder. Miranda gave a contented sigh. So Patti's cloud had a silver lining after all.

The auctioneer finished with tools and started on the kitchen. "First up is this vintage chrome table and chairs. Lots of wear left in these items, folks. Who'll give me fifteen dollars to start the bidding?"

Jason nudged her with his elbow. "This is your item."

"You need a better poker face if we're going to do auctions." She raised her number.

"We?" He smiled. "I like the sound of that."

She bought the kitchen set for less that it was worth, and glanced toward the garage to see if Patti had noticed. Mitchell was gone, replaced by a platinum-blond woman in a pink pantsuit. The woman exuded energy as she poked her finger into Patti's chest, talking rapidly. Patti was pale, her jaw set in a stubborn line.

Miranda nudged Jason. "Looks like Donna Davenport found Patti. She might need help."

"Right. I'm on it." But before he could move, Mitchell stepped from the crowd and placed himself between Patti and her accuser. Gently and firmly he took the woman's arm and escorted her toward the alley. She tried and failed to pull her arm free, talking all the while, her face bright red with wrath. When they reached the end of the property, he stopped and said something that silenced her. When he finally let go of her arm, she gave him a nasty glare and hurried away.

Jason nodded toward the alley. "Mitch's got it handled."

"So I see." Miranda was about to breathe a sigh of relief when somebody new approached Patti from the crowd. She nudged Jason. "What is Elaine Woodward doing here?"

"Who's that?'

"The music department secretary. She's an awful old witch."

Elaine spoke to Patti, who answered by pointing at the alley where Donna Davenport had just disappeared. The secretary hurried away, brushing past Mitchell in her haste to catch up with the author.

Elaine and Ms. Davenport? The connection rang alarm bells in Miranda's brain. "I have to go." She shoved her number into Jason's hand. "Win the Homer Laughlin china for me."

Before he could answer, she fled.

♫

Sam was talking Katherine Snelling through the bidding process when Miranda appeared at his elbow. "Elaine Woodward just left with Donna Davenport."

Sam drew a blank at the name. "Woodward? I don't know that name."

"Let me get this straight." Katherine looked puzzled. "Elaine was at the auction with Donna Davenport, the author? How do they know each other?"

"Ms. Davenport is writing a book about Lottie," Miranda said. "I think Elaine is selling information to her."

"If that's true, she'll lose her job."

"Lottie didn't answer her phone at the office," Miranda said. "I'm going up there to make sure she's all right."

Sam frowned. "What are you afraid of?"

"I don't want them to catch her off-guard. At the very least they could surprise her into saying something she'll be embarrassed about later."

"Do you want me to go with you?" he asked.

"No. Somebody needs to make sure they don't come back here."

"I'll go," Katherine said quickly. "Lately I've had my doubts about Elaine." She handed her envelope to Sam. "Could you please buy lot number fifty-nine for me? It's a purple dress in a picture frame."

Sam took the envelope with a sense of resignation. He'd already bought six boxes of cloth. He might as well take the whole dang sewing room. "Let me know what you find out."

Miranda walked away with Katherine in tow, and Sam decided to move closer to the front. He tapped a man on the shoulder. "Excuse me. I need to get by."

Bob Holt turned to grin at him. "How's it going, Sam?" The police chief lowered his voice. "Say, did you hear what happened yesterday over at the P.A.B.?"

"I did."

Bob shook his head in disgust. "It was the craziest thing. The guy was strung out on something. He didn't even know who Lottie Braun was."

"Was he working alone?"

"He said so."

"But you don't believe him?"

"Nope. His story didn't hold together right."

Sam leaned closer. "Did you search his house?"

"Of course."

"Did you happen to find a broken pocket knife?"

The police chief looked interested. "No."

Sam swallowed hard. "Bob, there's something I need you to do."

Lottie awoke to the murmur of voices crossing the atrium, rising as they came near, and fading when they passed. Through the palms she spotted Elaine Woodward leading a neatly coiffed blond woman toward the shadowy back hall. Their voices drifted back to her.

"This is an odd place for her office," the stranger said.

"Why? She's no better than the rest of the staff," Elaine answered.

Lottie sank deeper into the couch cushions, thankful she'd had the good sense to lock her office. If their purpose was to find Lottie, Elaine and her guest would be disappointed. Any minute now they would leave the way they'd come, and Lottie could return to her work.

Minutes passed. Not only did the ladies not leave, Elaine had no trouble unlocking Lottie's office. Their voices rose and fell in casual conversation as they turned on her light and made themselves at home.

As quietly as possible Lottie tiptoed across the atrium. Holding her breath, she slid along the wall to her office, but she didn't need to be so careful. The women inside were too intent on going through her desk to notice her.

"How much information do you need, Donna?" Elaine said as she searched a drawer. "You have all of Andrew's papers. He collected plenty of evidence."

The other woman's voice was matter-of-fact. "Your son had theories, not evidence, Elaine. I'll need rock-solid proof before I accuse a woman of her stature taking bribes. A letter asking Lottie to throw the contest, or a bank receipt for the money. Something tangible."

Lottie closed her eyes. Finally, the tax return made sense. 1976. The year of the infamous Philadelphia competition. The runner-up had challenged the decision in the Philadelphia contest, accusing the judges of taking bribes. An inquiry cleared Lottie and the other judges of the charges, but the decision derailed Andrew Wood's career, not to mention his mental health.

Lottie stepped into the light. "You won't find anything."

The stranger looked her over with interest. "Well, Lottie Braun. We meet at last."

She nodded. "The pleasure is all yours, believe me, Ms. Davenport."

Donna Davenport's laugh rang out. "Can I quote you on that?"

Lottie ignored her. "Hello, Elaine," she said to the secretary. "Are you planning to destroy my office again? Or just leave a nasty message?"

Elaine turned scarlet. "I don't know what you're talking about."

"I think you do. You slashed my tire, too, didn't you?"

The secretary's expression turned sly. "As far as the police are concerned, I'm innocent. My nephew will take the full blame as long as I keep supplying his drug habit."

"Hold on. What are you talking about?" Donna Davenport had begun to look alarmed.

Lottie kept her gaze trained on her opponent, who had begun to shake. "I was sorry to hear about your son, Elaine."

"You didn't know Andrew," Elaine spat. "You didn't even recognize his name."

"When you mentioned him the other day, it didn't immediately ring a bell. But nobody could forget the young man who took his own life because he lost a concerto competition. It was a senseless tragedy. I

215

can't imagine the pain you've gone through."

"You drove him to it." Elaine drew a ragged breath. "You and the other judges should have judged that contest fairly. Andrew clearly won."

"The judging was fair. On that day, with that music, another pianist did a better job. That's not to say your son wasn't a wonderful musician." Lottie turned to Donna Davenport. "Is this what you're writing about? You think I'm a crooked piano judge? Who's going to care about that?" She shook her head in pity. "You've fallen pretty far, from Elvis to this."

"There's always your affair with Sinatra."

This made Lottie laugh. "Yes, there's always that. Another phantom rumor about the Great Lottie Braun."

The author looked uneasy. "Or is that a lie, too?"

Lottie turned to Elaine. "There's one thing I want to know. Why did you work so hard to destroy my photograph? What earthly good did that do?"

The woman's voice rose on a hysterical note. "My son should have pictures like that, hobnobbing with Victor Horowitz at fancy award shows. You don't deserve those honors nearly as much as he did."

"Maybe you're right, but destroying my career won't bring Andrew back. You're badly mistaken about that."

"No, I'm not!"

Lottie couldn't help but pity the woman who was coming unglued before her eyes. "I hope you get the help you need."

"I don't need any help," the secretary shrieked. "This is all your word against mine. I plan to stay right here and make your life miserable. You won't last another month in this job."

"That's not true!" Katherine burst into the office with Miranda at her heels. "Elaine, you're fired." She turned to the police chief, who had followed Miranda inside. "I'm pressing charges against these two women."

The chief pulled a set of handcuffs from his belt. "I'm way ahead of you, ma'am."

"Wait." Donna Davenport backed away. "I'm not involved in this. I had no idea Elaine was crazy." She jerked her arms away from the police chief. "What are you charging me with?"

"Breaking and entering," the police chief said. "Criminal trespass.

Burglary, if we find Lottie's property in your possession."

The author tossed her head defiantly. "I've got nothing of hers. As far as I can tell, there's nothing interesting about her." She glared at Lottie. "You've got to be the straightest, most boring celebrity I've ever heard of." She turned to the police chief. "I want to call my lawyer."

He shrugged. "That's your right, ma'am."

Chief Holt carted the two women away, and Lottie sank wearily into her office chair. "The most boring celebrity..." She chuckled. "What a great title for a book."

Miranda looked concerned. "Are you all right?"

"I think so." She bit her lip. "How did you know I needed you?"

"Miranda connected Elaine with Donna," Katherine said, "and decided they added up to trouble."

Miranda looked thoughtful. "I don't know where Chief Holt came from, though. We didn't call him."

Lottie felt that familiar warmth start up in her chest. "I'll bet Sam had something to do with that."

Sixteen

he auctioneer was packing up his sound equipment when Sam tapped Patti's shoulder. "Looks like you had a good day."

She glanced at him. "I guess so. I noticed you bought a lot of stuff."

He nodded. "It'll come in handy for a project."

"You're going to do a project with Mom's fabric remnants?" Her voice held a teasing note.

"Something like that."

She touched his arm. "You must really miss Nancy."

His face grew warm under her sympathetic gaze. She'd jumped to the wrong conclusion, but now was not the time to straighten her out.

Before he could think of an answer, she patted his arm. "Thanks for helping out, Sam. It means a lot."

"Sure thing."

Patti stepped past him. "I have to get Sarah up from her nap. Goodness knows how she slept through all this noise."

Mitchell came around the side of the house as she walked away. "Hey, Dad."

"Mitch, I need your help with something."

Mitchell gave him a curious look. "What can I do for you?"

"I need you to distract Patti for a little while."

As Sam explained what he had in mind, Mitchell started to grin. "I'm your man, Dad." He started for the house, then turned to slap Sam on the back. "That's an awesome thing you're doing."

"It's not my idea, son. I'm just helping out a friend."

Lottie parked in her empty garage, and waved to the kids in the band. "Drop by later," she told them. "I'm ordering pizza."

They waved back but made no promises.

Cal Jefferson's car was parked on the lawn where the auction stand had been just a few hours earlier. Marmalade ran out from under it to rub his back against Lottie's legs. She leaned down to scratch his ears. "Have you been in hiding, old fella? Too much excitement today, I'll bet."

Jessie McCall crossed the yard, carrying a large cardboard box. "I'm going to miss that cat." She sighed. "On the bright side, Grandpa's house sold today."

Lottie looked up. "That's great, Jessie. Who bought it?"

"Some professor-type in a wheelchair. Do you want to meet him? He's in there right now with Diana Deering."

This surprised a laugh out of her. "I'll take a rain check." She could wait to welcome Nathan to the neighborhood. She pointed at the box in Jessie's arms. "Come inside and I'll reimburse you. How much did you pay, anyway?"

"Not much. Fireplace tools must be out of style in the antique world."

"Well, I'm grateful to you."

"Don't mention it." Jessie looked toward the house. "Sounds like there's a crowd inside. Are you having a party?"

Lottie shook her head. "People are just coming to drop off the things they bought for me. I thought I'd feed them pizza to thank them for their help."

"Food and people?" Jessie's face lit up. "So it *is* a party."

She laughed. "I guess you're right. And you're invited."

In the kitchen they found Sam opening a can of peaches for Sarah's dinner. "Mitchell took Patti off our hands for a while," he said in answer to Lottie's inquiring look. "Least I could do was take care of her kid."

Lottie smiled at her friend. "You're good at that, Sam. Taking care of people, I mean." He looked up, a question in his eyes, and she nodded. "I'm all right," she said softly. "The whole ordeal really is over now."

He raised an eyebrow. "Did they find the knife handle?"

"In Elaine Woodward's desk."

Something in him seemed to relax. "Good. Now, if you don't mind feeding your great-niece, I've got some furniture to move."

Lottie glanced at the little girl. "You want me to feed her? By myself?"

He looked puzzled. "Yes. Put the peaches on the tray."

"O-okay." She took the can and sat down in front of Sarah. "Hand me a knife, Sam. I've got to cut these things into smaller bites."

He gave her a table knife and turned to Jessie, who still held the box. "Follow me and we'll put those things away."

"You'll have to be patient," Lotte told her great-niece. "I'm a little out of practice at this. I hope you don't mind."

Sarah raised a fistful of peaches to her mouth, her blue eyes wide and trusting. Lottie's heart melted into a puddle of adoration. "You really are an extraordinary child."

When the peaches were gone, she wiped the child's face and hands with a washcloth and lifted her out of the high chair. Sarah settled onto her hip as if she belonged there, and they set off to see what their friends were up to.

Ed and Cal were adding a leaf to the dining room table while Martha and Teresa arranged Helen's wedding dishes in the china cabinet. Parson's desk once again stood in its accustomed place in the living room. By the sound of things, someone was moving furniture into place upstairs.

When Martha saw Sarah, she held out her arms. "Let me have her for a minute. I miss my grandbabies so much."

Lottie relinquished the baby and took a seat at the dining room table. Pulling a steno pad out of her bag, she said, "It's time to settle up, everyone. Tell me which items you bought, and how much you paid. I've got cash."

Ed and Martha exchanged glances. "We don't want any money," Martha said. "You had a great idea. We were glad to do our part."

"Same goes for me," Sam added.

She frowned. "I don't want my hare-brained plan to cost you anything."

Jessie raised a timid hand. "I need the money. Sorry, but I do."

Lottie pretended to glare at Sam. "See? This is how it's supposed to work."

Miranda and Katherine walked in a few minutes later, carrying bags of pop and cookies. "Pizza alone isn't much of a party," Miranda said, "so we stopped at the grocery."

Sam took Miranda's bags and nudged her toward the living room. "Jase is upstairs putting together a bed frame. I'm sure he could use some help."

Lottie shook her head. "Are you managing everyone's life again, Sam?"

He chuckled. "You're one to talk."

Patti had just spent the slowest two hours of her life. First Tina had gone over the auction account in painstaking detail, verifying which of the leftover items were to go to charity and which were to be thrown away, and itemizing the price of every lot sold. Then Mitchell had driven all over town, first to Goodwill to drop off the donations, and then to the construction office, where after a long delay he'd finally located some obscure document he claimed to need. By the time they got back in the car to go home, Patti was starving and exhausted. The only bright spot in her world was the size of the check in her hand. It exceeded her wildest hopes.

"We're here," Mitchell said as he parked in the alley.

"Finally."

Mitchell took her hand as they passed a couple of cars parked on the lawn. "Thanks for being so patient. I know you've had a long day."

She heard the affection in his voice and felt better. "I'm all right. At least we're together."

Light spilled onto the lawn from the open windows, and a dull roar of conversation met her ears as she climbed the porch steps. Was Lottie having a party? She stepped into the kitchen and sniffed the air. A piece of pizza would taste wonderful.

Sam walked through the kitchen with Sarah in his arms. "Hey there, Patti. You look hungry."

She looked past him into rooms filled with people—and furniture. Mother's furniture. "What's going on here?" she whispered to Mitchell. "Is that Mom's kitchen table?"

"Yeah. Isn't that great?" Mitchell's face was full of suppressed excitement. "Stay right here. I'll get Lottie."

Lottie had gone behind her back to buy her mother's things. Things that Patti would give her eye teeth to keep. The sense of betrayal nearly knocked her off her feet. She had to get out of here. Blinded by tears, she turned and stumbled out the way she'd come.

She was nearly to her car when Mitchell caught up with her. "You can't leave."

She shook off his detaining arm. "Why not?"

"Because whatever reason you've invented to feel angry with Lottie, it isn't true."

"I saw what I saw."

"No," he said. "You saw what you wanted to see."

She froze. "What does that mean?"

"Come back and find out."

Slowly she turned and gave him a long, measuring look. He waited, his gaze willing her to trust him. "What's this all about?" she said finally.

He took her hand. "You have to let Lottie tell you."

They walked back along the alley, Mitchell holding on tight as if she might change her mind and run. "I know how you feel about standing on your own two feet," he said quietly. "But once in a while we all need a helping hand. Remember that."

Lottie stood on the porch, framed in the light from the kitchen window. "Come inside," she called to them. "It's getting cold."

Mitchell gave Patti a little push in Lottie's direction. "Give her a chance," he said. "I'll be inside if you need me."

Patti climbed the porch steps and turned to face her aunt. "Why did you buy my mother's furniture behind my back?"

"Because you wouldn't let me do it up front," Lottie said gently. Patti opened her mouth to protest, but she held up a hand. "Hear me out." She waited for Patti's reluctant nod, then continued. "All the things you saw in that house—your mother's china and your dad's desk—those things are still yours. I saved them today because you were being so sacrificial, selling your past to secure your daughter's future. I couldn't stand to let you lose every tie to your parents. You're a brave girl, Patti, but you don't have to do everything alone."

Patti stared at her. "Dad's desk is in there?"

Lottie smiled. "Yes, along with your parents' bedroom set, and your mother's wedding china. All the things you told Miranda about the other day. And that's where everything will stay until you have room for it. Then, when you're ready, you can move it all to your house—or sell it, if you like. It's up to you."

"I can't pay you back, you know."

"I don't want you to." Lottie clasped her hands so tightly her knuckles turned white. "I have the means, Patti. Please let me do this for you."

She crossed her arms. "And if I don't?"

"Then I'll live in a house full of my sister's stuff until the day I die."

Tears filled Patti's eyes even as she fought a smile. "Well, we can't have that," she said in a voice that cracked.

They stared at one another for a moment, unsure of what to do next. Then Lottie stretched out her arms and Patti walked into them. "I'm glad you're home, Aunt Lottie."

Lottie held her close. "Me too."

After a moment Patti pulled away. "What exactly did you save?"

"Come see for yourself."

Lottie walked into the kitchen, arm-in-arm with her niece, her heart full to overflowing. Sam looked up from his seat at the kitchen table, a question in his eyes. The joy on her face must have answered it, because he gave a satisfied nod and turned his attention to his dinner.

Patti pulled her into the dining room. "I can't believe you kept the Homer Laughlin dishes. Mom always loved the ones with the roses."

"Miranda takes good notes," Lottie said. "To tell the truth, this pattern is more to my taste, too."

Their tour continued into the living room, where most of the guests had gathered. Katherine sat with Cal and Teresa, talking college politics, while next to them Martha and Jessie critiqued the store-bought cookies on their plates. Jason and Miranda sat very close together on the beat-up carpet, listening to Ed Williams tell a story.

Patti stopped to hug Miranda. "Thank you," she whispered.

Miranda smiled up at her. "It was all Lottie's idea."

Patti sat down and Mitchell joined her, dropping a casual arm around her shoulders.

"Hey, Lottie? You've got visitors," Sam called.

She hurried back to the kitchen, where Thomas and his band mates were taking up all the room. Clapping her hands together she said, "I promised you kids some pizza, didn't I?"

Thomas shook his head. "That's not why we're here. Chad bought a saxophone from the auction today, and he found something in the case."

The sax player stepped forward. "The lining was coming apart, so I started to pull it out. This was behind it."

Lottie took the picture from his hands. "Oh, Sam! It's the Neverland."

There they all were, recorded in sepia-toned ink: Johnny and Parson, Sam and Lottie. Mr. Schultz held the string bass to one side, his chest puffed out in his dark suit. The only person missing was Helen.

Patti stood at her shoulder. "Who are those people?"

Lottie glanced at her. "The Neverland Orchestra, of course." She smiled at her visitors. "Thanks for bringing this back, kids. Grab some pizza and stay a while, if you want. I'm going to tell these people a story that will knock their socks off." She turned to Sam. "You'll help me, won't you?"

"I sure will."

They all trooped into the living room, where Lottie called for everyone's attention. "Get comfortable," she said. "I've got something to say, and it's going to take a while." She looked from face to face, at all the friends she had made in such a short time, and began. "When I was ten years old, I won a talent contest in Des Moines."

A long while later she finished her tale. "The Neverland broke up in Shreveport, Louisiana. They didn't have the heart to go on after Monica married her soldier and left them without a singer. My sister moved Billy and me to California to wait for the war to end, and shortly thereafter I was accepted to the Dayton Conservatory of Music. The rest," she said with a flourish, "is history."

After a little silence, Thomas's girlfriend said, "What happened to the baby?"

Lottie took a deep breath. Lord, what do I say? In an instant, she knew. "Billy died in California." She gave Patti a sober nod. "The details of his death are better kept in the family. Afterward, Helen returned to Westmont to heal. Her husband died in the war, and she was alone for a few years, until she met David Parker again, and fell in love." She smiled around the room. "You people know the rest of that story better than I do."

When they were sure Lottie had finished, the kids in the band stood up as one. "Thanks for the pizza," Thomas said. "We should go."

Lottie walked them to the door and gave each a solid handshake. "Thank you," she told them. "That picture is the only one I've ever seen from those days."

Katherine walked out right behind them. "Thank you for sharing. I wouldn't have pegged you for a child star. Not in a million years."

Lottie gave her a nod. "I'll take that as a compliment."

"Great story," Cal said as he and Teresa took their leave. "I'd love to do more research on bands like the Neverland Orchestra."

"You do that, Cal." Lottie smiled at her friend. "I'll help you any way I can."

Jason and Miranda said good-bye, looking so filled with happiness that Lottie wanted to laugh. Mitchell gave Patti a quick kiss, and followed his brother out the door.

Patti scooped her sleeping daughter off the living room floor with a smile. "If anyone wants me, I'll be upstairs tucking this one in."

Sam started for the door. "I'd better be going, too."

"Wait." Lottie put out a hand to stop him. "I want to thank you for everything you did today. You've been looking out for me practically since I moved here." She gazed at him with grateful eyes. "I couldn't ask for a better friend."

"I'm happy I could help." His smile reached right into her heart. "Can I pick you up for church tomorrow?"

She leaned over and kissed his cheek. "I'd like that."

Sam scooted out the door as Patti came downstairs. "Did Sam leave?"

Lottie couldn't keep the smile off her face. "Yes. But he'll be back in the morning. Is Sarah asleep?"

Patti nodded. "She was exhausted. So am I, come to think of it."

"Do you have to go back to Chicago tomorrow?"

"I'm afraid so. But we'll come back often, if that's all right."

"You're welcome any time, dear. Your room will always be ready."

A look of concern passed over Patti's face. "What's going to happen with Donna Davenport?"

"I think she'll leave me alone from now on." Lottie smiled. "She's decided not to write that book after all."

"Why not?"

"She said I'm too boring."

Patti stared at her in disbelief. "Boring is the last word I'd use to describe you."

Lottie's heart swelled with happiness. "Does this mean you'll let me be part of your family?"

Patti squeezed her hand. "I think you're all of my family now. We need to take care of each other."

A lump rose in Lottie's throat. "I can't wait to get started."

Patti gave her an impulsive hug. "I think you already have."

JANE M. TUCKER

Jane M. Tucker is a lifelong reader and writer who has a deep love for the art of storytelling. In fact, her favorite job at church is telling Bible stories to children. She's been a dedicated follower of Jesus since she was nine years old, and you can find strong Christian principles throughout her stories. Jane proudly hails from the great state of Kansas and her weekly blog, "Postcards from the Heartland," is about her life in the Midwest. Having lived in Wisconsin, Iowa, and on the Kansas/Missouri line, she has a deep love for the region. Her blog is filled with stories about her micro-travel adventures as she introduces her readers to places even she didn't know existed. Jane lives with her husband and three children in Overland Park, Kansas.

www.JaneMTucker.com
Facebook.com/JaneMTuckerAuthor
www.Twitter.com/JaneMTuckerAuth

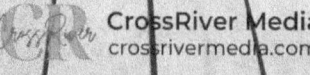

Discover more great books at
CrossRiverMedia.com

SURVIVING CARMELITA

Josie was driving. Her foot on the pedal, her hands on the wheel. Her fault. Sweet Carmelita will never see her fifth birthday. Overwhelmed by guilt and unable to function, Josie flees to Key West, seeking refuge with her cousin. But her journey is guided by an unseen hand, leading her to unexpected encounters—a trailer park pastor, a battered horse, a pregnant teen, and a mysterious beachcomber. Together, they might just show Josie the way to unimaginable hope and redemption.

LOVE FINAL SUNRISE

Ruth Jessup, a New Yorker, and Joshua Stutzman, an Amish man, couldn't be more different—yet their lives collide as they face a psychopath and the chaos of the New World Order. Struggling with amnesia, Ruth awakens in a world of buggies and lanterns, far removed from modern life. As the biblical seven-year tribulation unfolds, an unexpected bond grows between them. Can Joshua's Amish ways help them endure the next three-and-a-half years without taking the mark of the beast?

ANTS ACROSS THE PAGE

Set in the 1960s, Ants Across the Page follows eleven-year-old Luke, a motherless, undiagnosed dyslexic boy, as he hatches a plan to spruce up his grease-stained father and win the heart of "the Sarge." Through Luke's eyes, this heartwarming story shows that whether you're a kid whose letters dance on the page or a man awkwardly chasing love, there's always hope. Filled with laugh-out-loud moments and heartfelt tears, this tale will charm you from start to finish.

Claiming Her Inheritance

She just inherited a fortune... but the
strings attached could unravel everything.

Discover more great books at
CrossRiverMedia.com

Obedient Unto Death

Sinister forces are at work to destroy the fledgling Christian faith in Ephesus, and Sabina is in their way. A young scribe is murdered during a covert Christian worship service. Sabina, a member of this outlawed religion, can't believe a member could be the killer. But when her Roman magistrate father arrests the church bishop for murder, she realizes all is not brotherly love among the faithful. Racing to stop the bishop's execution, Sabina scrambles for proof of his innocence. Will she discover the truth in time, or will she be thrown in prison herself for her faith in Christ?

ROOTS REAWAKENED

Robbed of the only family she has left, Justine Davidson escapes to America to outrun her pain and loneliness. Penniless and homeless, both fortune and misfortune, love and terror twist Justine's road in new and unexpected ways. In the midst of finding herself surrounded by new friends and being pursued by two very different men, Justine's heart is torn between trusting a sovereign God and trusting in herself to avoid painful change. Will deception and the reignition of an old passion bring Justine to the brink of hope or destruction?

Swept into Destiny

Maggie Gatlan may be a Southern belle on the outside, but a rebel on the inside. Ben McConnell is enchanted by Maggie's beauty and fiery spirit, but for him the South represents the injustice and deprivation he left behind in Ireland. As the country divides and Ben joins the Union, Maggie and Ben are forced to call each other enemies. Will their love survive or die on the battlefield of South against North?

Bold faith starts here.

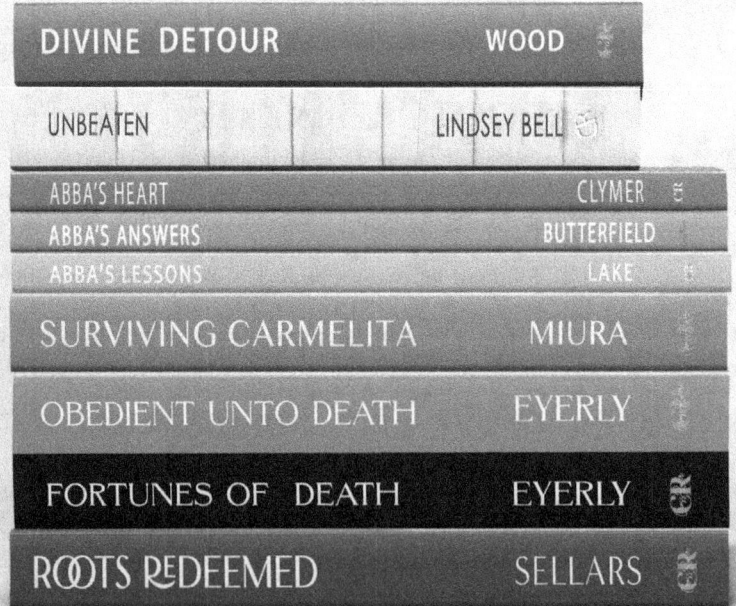

If you enjoyed this book,
will you consider sharing it with others?

- Please mention the book on Facebook, Instagram, Pinterest, or another social media site.

- Recommend this book to your small group, book club, and workplace.

- Head over to Facebook.com/CrossRiverMedia, 'Like' the page and post a comment as to what you enjoyed the most.

- Pick up a copy for someone you know who would be challenged or encouraged by this message.

- Write a review on your favorite ebook platform.

- To learn about our latest releases subscribe to our newsletter at CrossRiverMedia.com.

www.ingramcontent.com/pod-product-compliance
Lightning Source LLC
Chambersburg PA
CBHW060635260626
47161CB00008B/2894